A New

At Home and at Sea

1803

by

John G. Cragg

Beach Front Publishing House

A New War: at Home and at Sea – 1803

Copyright © 2016 by Beach Front Publishing House

BeachFrontPress@gmail.com

Dedicated to

My most encouraging and helpful critic

Olga Browzin Cragg

Special thanks to

Joan Lundell
Dawn McDougall

Chapter I

It is astounding how important news spreads through the countryside without any intervention from newspapers. Almost as soon as old Mr. Charles Gramley of Dipton Hall died, it was known that the estate was heavily in debt, while his heir, James Gramley was known as a profligate. Somehow, the news then spread that each had been borrowing on the same security so that when his father's debts were added to his own, Mr. James was in no position to occupy and maintain his inheritance.

Presumably, this meant that Dipton Hall would have to be let. The circumstance was regarded as no great loss by various young ladies in the area for, even on the infrequent occasions when he had been at Dipton Hall, Mr. James had shown no interest in their charms, while even the mothers who were most eager to see their offspring married had looked with little favor on the spendthrift, uncouth and ill-appearing heir to Dipton Hall. Instead, the news inspired lively, though uninformed, speculation about who the new tenant might be and whether the new household would include any unmarried men who would provide suitable targets for the marriage maneuvers of the young ladies and their mothers. Indeed, the next rumor was that the Gramley financial situation was so serious that the estate would have to be sold – and with it the dower house and even the right to appointing clergymen to the livings in Upper Dipton and Dipton. The second of these church positions was currently vacant, filled temporarily by the incumbent of Upper Dipton while Mr. Gramley collected the tithes and rents.

The news of the sale of Dipton Hall met with mixed reaction.

"Now we'll have some jumped up manufacturer pretending to be a gentleman living at Deepton Hall," complained Mr. Sandforth of Deepling Hill. "Or worse still some shoddy Army contractor."

"Well, it would not be a bad thing to get some more active people in the parish, and, anyway, many of the now landed gentry can trace their fortunes back to people in trade or commerce," countered his daughter, Miss Penelope Sandforth, "and often their sons have been to good schools and are perfect gentlemen." She had yet to secure as a husband one of the gentlemen of the neighborhood and she was not averse to having a wider hunting range.

Widening the supply of possible suitors was, indeed, the hope of many of the young ladies of the area, for there seemed to be many more who needed well-to-do husbands than there were well-off men looking for brides. So excitement grew as it was learned that a naval captain had shown serious interest in the estate and had visited with another captain on a hurried visit of inspection. Soon it was learned, through a circuitous route starting with a solicitor's clerk in Dorchester, that the Captain was named Giles and his companion was called Bush.

When the rumor reached Mr. George Butler, who took a keen interest in everything naval, he looked the captains up in the Naval List. Unfortunately, either from inaccuracy of the transmission of the news, or because Mr. Butler was rather deaf, the captains he sought had the names Miles and Rush. His search revealed that Captain Rush was a very senior officer, who had been made Post in 1775, so he could not be a young man. There was no Captain Miles; all that Mr. Butler could find was a rather elderly Lieutenant Miles.

"I suppose," Mr. Butler told his two nieces, Catherine and Susan, "that the man must have been given command of a cutter or sloop. "Naval custom is that those who are in command of a vessel, even a very humble one, are given the honorary title of captain. I confess that I have never heard of Captain Rush. He must have inherited his money; I do not believe that I would not know of him if he had earned a great amount of prize money."

Mr. Butler then had to explain to his nieces that prize money was the money paid to the officers and crews of ships for prizes; then he had to explain that prizes were enemy ships captured by vessels of the Royal Navy. He felt no need to elaborate on the terms further to explain that the same terminology was usually used for the reward for a privateer capturing an enemy vessel.

The information that Mr. Butler had discovered did not sound encouraging to the young ladies, for Catherine at age 21 had been in high hopes of finding that the captains would make suitable mates, and Susan, aged 19, was at least as keen as her sister to land a well-to-do catch. Their opinion might well have been altered had they paid enough attention to realize that Mr. Butler had the names wrong. However, they took this news as gospel and, with some embellishments, spread the word among all the young ladies of the neighborhood that the new residents of Dipton Hall were a great deal less interesting than they had hoped they would be.

So the news that the captains were staying at the Dipton Arms, though of considerable interest to all, was greeted with only rather limited enthusiasm by many.

"Why are they staying at the inn," asked Susan Butler when the subject arose at tea. "Why aren't they at Dipton Hall?"

"Because, you ninny, Mr. Gramley sold most of the furniture, don't you remember? And he let most of the staff go before he sold the estate," answered her sister with a superior air.

"Well, that won't be made easier now that Captain Giles has sacked the butler and the housekeeper," said their mother, glad to have some news that her daughters hadn't yet heard.

"Where did you hear that?" asked Mr. William Butler, her husband and father to the two young ladies.

"Ellie had it from George who heard it from Roger, the gamekeeper at Dipton Hall, when he was in the Dipton Arms. Ellie says that they were sacked because Captain Giles was going over the household accounts and found they had both been stealing. And that half the cellar had disappeared before it was sold at the auction."

"That doesn't surprise me," said Mr. Butler, "I never did like the look of that man. Though old Gramley never served very good wine anyway, and I heard that the cellar fetched next to nothing."

"Well, without the senior staff, the new residents will have a hard time choosing staff and furnishing the place. Perhaps we should offer to help. Papa you must pay them a call at the Dipton Arms and invite them to visit us." Susan saw no reason to abandon all hope when there was no other prospect on the horizon.

"Oh, they'll get some London arranger to furnish the place, no doubt," said Mr. Butler.

"Getting good help is more of a problem, especially when they don't know the neighborhood. Mr. Butler, you really should go," said Mrs. Butler, who also saw the advantage in getting ahead of the competition.

"Not till they are settled," said Mr. Butler firmly. "We could be of no help in decorating and I am not going to make recommendations on staff. If my suggestions don't work out, we would just be blamed for their hiring them."

There the matter rested for the Butlers. Similar conversations were held in other houses around the neighborhood, with similar results. The new inhabitants were to be ignored until they had properly taken occupancy of Dipton Hall – when it would be each eligible young lady for herself – and in the meantime, they would pump their servants for news through the web of information that circulated among those who kept the gentry's economy running.

Daphne Moorhouse was one young lady who had not shown much interest in the news of the new arrivals. This indifference was not because she was not fully cognizant of the rumors and speculation surrounding them. It was rather that she was a good listener who herself did little to add to rumor or to speculate on events. And she did not exhibit the keen interest in the suitability for marriage of the various young men about whom so much of the speculation by other young ladies centered. Indeed, it was widely supposed that, having not simpered properly when she first came out – instead rather frightening off several possible suitors by her directness and willingness to hold firm on a large number of subjects many of which were not widely considered suitable for young ladies – she was undoubtedly condemned to spinsterhood. Indeed, this might be expected in any case since as the youngest daughter, her proper calling would be to care for her father in his old age and not abandon him for another man. The likelihood of this outcome was accentuated by her eccentricity in not adhering to minor social customs if they appeared to have no merit in particular circumstances.

Daphne was indeed the youngest of Mr. Moorhouse's offspring. Her brother, and Mr. Moorhouse's presumed heir, was well established as a barrister in London, and her two sisters were married with several children each. Her mother had died when she was fourteen, and as she grew up she indeed had steadily taken over more and more of the duties of running the Dipton Manor house, and taking the myriad decisions involved in managing the estate. She was devoted to her nieces and nephews who delighted in her willingness to indulge in play and to romp with them in quite undignified ways. All in all, the role of the valued, independent spinster, pillar of the community, and beloved aunt was one that she seemed to be assuming most willingly even though she was now only twenty-one.

On the morning after the news spread about the visitors at the inn, Daphne Moorhouse was walking at her usual brisk pace from Dipton Manor to St. Mary's Church, Dipton, to ensure that all was in readiness for the service on the coming Sunday. To her mild surprise and interest, she saw a man – clearly a gentleman – standing at the side of the path first apparently gazing off into the distance and then consulting a sheet of paper in his hand. Since she knew all the gentlemen for miles around, she presumed that he must be one of the captains. Completely ignoring the fact that they had not been introduced, she hailed the man with the cry, "Can I help you, Captain?"

Richard Giles, startled, spun around. Before him he saw a slim woman, from her clothes clearly a lady and an attractive one at that, looking at him directly from corn-flower blue eyes without a hint of that bashfulness so often assumed when a young lady met a gentleman for the first time, though she curtseyed as he bowed to her.

"Madam, allow me to introduce myself. I am Richard Giles." In the Navy, Giles had insisted on not being addressed as 'Lord Giles', using instead the title "Captain", and he would never have dreamed of mentioning the knighthood that had been awarded to him just before he came down to Dipton. "And in answer to your question, I was just reflecting on how much it appears that this land has been allowed to deteriorate."

"Oh, dear," Daphne thought to herself. "Have I done it again? I suppose I should have waited for a proper introduction. However, I'll just have to make the best of it. I hope he won't hold it against me."

"I am Daphne Moorhouse," she announced, "from Dipton Manor. And yes, in recent years Mr. Gramley has not really kept up the drainage or hedges on his land."

"So are those fields to the left, which seem to be in better condition, on your land?"

"Yes – or at least on my father's. He has kept up – and indeed-- improved the drainage." Daphne saw no need to mention that in fact the initiatives for the maintenance and improvements all came from her. Indeed, her father had so little interest in farming that she was actually in charge of all these operations, except that usually her father would resist for a time any suggestion that he spend money on improvements and make her justify them clearly.

"I am about to return to the village. May I accompany you?" Giles asked, holding out his arm for Daphne to take.

Daphne was more than willing to have company, and they were soon talking animatedly about requirements of the land and how best to farm it. Giles was astonished to meet a young lady who was perfectly willing to express strong opinions, even ones at odds with his own. Daphne was equally surprised to find a naval captain who seemed to be well informed about farming problems, even if some of his ideas were a bit muddled. But before the conversation could become heated, they reached the inn which was his destination. As they were about to part, Daphne impulsively ignored all proper behavior.

"Captain," she smiled, "I have enjoyed this walk. I don't know if you and Captain Bush have an engagement tomorrow. But if you don't, I – and, of course, my father – would be delighted if you could come to dinner after church."

Giles looked startled at the invitation, but wasted no time in accepting.

Daphne proceeded towards the church, thinking wryly, though without regret, about her impulsive invitation. She knew that Mrs. Hancock, the family cook, would have any needed provisions and that she could easily square any objections that her father would certainly make, for he always shunned the unexpected.

Daphne's invitation produced greater consternation in the Inn Yard. Giles turned in to find Bush and Carstairs, his coxswain, in conversation with the innkeeper.

"Captain … ugh … Richard," Bush hailed him, still not used to addressing Giles as an equal rather than as his commanding officer, "The axel on our carriage was cracked on that last bump we hit getting here. Carstairs tells me that it can't be fixed for a couple of days, and the innkeeper has no carriage for hire – and knows of none in the immediate area. So we shan't be going anywhere for a day or two and we will have to postpone our visit to the farms."

"Well, are there any horses for hire? We could easily ride for our visits. And I have just accepted an invitation to dine tomorrow. We will need some means of getting there since your leg is not up to walking that far yet."

"We do have several horses for hire, sir," interjected the inn-keeper. "Fine steeds!"

"And how do you expect me to ride with only one leg and one arm," grumped Bush. "I just don't think riding a horse is the solution to our problem."

"Nonsense. You'll have to learn to ride despite your injuries if you are going to live in the country. And there is no time to start like now, with Carstairs and me here to help you. Think of all the peg-legs you've seen on ships, and that is much harder than riding a horse."

Bush was ashamed to admit that he had never ridden a horse even when he had had two legs and two hands, and that the prospect rather terrified him. Instead, he said, with rather bad grace, that since they had decided to go by horse, he had better start by practicing getting on and off the beast. To his dismay, Carstairs promptly headed into the stable and quickly emerged with a large, black horse.

"This, Captain Bush, seems to be the most docile of the mounts here. Let's get you aboard."

Carstairs boosted Bush into the saddle. Unfortunately, the horse took exception to this; only Carstairs' quick lunge to grab the head harness stopped Bush being ignominiously bucked right off. Even so, he had trouble grabbing the pommel with his one hand and was only just able to hang on.

When he had the horse under control again, Carstairs said, "See, sir. That wasn't so bad. We'll walk around a little to get him used to you. Just hold the reins in your hand, tight enough so that you can pull on one or the other or both."

They proceeded slowly around the inn yard two times. Bush was just getting to feel a bit more confident that he wasn't about to fall off when Carstairs stopped.

"Now you had better try getting off, sir. Just swing your leg over his back – no, the good leg, he is used to people mounting him on the port side."

Bush complied. Just as his right foot touched the ground, the end of his wooden leg slipped through the stirrup, in such a way that he could not extract it. The horse, alarmed by this development, started shifting around despite Carstairs hanging on to his head harness, leaving Bush hopping around on his good leg while clinging to the saddle to prevent his falling over. Only Giles's coming to the rescue and getting the wooden leg out of the stirrup prevented a rather nasty accident.

"I told you this wouldn't work," said Bush decisively.

"Nonsense. What you need is a groove in the bottom of your leg. Carstairs, can you cut it?"

"Aye, aye sir. Just let me have the leg, Captain Bush."

So, still grumbling about the futility of the exercise, Bush passed the leg to Carstairs. When it was altered, up on the horse Bush had to go again, for he still was unwilling to confess that he had no wish ever to ride or that he had never before been on a horse.

Another couple of trips around the inn yard, and mounting and dismounting without further incident, did give Bush a measure of confidence.

"I think that now you are ready to try riding by yourself," announced Giles. "Let go of the horse, Carstairs."

"But how do I steer?" asked Bush.

For the first time Carstairs realized that Bush had no experience riding a horse. "Pull on the starboard line to make him go to starboard and on the port one to go to port. Pull on both to get him to stop. And, Captain, until you are more used to the horse, I had better come along to help. If you get your own horse, he can be trained so that you mount from starboard, but mounting from port is the usual way, and that's what most horses expect."

This rudimentary instruction was sufficient so that next day Captains Giles and Bush were announced as visitors at Dipton Manor. After introductions, Daphne asked, "Did you walk? I didn't hear a carriage."

"Why no. We rode," replied Bush nonchalantly.

"How very brave of you!" Daphne, as usual, spoke without regard to customary proprieties. "I can't imagine how you do it with your injury. Is it recent? And how did you get it?"

"Oh. I was wounded in our last engagement with the French, four months ago," For the first time Bush felt proud and was glad that someone recognized openly his problem rather than nervously skirting around it. "But I've only had the peg-leg for three weeks and am still getting used to it. Captain Giles' cox'un came with us to help me on and off the horse."

"Cox'un? I've heard the term, but what does it mean?" asked Daphne.

"It's short for coxswain, who is the petty officer in charge of a captain's barge -- that is, his boat. But a good cox'un is much more, for he is often the informal channel between a good captain and his crew, so that the captain is aware of feelings on the lower deck which would not reach him through the usual chain of command. And he often goes with his captain rather than staying with the ship. Carstairs is one of the best."

"Where is Mr. Carstairs now?" Daphne asked.

"He is waiting for us with the horses outside, I imagine," said Giles.

"Well that won't do. The stable boys can deal with your horses, and Mr. Carstairs must come inside. See what Cook can provide him, Tisdale," she instructed the butler.

"Captain Giles, you really must do something about Mr. Twilgate," announced Mr. Moorhouse, abruptly changing the topic.

"Mr. Twilgate?" murmured Giles, looking puzzled.

"Yes, yes. The rector from Upper Dipton. You heard him this morning and a greater load of twaddle I've never heard, except in other of his sermons. Why he can't just use ones properly written, I don't know. It is like that every Sunday. And anyway, the parish needs a proper clergyman."

"Ah," said Giles, who, as was his usual custom, had let his mind wander the moment the preacher entered the pulpit and so had not noticed whether the sermon was good or bad, "ah, yes, I suppose so. I'll have to look into it. Though I really know nothing about how one finds good clergymen. But I don't suppose that I could just toss Mr. Twilgate out of the living of Upper Dipton."

"Oh, I'm sure the Bishop could find him something," said Mr. Moorhouse dismissively, "and to be selfish I only care about Dipton itself. But tell me, Captain Giles, when will your wife be joining you to see the Hall?"

Daphne gave a little gasp at her father's audacity in asking the question whose answer was the subject of speculation by every young lady in the neighborhood who had learned that Captain Giles was far from being some ancient dullard. Even Daphne had realized that she couldn't very well ask the question, but had hoped that Carstairs would provide the information in the servant's hall. Giles, however, seemed not at all surprised by the question.

"I fear, Mr. Moorhouse, that I have not had the good fortune to find a wife."

"You astound me, sir. Why would a young man, who is unmarried with an active naval career, want a remote residence in the country?"

"There are a number of reasons. Before I was sent to be a midshipman, I spent much of my time with the tenants on my father's estates and became fascinated with farming ways. Then when I became a lieutenant, and even more when I was made Post, I found that I greatly enjoyed spending my idle time reading works on modern farming and husbandry. So I very much wanted to have some land of my own for when I am ashore. I have been very lucky in the matter of prize money, so I found that now I can afford to indulge my interest by actually carrying out agricultural improvements. And, I won't be alone here. My older sister is in need of a place to live, so she and her two daughters will be living in Dipton Hall."

"How old are you nieces?" asked Daphne, though, if even she hadn't realized how rude it would be to ask, she would have preferred to explore the strange way in which Captain Giles referred to his sister's lack of a home.

"The older one, Catherine, is nineteen and Lydia has just turned eighteen."

"And you, Captain Bush, are you married?" Daphne's impulsiveness once more got the better of propriety.

"No, Miss Moorhouse. But I do have to provide a home for my mother and two sisters. My father was rector of a parish in Harwich, and he died two months ago, so they have to leave the rectory. My mother does not want to remain in Harwich, so I had hoped to find something where I could be close to Captain Giles."

"Captain Giles," Mr. Moorhouse broke in, "I was surprised that you spoke as if you had a great deal of idle time while at sea. I was always of the impression that naval service is very active."

"That is, of course, the case when we are in battle and sometimes in a storm, but the truth of the matter is that very often there is very little that actually needs to be done by the captain. The crew of a man-of-war is very large for the tasks that are necessary on a regular basis for we need them in battle and to make sure that even with significant injuries, we are still an effective unit. We keep the crew busy with drills of various sorts – and these drills are important for developing a crew that is as efficient as possible in battle. But they largely involve the other officers, rather than the captain. And the officers standing their watch have to be on deck usually, in case they are needed, though in truth there would be no great difficulty in requiring much less of their time. A captain doesn't have even those duties. He can either be on deck making every one nervous about what he may be thinking and interfering with what the other officers are doing or he can find other uses for his time in his cabin. So I spend quite a bit of time reading and playing my violin. The fiddle is one of the benefits of command. When I was a lieutenant, no one wanted to hear my attempts at trying to master new pieces, but now they can't object."

"And how do you spend your off-duty time, Captain Bush?"

"I enjoy reading classical history, especially military history. Though until recently, I was only a lieutenant and so did not have as much spare time as Captain Giles indicates is the lot of a commanding officer."

"Dear me, classical history is one of my own interests," declared Mr. Moorhouse.

At that moment dinner was announced, and when the party was seated, conversation drifted into other areas. Indeed, Giles kept his host talking animatedly about the locale in which he was going to settle, and both Mr. and Miss Moorhouse were more than happy to regale their visitors with the oddities of their neighbors. Just before the final course was served, the conversations diverged and Captain Bush and Mr. Moorhouse began a spirited debate about the Battle of Cannae, while Giles and Daphne discussed the possibilities for draining the low-lying fields where their properties met. Their discussion proceeded so rapidly that they agreed to meet the next day to examine the possibilities more specifically on the site. When Daphne arose to leave the gentlemen to their port, Mr. Moorhouse protested that there was no reason to leave and spoil the good conversation. Daphne stayed, but noting that Captain Bush seemed to be fading rapidly and remembering that he had been injured but recently, she soon suggested that it was time to let their guests depart.

"Well, Daphne, you have certainly landed a whale where I expected only a trout," declared M. Moorhead.

"Whatever do you mean, father."

"I was led astray by that old fool George Butler, even though I supposed he had probably got things wrong, or I would have warned you earlier. Your Captain Giles is actually Captain Sir Richard Lord Giles, or some such combination of titles, with the knighthood won as a result of his own activities. He's the son – third or fourth I think – of the Earl of Camshire."

"He's not *my* Captain Giles. But he did seem perfectly nice to me"

"There is no reason why an earl's son should not be 'perfectly nice'. Anyway, you have certainly stolen a march on the other young ladies."

"I don't know what you mean," though Daphne's smile indicated that she knew perfectly well what her father was suggesting, and felt rather pleased with it, even if she had ruled herself out of the matrimonial steeple chase.

"It did strike me as odd," continued Mr. Moorhouse, "that Captain Giles – I suppose we should call him that since that is how he chose to be introduced – should be providing a home for his sister. The Earl is still active and Ashbury Abbey should have any amount of space to provide for her. I do seem to recall some bitter scandal involving the Earl about the time you were born, but the details all escape me. Maybe you can find out more about Captain Giles' circumstances and why he is making a home for his sister from Elsie."

Elsie was Daphne's maid, and Daphne was mortified to realize that her father had seen through her insisting that Carstairs be well entertained, knowing that Elsie was a past master at prying gossip out of the servants of others. But she discovered, when Elsie came to help her when she retired, that this scheme had resulted in nothing. While Elsie was full of what a splendid man Carstairs was and how he had ambitions to keep his own public house, she had found out only that Carstairs had not accompanied Captain Giles either to Ashbury Abbey or to Ripon and knew no more about the circumstances of the Earl and his daughter than her father had already imparted. She could look forward enthusiastically to the meeting on the morrow, but she knew that it was not likely to produce answers to any of the social questions that were running through her mind.

That rendezvous was not to be kept. Giles and Bush arrived back at the inn to find a courier with a message from the Admiralty for Captain Giles. The message was crystal clear, though its import was totally mysterious. Captain Giles was requested to present himself to the First Lord at the Admiralty as soon as convenient. The polite form was belied by the method of delivery of the request, and on a Sunday no less. In plain English, Captain Giles was to get to the Admiralty as quickly as possible.

"It must be a ship." Bush was full of enthusiasm for his friend, the very tender nature of his backside, produced by bouncing around on the horse, quite forgotten.

"That doesn't explain the urgency," replied Giles a bit morosely. "Maybe they have found some inconsistency in my last report or something equally stupid. But I should go first thing in the morning. Carstairs will come with me. I hope that you can look after some things here that we have started."

"Gladly. But that doesn't include the drainage you have been talking about." Giles had spent most of the ride back talking about the meeting he was to have with Daphne and what needed to be done about drainage.

Chapter II

Early on Tuesday morning Giles alighted from a carriage at the main entrance to the Admiralty. He had spent the night at his father's London house – to the consternation of the servants since it was not officially "open" -- and took one of the Earl's carriages to the Admiralty. He rightly supposed that the crest on the door might help him to get past the notoriously unhelpful doorkeepers. Even so, he was surprised when he was whisked away right past the usual waiting room where naval officers from lieutenant to admiral invariably spent considerable time before being seen by any official of the Admiralty. It was rumored that the officers had to endure the wait so that they would know their proper place. Instead, Giles was ushered directly into the vestibule of the First Lord's room. Moments later, he was shown into the presence of the great man.

"Thank you for coming so quickly, Sir Richard. We have urgent need of the best frigate captain available. And we need to show that we have taken vigorous steps before news of the situation spreads. I've already ordered the Channel Fleet to take action, but we also need a specially commissioned vessel with the sole task of dealing with the situation. Three frigates! Three Frigates!"

"My Lord," interrupted the Second Secretary. "We hope that Captain Giles has no idea of the subject about which you are talking."

The First Lord seemed to swell as his face turned red and Giles expected a violent explosion aimed at the Second Secretary. Instead, suddenly, the First Lord grinned, relaxed and took a pinch of snuff from the box lying on the table in front of him. Giles was much more astounded to see that the fearsome First Lord could grin than he would have been by the explosion that had seemed imminent.

"Quite right, Newsome, quite right. I can't expect Sir Richard to be clairvoyant, though it would be most helpful to the mission we have for him.

"There is a French ship – pirate, privateer, national ship, we don't know which – which has been taking a large number of vessels in the area of the mouth of the channel. She is fast, powerful and very well handled. Her success against merchant shipping is very worrying, but what renders the situation a crisis is that she has defeated, and in most cases taken, three of our frigates – at least. Another one has gone missing when on route home.

"Only in one case was her battle with one our frigates such that our ship was sunk. In the others she took them, usually after a short battle that made it quite easy for her to board and make repairs in order that her prize could be safely sailed away.

"The worst case, and the one that is going to cause the ministry problems if we are not seen to be taking swift action, occurred ten days ago. The frigate *Artemis* – a thirty-six, I don't know if you know her – Captain George Ferguson -- was on passage from Portsmouth to Gibraltar in company with the sloop *Squirrel* when she encountered a large frigate apparently closing on a group of three merchantmen. When the strange frigate did not respond to the private signal, *Artemis* signaled *Squirrel* to support her in attacking the stranger. *Artemis* and the French vessel sailed towards each other, *Artemis* close hauled while the Frenchman was on a reach on a course that would lead her to pass to windward of *Artemis*. Just before they would meet, the French vessel opened fire with her bow chasers. They were well aimed – and we have reason to believe that the bow chasers were heavier cannon than is usual on our own ships – with the result that it took the fore topmast. The wreckage in the water slewed *Artemis* around so that her broadside could not bear on the enemy which was about to cross her bow and presumably fire her full broadside. *Artemis* at that point struck her colors."

"Without firing a shot?"

"Without firing a shot! That's where the scandal lies. Commander Stevens, in command of *Squirrel,* tried to interfere with the French ship's taking *Artemis*, but a well-placed broadside into her meant that all *Squirrel* could do was to make emergency repairs and try to avoid being taken herself. The French ship was not interested in *Squirrel* further. The wreckage was quickly cleared away on *Artemis*, and the French got her under way with the French frigate placing herself so that *Squirrel* could not interfere. They headed to where the merchant ships had disappeared over the horizon. Commander Stevens decided to follow, though keeping a safe distance from the French frigate. They soon overhauled the merchantmen and it then became obvious that, far from the arrival of *Artemis* preventing the capture of the ships, it had simply induced the French frigate to draw *Artemis* and *Squirrel* away from ships that the

Frenchman had already captured. The French then set a course towards the French coast. Darkness by now was approaching and *Squirrel* lost sight of them during the night.

"We cannot let this continue. Quite apart from the stain that *Artemis*'s surrender puts on the Navy, this ship is wreaking havoc in the merchant fleet. An adequate convoy system would require many escorts – more than we can really spare – and would still be subject to the basic problem that this ship presents us…"

The First Lord paused, clearly expecting Giles to fill in the gap. For a moment he felt again like a fourteen year old midshipman confronted with a loaded question from his captain. As was the case then, he guessed that a wrong answer would be better than no answer at all or even worse a toadying answer that merely tried to draw out the questioner. Anyway, Giles thought he had a good answer. "Any ship stronger than her, she can out sail; any ship faster than her, she can defeat."

"Yes. Furthermore, we usually have the advantage that our ships are at sea and well-practiced, while the French ships have usually been bottled up in harbor and so are inexperienced. That is clearly not the case here."

"What do we know about this ship?"

If the Earl of Finisterre was surprised at the temerity of a junior captain asking a question, he did not show it.

"Quite a bit – at least if we have identified the type of ship correctly.

"A while back, an émigré from France showed up with what he claimed were the plans for a new type of frigate that the French were building. The design was somewhat radical and most ship builders who saw the plans labeled it as completely impractical. Here, I have the plans on that table. Have a look."

Giles joined the First Lord as he unrolled a set of plans. The first was a deck plan, the second was an elevation including a sail plan. Presumably subsequent sheets gave more detail.

After studying the plans briefly and referring to the scale, Giles remarked. "She is certainly different from your standard 36. A good bit longer and a bit narrower. And it looks as if she has a deeper draft. That's what strikes me. I expect that those features would make her faster than any of our frigates of similar size. She is almost more like a sloop – though with very different rig – than a frigate. Speed does seem to me to be more a function of how well a ship is designed – and how clean her bottom is – rather than how she is rigged. I would fear, however, that the narrow beam would make her somewhat unstable, particularly when she tried to fire a broadside. It does look as if she is designed to have larger bow chasers than usual, but I'd have to see how that is to be achieved."

"That's what most of the experts we consulted thought. Indeed, most were quite contemptuous of the whole layout of the ship, predicting that she would be slow – something about the amount of hull in the water – crank and, indeed, useless in a fight or for any other use. There were one or two, however, who doubted the analysis of the other experts, and made a case that she would be faster, and that the instability in battle could be effectively and efficiently overcome. One man even went so far as to predict that she would be the better ship in a scrap with another 36 or even 42.

"The argument went back and forth, focusing on whether we should try to build a ship from the plans. I was swayed by two considerations. The traditionalists became quite shrill about how right their evaluation was and what a silly set of notions was embodied in the French plans. Those who saw merit in the plans were much less dogmatic about the superiority of their views and that in itself made me think they might have considered the matter more objectively. But more importantly, I realized that if we were to build to this plan and the ship was a failure, it would not be the first poor ship we have built nor would it be the last. If it were a success in French hands, and we had done nothing, we would be vulnerable for a while to the damage that the ship could do – and any others they might build. Presuming that the ship, which is causing all the problems I have mentioned, was built to these plans, that danger is now realized, though we are not completely caught out. I was finally persuaded by the argument that the French have long tended to build better ships than we do, and that their advantage has only been overcome by capturing large numbers of them.

"One of the most level-headed of the supporters of the vessel was Joshua Stewart of Baker's Yard at Butler's Hard. He thought it would be worthwhile to experiment, but he also pointed out some things he thought could be improved. His feeling was that in trying the new approach to design, it makes sense to take the new concepts as fully as feasible to the new design. As he put it, 'in for a penny, in for a pound.' He suggested some modifications to the plans – primarily, lengthening the vessel still farther, and putting more emphasis on those bow and stern chasers – *Artemis*'s fate suggests that they may be a crucial aspect of the design. In this he was aided by the Ordinance Office which showed interest in using longer and heavier guns for this armament than had even been tried before.

"This is where you come in. Baker's Yard has been building the new ship and she is ready for commissioning. She will be called *Patroclus* and be listed as a 36 gun frigate. The Admiralty is giving you her command, and your orders after getting her seaworthy is to search out and destroy the French frigate that has been causing all these problems. If you can capture her, so much the better, but we do not want you to end up with the fate of other frigates who have met you. But…"

Newsome cleared his throat. "My Lord, the time…"

The First Lord glanced at the clock. "You'll get your detailed oral instructions and written commission and orders from Newsome here. I have to see Addington and am already rather late for my appointment. Good luck with her, Captain Giles."

The First Lord disappeared in a flurry through the door, leaving Giles to wonder what he had been about to say.

Newsome took over the instructions smoothly: "*Patroclus* is ready to be handed over by the Yard. You are to take command of her. Details and your commission are in this packet. Our experience with Baker's Yard has been very good, so you can expect that she will be ready to go to sea as soon as she is provisioned. I have arranged for supplies to be lightered over from Portsmouth and they are due to arrive in a couple of days. Crew may, of course, be a problem. As you know, *Phoebe* wasn't condemned, but also hasn't been scheduled for repair. As a result, your old crew is available, except for a draft of 25 that Admiral Cork succeeded in wangling out of the Port Admiral. Your crew will be transported to Baker's Yard and they should be there by tomorrow. *Phoebe* now will be condemned and broken up. *Patroclus*, of course, has a larger nominal crew than *Phoebe* had, and your company was already short by 70 seamen. So you have a total deficiency of 125 men. I can't help with that: you'll just have to rely on your press gangs. You should have a large enough crew to sail, and the Admiralty can brook no delay for lack of crew.

"The warrant officers from *Phoebe* have all been re-assigned to *Patroclus*. This includes, of course, your master, Brooks. I hope he is not one of those hide-bound masters who are leery of change -- if so, you may want to think about getting a more malleable master, but I warn you that time is short."

"No, Mr. Brooks has always been open to new ideas and does not think that our present ships have reached perfection. When we were on the Halifax station, he muttered several times that the Admiralty would do well to learn from the design of Nova Scotia schooners, so he should welcome the chance to see how this new design sails."

"Good. Your officers may be more of a problem. Bush, of course, has been promoted. How is he, by the way?"

"Recovering very nicely. He should be ready for service very soon."

"I'm very glad to hear it. Evans, your second, got a position in a 74 as soon as he had brought that prize home – I cannot imagine why he thought that would advance his career rather than staying with you..." The Second Secretary paused, obviously hoping for some information, but Giles pretended to be oblivious. "Davis is now the senior – indeed the only – officer in *Phoebe*, but he is pretty junior. Miller, your mid, has passed for lieutenant and is available. I have his commission here if you don't object."

Giles nodded his agreement. He was about to make a suggestion for First Lieutenant, but Newsome continued firmly.

"We have had to assign you a first lieutenant. Lieutenant Foster who most recently was first lieutenant to Pritchard in *Thunderer*."

Seeing the look of dismay on Giles face, he hurried on. "Lieutenant Foster has some powerful interest behind him, and the Board felt obliged to appoint him. He's experienced; you should get on together very well. His commission has already been sent to him at Portsmouth and he should be on board in a day or two.

"Now, there is some urgency. You'll want to arrange your affairs as fast as possible. Today? Hopefully you can post down to Portsmouth and proceed to Baker's Yard tomorrow. Your orders should explain everything. You are to have a make-up cruise down the Channel with a Mr. Hughes of the ordinance Board, and drop him at Falmouth before proceeding to find this French nuisance. Good luck."

Giles found himself ushered without further pause from the Second Secretary's presence, the reason becoming clear when Giles passed a senior admiral clearly being escorted to the same room. The Second Secretary was undoubtedly aware that it was more important for him to accommodate promptly an officer who could directly affect his own well-being rather than a somewhat junior captain. This would be the case even though Giles was a captain with good connections and in whom the First Lord had shown very considerable interest, a situation especially remarkable for one who was not the First Lord's own client. Not that Giles didn't suspect that Newcomb had delayed imparting the unwelcome news about his first lieutenant until he could assure himself of no time for a protest.

Pritchard and the *Thunderer* had been notorious in the fleet for sloppy seamanship. It was reported that Pritchard had ordered more floggings than any other captain, even though *Thunderer* was not one of the larger ships. It was also rumored that Pritchard was shy. Indeed, the rumor was that Thunderer had been taken out of service for a complete rebuild in the dockyard only to prevent a mutiny and not because she needed it. However, Giles reflected, there was nothing he could do about the appointment, and he had a lot to accomplish if he was to post down to *Petroclus* on the next day – how he wondered would the crew mangle that name? –while leaving his own affairs in some semblance of order. He had to see his prize agent urgently, but equally important, he had to see his brother, David, who had arrived at the Earl's London House yesterday evening, before he went out again.

"Is there somewhere I can write a couple of notes," Giles demanded of the servant showing him out.

"Yes sir, this way." It was a sign of his standing in the Admiralty that he was promptly shown to a large room with a table and stationary at hand. It was the task of a moment to write a note making an appointment with his prize agent for that afternoon and passing a coin to the servant to arrange the note's prompt delivery. It spoke even more highly of his standing – and possibly his father's – that his father's coach was waiting for him when he emerged from the entrance. It did save him having to find a cab.

Giles arrived at Compton Square to find that the butler had a very long face as he opened the door.

"Whatever is the matter, Steves?"

"Nothing, my Lord."

"Nonsense, Steves. I've known you all my life and have never seen you look so glum. Something's not right."

"Well, my Lord. Mr. Guildford, the Earl's man of business, was just here. The house is to be sold and we are all to be let go."

"What? Sold? When will the transition take place?"

"Immediately, my Lord."

"Well, what provisions is he making for you and the others?"

"None, my Lord."

"None? But surely he at least is paying you a month's wages and making other payments as well."

"No, my Lord. Mr. Guildford said that we could have two-weeks' wages, but then his Lordship would not give us good characters, or we could have nothing and he would provide good characters."

"I see. Well, this won't do. Is Lord David still in the house?"

"Yes, my Lord. He is in the library."

"I must see him immediately. My conversation with him will take a while, but then I'd like you to see you and Mrs. Wilson in the drawing room in about an hour. We might as well include Mrs. Darling as well."

"Very good, My Lord."

Giles crossed the entry to the library, knocked, and went in. His brother looked up from the book he was reading. Giles realized that he hardly knew David. Growing up, the age difference between them had been such that David was more of a nuisance than a companion. After Giles had gone to sea, their paths rarely crossed; on the few occasions when Giles had been to Ashbury Abbey, David had been at school or at Cambridge.

After exchanging greetings, Giles decided to approach matters a bit obliquely, "David, now that you have graduated from Cambridge, how did you like your experience there?"

"I started out being resentful, partly because my school hadn't been the most prestigious and Selwyn isn't a very fashionable college. I didn't like the presumption that the Church was to be my profession. But that changed because of a really good college tutor who led me into philosophy and then theology. And I got into a more serious group than I first wanted and so became interested in what I was doing. As a result, I became quite keen on being a parish priest, while at first I resented the idea."

"So quite different from Ashton, who was rusticated in his first term at Trinity and called it quits for further learning. So what is next?"

"Mother wants me to become secretary to the Bishop of Winchester, as a first step to becoming a bishop myself, but I would prefer to be a parish priest, preferably – much preferably – in a country parish. But the livings that Father controls are all given out and he doesn't seem ready to use his influence to help me."

"Well, I may be able to help there. Dipton needs a vicar, and it seems that when I bought the Hall, I got the rights to the major tithes of the parish and to appointing the vicar. You might be interested. Think about it."

"I do not need to think about it. A good country parish living is just what I was hoping for."

"Good, then it's yours. I am not sure exactly how the appointment is made – you may know more about it than I do, and my man of business, Edwards, may have some knowledge. I have to go to my new ship as quickly as possible, but he will probably be going down to Dipton very soon. And my friend Bush is there right now, though I don't know how long he will be staying. You may want to go down to Dipton in order to see for yourself what it is like before committing yourself fully.

"Now on another matter entirely, you may be able to render me a great service. It concerns our sister Marianne."

"You know," said David, "I have never met Marianne, and I know almost nothing about her. Indeed, she has always a great mystery. Even that we have a sister. And no one would tell me about why we never saw her. Even Mother wouldn't enlighten me, and when I once asked Father, he became very angry."

"That was the same for me. I did know Marianne, I suppose, when I was a very small child, but I don't remember her at all and I never understood why she disappeared and no one talked of her. I only found out the story very recently – and largely because Mother felt we had to do something and Father absolutely refused.

"As you know Mother is Father's second wife. With his first wife, he had three children, our half-brothers Ashton and Thomas, and a sister Marianne. She was the middle child – and now must be about forty-five years old. Their mother, Father's first wife died. Marianne must have been about ten then and Thomas eight years old. A few years later, Father married Mother so she became the step-mother to Ashton, Marianne and Thomas. However, Father allowed Mother have little do to with their upbringing – indeed, they must have been pretty well full grown -- and he himself was not much concerned. Ashton and Thomas were sent off to Eton as soon as possible, and Marianne was brought up by a series of governesses. Mother confessed to me that she never liked Marianne and did not pay much attention to her. When she was 18, Marianne became involved with a territorial officer, Lieutenant Crocker. He basically seduced her and got her to elope with him, probably expecting that Father, faced with a *fait accompli,* would then provide a handsome dowry.

"This Father refused completely to do. The most he would do, and on the firm understanding that he would do nothing more for them, was to buy Lieutenant Crocker a majority in a not very fashionable Yorkshire regiment. Possibly he would have done more if Crocker had agreed to go to Canada, but he wouldn't. That was the last our family had anything to do with them for a long time.

"Major Crocker came into a small inheritance that, together with his army pay, allowed them to live in reasonable comfort. But that come to an end when Major Crocker died – from some sort of sickness. It turned out that they had gone through his inheritance and were deeply in debt. Marianne wrote to Father asking for money and including the information that he had two grandchildren: Catherine, aged 19, and Lydia, aged 16.

"Father absolutely refused to give Marianne a penny, but Mother felt that she should be helped, especially since there were granddaughters. Mother sent Marianne enough to last her a quarter (or so Mother thought) expecting that over that period she could talk Father into seeing that support was his duty – though we both know that when it comes to supporting his children, Father's idea of his duty is very limited.

"Unfortunately, within a month Marianne wrote again asking for money. And Father saw the letter which was the first time that he had heard of Mother's sending her money. Amid a great many recriminations – you know how they can row – Father absolutely prohibited Mother from sending more money – and, of course, there was nothing Mother could do about it. I had just returned to Ashton Abbey when this blew up, and Mother asked me to do something about Marianne.

"So I went up to Ripon and found that the situation was worse than I expected. Marianne had used Mother's money to pay some of the most urgent debts, but not all, and she had not paid the rent for their lodgings. She had spent the rest and had borrowed still more. I paid the rent up to the end of this quarter, paid off all the debts I could find, paid some of the tradesmen in advance, indicating that there would be no more money when that had been exhausted, and generally warned all and sundry that they would not be repaid if they lent Marianne more money."

"I imagine that Marianne was not too pleased with that," David remarked.

"She was not. Nor with anything else I proposed, but she had little choice. I had just bought Dipton Hall, and realized that the best solution, at least for the interests of our nieces, was to move the family to Dipton. I thought at first that they could occupy the Dower Cottage, but now I think that it might be better if they were in the Hall itself, where I shall be better able to control expenditure.

"Now to the favor I want to ask of you. I was intending to go back to Ripon to bring Marianne and her two daughters to Dipton -- in about a month or at most by the end of the quarter. I now have a new ship and so I will not be able to perform this task. I could ask Edwards, my prize agent who also looks after my affairs, but it would be better if a family member could do the job."

"I'll be very glad to help out in this way, if that is what you mean. I don't imagine you had either Ashton or Thomas in mind for the job."

"Quite right! Edwards will of course advance you enough to see the journey through – and he'll also provide some funds to cover any debts Marianne may have succeeded in arranging despite my efforts. Are you dining here tonight?"

"I hadn't really thought about it. If you are going to be here, I most certainly will so that we can get to know each other a bit better."

"I'd like that. Yes, I'll dine here. Now I have to see Steves and the rest of the servants before I go out. You might as well come too. Don't hesitate to interrupt if you think I am being preemptory."

In the drawing room, they found Steves together with Mrs. Wilson, the housekeeper and Mrs. Darling the cook. All three were standing and looking most uncomfortable. Giles wasted no time.

"I was appalled at Steves' news about my father closing this house and letting you all go. But from my own point of view, it may well be good news.

"As you may have heard, I have bought Dipton Hall. It is, of course, not as big or grand as Ashton Abbey – possibly more of the size of this house, though again not as grand. The previous staff were all let go. I would be very pleased if you could take on the positions you have been holding here for me at Dipton Hall. I will probably be away at sea quite a bit, but Lady Marianne and her two daughters will be living at the Hall. I would also be pleased to take on any of the other servants here who would like to come and in whom you have confidence. Lord David will be occupying the vicarage and will also need servants. And Captain Bush, together with his mother and sisters, may well be in the Dower Cottage at Dipton and they will also need servants.

"I can't expect you to answer now. But I wanted to tell you about the possibility, and ask you to tell the other servants about the situation."

"My lord," said Steves. 'This is most gracious of you. I confess that I didn't know what would become of me. I most gladly accept –I need no time to think it over."

Mrs. Wilson and Mrs. Darling murmured their acceptance as well.

"Good. Lord David and I will be dining here tonight. Now, I have to go out."

Giles' afternoon was both busy and productive. His meeting with Mr. Edwards started with the good news that his prizes had brought in more money than expected. He was more than happy to oversee the furnishing of Dipton Hall and to make sure that the financial matters went smoothly. He even volunteered to stand as scapegoat should Lady Marianne's demands run counter to Giles express wishes for restraint and to back Steves up if she should cause any problems. He would furthermore go down to Dipton himself with a Mr. Walters, whom Edwards described as being very good at prescribing furnishings in the latest and most elegant style. He would see to the Dower Cottage and the vicarage at the same time.

Edwards, however, balked at being involved in the running of the estate. He was rather horrified to learn that Giles had sacked his bailiff, and had no immediate replacement. The problem came to a head when Giles mentioned that he had been in discussion with Miss Moorhouse about draining some common fields and saying that he wanted her to go ahead with the project.

"Is that wise, Sir Richard? Surely you will want to have your steward look into the project before going ahead."

"Yes, but I don't have any reason to trust the steward. Indeed, I have no one to look after the management of the estate in whom I have any confidence. Miss Moorhouse has very well formed plans for the area. And she has the reputation for being the best farm manager in the county."

"Well, if you are sure, Sir Richard, I will arrange for your share of the funds required for the improvements to be made available. But I still do not think it wise."

"If you can't help with a steward or bailiff, I think I might ask Miss Moorhouse if she knows anyone suitable. Indeed, if she would be willing to do it, I would have her supervise anyone who might be able to undertake the tasks. Indeed, I don't suppose that she would be able to act in those positions herself."

"A woman – managing an estate?" Edwards was quite horrified by the idea.

That was enough to prod Giles, "Indeed, if she is more capable than others, I don't see why not. I'll suggest it to her. And authorize improvements to be made at her discretion up to – oh, up to 2000 pounds. I can afford that, can't I?"

"Yes, Sir Richard. But I must again point out that I think it is very unwise. But yes, you can afford it. But I must add that if you want to keep adding to your expenditures at the rate you have done today, it would be a good idea to capture some very valuable prizes."

Giles laughed. "I might just do that, since my next command is again a frigate. But rest assured, Evans, when I come ashore, I hope to live a quiet country life and expect my holdings to meet my needs fully."

It was a tired but contented Richard Giles who finally got to bed that evening. He had written all the letters arising from his activities of the day, he had arranged for the opening and running of Dipton Hall, and had even found Dipton a vicar, and one who it turned out he liked. He knew that once aboard ship, his concerns about Dipton would fade into the background and he would have found it difficult to focus on needed decisions – just as he realized that his concerns about *Phoebe* had retreated into the background when at Dipton to the extent that he had felt guilty about not being concerned about the crew when Newsome had mentioned them. He did not fall asleep immediately, however, an unusual state of affairs for someone raised in the midshipmen's birth where sleep had to be snatched whenever it was possible. Instead, Giles found himself thinking about how he had to learn more about managing his estate and hoping that he could find some congenial expert to provide instruction, and wondering if Miss Moorhouse might happen to be that expert.

Chapter III

Captain Tobias Bush was feeling sorry for himself. Indeed, he was wallowing in self-pity, and quite enjoying being miserable. He was sitting at ease in the parlor of the Dipton Arms with the remains of a satisfying breakfast in front of him, the sun beaming through the rather distorting glass of the windows, but still he was miserable.

Not that he didn't have good reason to feel sorry for himself. Here he was left in the lurch by his friend, indeed his patron, his former captain and a man to whom he was indebted for much of the professional progress and wealth that had come his way. The search for a suitable house had so far come to nothing and his need to find accommodation for his mother and sisters was becoming pressing. And his missing foot itched abominably.

That brought him to his career. He was a very junior post captain and even with Giles' influence, if Giles was willing to extend it to Bush, he could hope at most for a small frigate, say a 28. And he had trouble imagining himself as a frigate captain with only one leg and one arm. He certainly could not go aloft and he could not imagine being a frigate captain who did not mount the rigging when a reason for doing so arose. In his present, melancholy state, it did not occur to him that there were many captains who never went aloft. Bush was modeling himself after Giles, who frequently climbed to the masthead.

Indeed, Bush wasn't even sure he wanted to go back to sea. His father had used his one small bit of influence to secure Bush a midshipmen's berth since he could not afford to provide his son with an education suitable for a gentleman. Bush had been an excellent officer, but he had never really liked the sea and he had never relished a fight until he was actually in one. Then he was transformed into quite another man.

He had thought how pleasant it would be to settle down in some country place and never go to sea again. But that hope was coming to nothing. He and Giles had been exploring the possibility of some suitable place for Bush at the same time they were looking for an estate for Giles himself and they had found nothing. He would have to move into lodgings with his mother and sisters and he didn't know where to start looking for them. His mother did not want to remain in Harwich and he did not want to live in the only other town he knew at all well, Portsmouth.

It was not at all what Bush had expected to happen when the time came for him to set up a home on shore. He'd vaguely thought of a modest house in a pleasant village, with a wife, where he could live contentedly on half-pay. Now the idea of a wife ran into the fact that he was a cripple – no one would love him or want to marry him. And his father, in dying, had left him with the responsibility for his mother and two younger sisters.

His father had been the rector of a poor parish in Harwich. He had had just enough money to take care of his widow if the need should arise and to provide his two daughters with modest dowries, but little more. He had been able, through a third cousin, to secure for his son a midshipman's birth at age fourteen, thus alleviating the need to pay for Tobias's education and to set him up in a career. What his father had not counted on was becoming ill with consumption. His imminent death would leave his widow and daughters with inadequate income and no dowries. When a man of his acquaintance had approached the Reverend Bush to participate in a venture that would certainly yield sufficient returns to solve these problems, the naïve cleric had jumped at the opportunity. Unfortunately, the venture had failed, leaving the Reverend Bush's widow with hardly enough money to pay for his funeral.

This saga had happened just before Captain Bush returned, injured, from his last voyage. The wife of the new rector in his father's old parish insisted that Captain Bush's mother and sisters move out of the rectory immediately. They were at present living in not very comfortable lodgings in Harwich. Furthermore, the new rector's wife was making life a misery for his mother by constantly criticizing to others how Bush's father had acted in the parish and how his mother had kept up the rectory. The result was that his mother desperately wanted to leave Harwich. Bush had no idea of how or where he might find a better situation for them.

He would have to go to Harwich soon – but not today. He would stay in Dipton where he didn't have to do anything right away. With that decided, he summoned the serving man to order another mug of small beer to complete his breakfast. When the servant responded, he handed Bush a letter from Giles that had just arrived.

Dear Bush:

I write in haste. The Admiralty has given me a new frigate, Petroclus, a 36 built to an experimental design. I take command of her at Butler's Hard and then take her out for a mission of some urgency. The Admiralty kept most of the crew of Phoebe together and are letting me have them, together with Phoebe's warrant and petty officers, but we will still have to get the press gangs out. Poor old Phoebe is being condemned. I've got Davis and Miller as Lieutenants and a John Foster as first lieutenant. I don't know him; his last ship was Thunderer. There will also be a fellow from the Ordinance Board to begin with to look into the effectiveness of our cannon. We are supposed to drop him in Falmouth before proceeding with our mission. That will be in three weeks, I hope.

I am sorry to have left you in the lurch so suddenly.

Bush reflected guiltily that Giles had not left him in the lurch at all. Instead, he had invited him to come to London on the way to Harwich, but Bush, still aching from his riding experience, had stated that he preferred to spend some more time at Dipton. The truth was that not having found a place for them, Bush was delaying seeing his mother and sisters. He returned to the letter;

I have been thinking about the arrangements at Dipton. As you know, I intended to have my sister Marianne and my two nieces live in the Dower Cottage. But I realize that Marianne is bound to spend out of control if she has her own establishment. Instead, I will have them live in Dipton Hall with me. Even when I am away, my butler – I've retained my father's London butler, Steves – and he and Edwards should be able to keep control of things. But having thought of having Marianne at the Hall, I realized that the Dower Cottage would be ideal for you and your mother. It strikes me as being very much the sort of thing you have been looking for. And you would be doing me a great favor if you would take it. It would be a comfort to know that Marianne could count on my good friend if some troubles arose.

Bush warmed to Giles' referring to him as his good friend even more than he had to the offer of the cottage,

While my brother David is going to be vicar of Dipton, he is very young and I am not sure how he would stand up to the sort of challenge that Marianne might pose. Actually, if you could live at Dipton until you get a command, you would undoubtedly be able to give David good advice on any problems that he faces, for he too will be alone there and he is totally inexperienced.

Edwards will be going down to Dipton on Monday with someone who is an expert on furnishings and houses. I have asked him to consider the Dower Cottage as well. If you should take up my invitation, he can undoubtedly help in setting the cottage up. I think that Edwards also has some good news for you.

I do hope you will take up my offer. Next to having you with me on Petroclus, there is nothing I would like better than to have you as a neighbor at Dipton when I am ashore. It's a pity you got promoted! I could use a really good first lieutenant.

I remain your good friend,

Giles

The penultimate remark amused Bush. He was sure that the only reason he had been promoted was the very firm advocacy of Giles himself.

The offer of the house would appear to solve all his problems. Of course, Giles hadn't mentioned the rent, but Edwards would know what it would be and Giles wouldn't make the offer if he wasn't certain that it was within Bush's means. The offer of the cottage was actually quite exciting.

Bush glanced at his almost full tankard of beer. He didn't want it any more. Instead, he was thinking of what arrangements he would need to make about the Dower Cottage. He had only seen it at a distance, and he didn't think Giles had seen it either. Giles had been concentrating on Dipton Hall: what it needed and how to get servants. It sounded as if he had both problems well in hand and was letting Bush piggy-back on those solutions.

Out of the corner of his eye, Bush saw someone outside peering in the window, but couldn't make out the features against the light. Minutes later Daphne Moorhouse burst into the room.

"Oh, Captain Bush..." Daphne stopped as Bush struggled to his feet to bow. Remembering that she should have curtseyed first, she rectified the omission before ordering, "Don't get up."

"I'm not a total cripple, Miss Moorhouse," Bush replied testily, after he had bowed, "and the more times I do normal things, the easier they will become."

"Oh, I didn't mean to imply that you cannot do anything that is usual.

"I have received a letter from Captain Giles. He mentioned that he has invited you to take over the Dipton Dower Cottage. I do hope that you do. Father thoroughly enjoyed talking with you on Sunday. There is no one around here with whom he can discuss his passion – I am afraid that I can't keep any of those old generals and battles straight in my mind -- and the gentlemen around here can't tell the difference between Themistocles and Thermopylae. So we would really like you to settle here."

"That's very kind of you, Miss Moorhouse, but surely Captain Giles didn't write just to tell you that."

"No. The real reason was that he wants to go ahead with the drainage of the joint fields that we were supposed to look at before he had to rush away. That's what I am so excited about. To do it properly really requires doing the drainage on both properties. I was so afraid that Captain Giles's having to go away meant that it would not get done, at least not soon, since he didn't have a chance to inspect the area closely himself. Captain Giles says that a Mr. ..." Daphne fumbled in her reticule to try to extract Giles' letter. "Mr. Edwards, his prize agent, will be coming to Dipton on Monday and will arrange that Dipton Hall's share of the drainage will be paid for. But I am to be in charge completely. Oh, it's so exciting! But why is Captain Giles's prize agent coming?"

"Mr. Edwards is also Captain Giles's man of business as well mine. I am surprised he is coming himself rather than sending one of his junior associates. Captain Giles must have given him some important commissions – of course, one of them must be your drainage project. But there is a great deal more probably in arranging for the Hall and also there may be some provisions to be made for Lord David, Captain Giles' brother."

"Yes, Captain Giles mentioned that his brother would become vicar here. What he actually wrote was, 'Tell your father that there will be a new vicar at Dipton, but since it is his first parish, I cannot guarantee that this vicar will really be an improvement over the parson who has been handling the services at Dipton. But since he is my brother, I must hope for the best from him.' Well, he can't be worse than Mr. Twilgate."

"Have you seen the Dower Cottage, Captain Bush?"

"Only from the road, and even then I only got a glimpse of it. Until I received Giles' letter a few minutes ago, I had no reason to be interested in it."

"I have never been in it. It hasn't been let for the last few years, and my father developed an intense dislike for the previous tenants and forbade me to have anything to do with them. Would you like to explore it with me now? That is, if you..." Daphne paused, before she blurted out what she was going to say: "if you can walk that far", a statement that would likely be seen as even more insulting than the suggestion that Bush should not rise when she entered the room. Instead, Daphne continued, "... if you think there is any chance that you would like to live in this neighborhood."

Bush indeed wondered whether he could walk the few hundred yards that separated the inn from the Dower Cottage – and then walk back again. His leg had been troubling him and even short walks made the stump of his leg sore and inflamed. However, his previous ill-tempered remark made him reluctant to suggest that he was physically not able to make such a short journey.

"I'd like to see the cottage, indeed I would. But can we get into it on the spur of the moment?" Bush felt he had overcome his dilemma rather well, but that satisfaction was short-lived.

"I know that Tom, the innkeeper, has a key, kept from the times when Mr. Charles Gramley hoped to rent the cottage while he did not want to trouble himself to show the house."

At that moment, the innkeeper entered the room, intending to ask if Miss Moorhouse would like some refreshment. But before he could ask, Daphne addressed him: "Tom, do you have the key to the Dower Cottage?"

"Yes, Miss, I do."

"Well, Captain Giles has asked Captain Bush to stay in the Dower Cottage with his family and he would like to see it. Could we have the key, please?"

"Certainly, Miss. I'll just get it."

Within minutes, Bush was on his feet, hat on his head, and stout stick in his hand.

It was only a short distance to the Dower Cottage, which was partially hidden from the road by shrubs and trees. When they turned into the drive leading to the establishment, Bush was confronted with a large and elegant house in the style of 80 years previously in red brick with white trim and cornices. It featured large windows on the ground and first floors. It was also notable for an imposing main entrance. The unkempt grounds spoke of long neglect.

"I had no idea the Dower Cottage was so large," Bush exclaimed.

"Yes, it really isn't a cottage at all, though that is what everyone calls it," responded Daphne. "I have heard that Mr. Gramley's grandfather inherited the estate when he was quite young. His father had married a second time, and his second wife had borne him several children. Mr. Thomas, for that was the Mr. Charles's grandfather's name, or rather more likely Mr. Thomas's wife, had no desire to share the Hall with his father's second family, and so he built this house to accommodate them. Since there was a large number of children, he had to provide a much larger house than would be the case if it were just his step-mother who had to be housed. Hence, while tradition makes the appropriate name 'the Dower Cottage', in fact it is quite a substantial house. There should be plenty of space for your mother and two sisters as well as yourself."

Bush was flattered that Daphne had remembered what he had mentioned about his family. He was also pleased to find that the house was substantial, for while reveling in Giles's offer, he had been afraid that his family would be a bit crowded in a cottage.

The key grated roughly in the lock when Daphne tried it, but the lock did yield and she was able to wrestle the door open. Neglect was immediately obvious. There was a damp smell, cobwebs were evident in the corners of the ceiling of the entry way and in the windows that flanked the door, and there were mouse tracks all over the hallway. The same was true elsewhere as they explored the rooms. But even so, the basic attractiveness of the house was evident, even though there was no furniture of any kind.

"I had heard that Mr. Gramley auctioned off the contents of the Cottage," remarked Daphne, "but I had no idea of how completely he had cleared the place out. It certainly gives you the chance to furnish it exactly as you want, Captain Bush. Or does your Mother have her own furniture?"

"No, only one or two favorite pieces. But this is a daunting challenge." This from a man who had faced French gunfire without flinching.

"It is, but not so great as it might appear. A good cleaning is needed first and then some paint or paper on the walls and brightening up the trim. Then it will be quite a different place. But let's explore upstairs."

The first floor was as pleasant as the main floor, with light streaming into the main bedrooms. There was indeed enough room for Bush, his mother and each of his sisters to have their own rooms, with the two main rooms having separate dressing rooms. There was even a couple of extra rooms that would serve for guests.

"This is wonderful," enthused Bush, "I am sure that my mother and sisters will love the house. But how do I get it furnished and ready? I suppose that Edwards might have some ideas. Captain Giles mentioned that he was arranging for the Hall to be brought to order and furnished."

"If Mr. Edwards doesn't come through, I am sure there are contacts in the village who can set you on the right path," said Daphne a bit testily. She had had in the back of her mind that she could guide the preparation of the Dower Cottage, and had been excited by the prospect. "But I would think that the first thing is to get it cleaned up – that is if you have made up your mind to take it."

"Yes, I think I will. But how in the world do I manage to get it cleaned up before Edwards and his arranger arrive?"

"My maid, Elsie, has a cousin living in the village. She's married to the hostler at the inn, who can organize several women to do the job. I'll ask her if you like."

"Please. It is very good of you to be so concerned."

Daphne carried most of the conversation as they completed their inspection and walked down the drive, chattering on about her hopes for the drainage project and about the possibilities of refurbishing the Dower Cottage. She did not notice that she was getting ahead of Captain Bush, until he called a halt, saying, "I'm sorry, but I have to rest my leg a while," as he sank down onto a convenient, low, stone wall.

Daphne was horrified. "Oh, no! What is it?"

"I am afraid that my stump has become too painful to continue immediately. And my other leg and my back are aching terribly."

"Stay right there. Mr. Jackson, our apothecary, is just across the road. I will fetch him at once."

Daphne scurried off and returned in a few minutes with a tall, rather grizzled man.

"So, your stump is giving problems. Let's see it. I'll need some help to get your trousers down. Daphne, please go and tell Jake to come

"A remarkable girl that," Jackson continued after Daphne disappeared on her errand. "She is the best assistant I can get, but her father only lets her help – because he can't stop her – when it involves one of the people on his own estate. If she were a man, she would make the best doctor in these parts. But then, she already is the best estate manager."

He broke off when a burly young man came through the gateway and up the drive.

"Jake, give me a hand here, I want to see Captain Bush's stump so we have to get his trousers out of the way. Oh, Captain Bush, this is Jake. He is a carpenter by trade and there is no one better at making artificial limbs and crutches and sticks to help in walking."

With Jake's help, Jackson soon had Bush's trousers down, the peg-leg unstrapped and the red and swollen stump revealed. Jackson delicately pushed and prodded at the stump causing some more pain even though he clearly was trying to be gentle.

"When did you suffer the injury?" asked Jackson.

"It must be six months ago, now."

"You have more of a pad over the bone than most surgeons seem to leave, so there is no basic trouble. But the peg-leg was not fitted properly. It doesn't conform to the shape of your stump. That's why it is causing so much pain. It is also too short. That and your stick being too short also account for your other leg being sore and your back aching.'

Jackson dug into his pocket and produced a jar of ointment which he rubbed onto the stump.

"I'll give you this salve to help soothe the stump. Apply it every few hours. When the swelling is down, Jake here can craft you a new peg-leg. He'll make you a new cane as well – of the proper length. You'll have to go easy for a while, but after that you should have no more problems. You will have to be pretty immobile until the swelling goes down and Jake can fit the new leg. I don't want you using the old leg – it will just slow the healing down. Now Jake, go and fetch the cart and we'll get Captain Bush back to the inn."

Raising his voice, Jackson called, "Daphne. You can come out now."

Daphne showed up almost at once.

"How did you know I was there?"

"I heard you talking to Mrs. James. We will take Captain Bush back to the inn and he has to avoid using his leg for a few days. Don't try to make him go on any more excursions with you."

"Daphne didn't make me go with her." Bush protested. "I was eager to see the cottage when she suggested it."

"Yes. Well I know how persuasive her suggestions can be," replied Jackson, "and the more you use your leg right now, the longer it will take before you are really mobile again."

Jake returned with a horse-drawn cart. Jackson and he lifted Bush into the cart. Jackson and Daphne accompanied the cart to the inn where again Jackson and Jake carried Bush in and deposited him in a comfortable chair in front of the fire.

They left, and so did Daphne explaining that her father would be expecting her and would get very worried if she was away much longer than expected.

Bush settled into his chair comfortably, leg up on a stool. He was contemplating what to have for luncheon when into the room came Mr. Moorhouse followed by two husky men dressed like farm laborers.

"Daphne told me of your problems, Captain Bush. It makes no sense for you to remain at the inn. They will have an awful time getting you up the narrow stairs to your room and there are no decent rooms on the ground floor. The only solution is for you to come and stay with us. Harry and Gordon here can easily carry you to the carriage and up and down stairs, which you may recall are quite wide. No, I won't take 'no' for an answer. Quite apart from the fact that I will be delighted to have you as a guest for a while, Daphne won't hear of your not coming."

Bush's protests went for nothing. Before he knew what was happening, he was bundled up, carried to Mr. Moorhouse's carriage by the two strong laborers, and placed inside where he was joined by Mr. Moorhouse who promptly gave the signal to proceed.

Daphne was equally firm when they reached Dipton Manor. "You'll be no bother at all, Captain Bush. Father is delighted to have a fellow enthusiast in the house. You can't stay at the inn while waiting for your new leg to be fitted – too uncomfortable – and you cannot think of proceeding to Harwich until you have seen Mr. Edwards. But you must write your mother at once to tell her the news and prepare her for the move. Here, we have a portable writing desk that you can put across your knees."

Bush decided to accept the hospitality with good grace. It was just what he wanted, and there was no point protesting out of politeness something that his hosts so full heartedly offered.

Chapter IV

Giles and Carstairs arrived at Butler's Hard at 10:30 a.m. in a gig from Portsmouth. It had been a slow trip since the coach from London had lost a wheel on the way and many hours passed before a replacement was found. They had needed to stay at a cramped inn in Portsmouth before being able to hire the gig to take them on their way. The sight that greeted them as they rounded the final curve seemed to compensate for all the discomfort and annoyances.

The sun was breaking through the clouds which had recently delivered rain. Shafts of light illuminated the scene. The river, somewhat muddy from the recent rains, seemed to ooze through the countryside as the rising tide met the current, producing only lazy swirls to show that it was alive. Beyond, flat, semi-marsh land gave way to forest trees, with a few ponies grazing in the distance. The centerpiece of this idyll was a frigate, obviously new, painted black with white paint outlining the gun ports, and decks still showing new wood, floating high, anchored in the middle of the river. It was almost finished from all appearances: the masts were stepped, the standing rigging in place and the yards crossed, but it was still lacking sails and some running rigging. A swarm of men was working on her, some aloft, and more on the main decks, some in laborers' clothes, others clearly sailors. Despite this bustle, the glass-like river gave the scene a feeling of peace with the frigate reflected in it, and the country side still. The frigate was the only vessel anchored in the river, but three ships were on the ways in various stages of completion.

Giles went directly to the works office where Joshua Stewart greeted him enthusiastically, "Captain Giles, *Patroclus* is ready. A few details and changes, which your master and bosun suggested, are being completed as we speak. Water's aboard, and provisions are supposed to arrive today, or so the Admiralty says. You can be on your way once your people get the sails bent on and the guns are in place. The Admiralty took the unusual step of bringing the guns to us rather than having you take them on board in Portsmouth. Something about not providing information to any spies there. Probably because of your bow chasers. They are twenty-four pounders, and I cannot guarantee that she can carry more, though the chappy from the Ordnance Board is talking thirty-four's. Your powder's not on board either. You should find her a fine ship, Captain."

"I'll need to inspect her fully, Mr. Stewart, before I can take possession," Giles interrupted his flow of words.

"Of course, Captain, of course. I think I saw one of your boats at the jetty, but if it's not there, I'll easily arrange a boat to take you out to her right away. Perhaps you can dine with me when your inspection is finished."

One of *Patroclus*'s boats was indeed at the jetty, under Midshipman Correll. Giles greeted him warmly, and nodded at the crew, all of whom seemed delighted to see him. They rowed smartly out to the anchored frigate, where Giles was properly piped on board, though even the boatswain's mates seemed to have trouble withholding their grins until the calls were ended.

"Mr. Davis, it's good to see you," Giles greeted the officer who stepped forward to meet him, "Has the First Lieutenant not come aboard yet?"

"No sir. And we've received no news of when he will arrive."

"Very well. Be so good as to assemble all hands so I can read myself in."

Giles greeted the other officers, and warrant officers, all of whom were well known to him, while the crew gathered. He then pulled from his coat the sturdy commission which gave him the authority to command the ship and gave him virtually the power of life or death over those before him. Those awesome words in no way seemed to disturb those who heard him. Giles, as always, felt qualms about his ability to truly fulfill all aspects of the burden he was taking up.

"I need to inspect the ship completely, from keel to topmast cap, before I can sign for her. Mr. Davis, come with me together with the Boatswain and the Carpenter. The little group formed and started to go over the ship carefully, noting every joint, rib and plank. The bilges were almost dry, having been pumped in anticipation of the Captain's inspection, and hardly smelled at all.

"A bit of vinegar in here, Mr. Shearer, I think."

"Aye, aye, sir. Though we already emptied two casks into it after pumping her."

"Very good, Mr. Shearer. I don't really need to tell you your business, do I?"

"No sir. I mean…"

"I know what you mean, Bill, and you are quite right."

They continued on their way, noting the few things that the others had already pointed out to the men from the yard who were still working to fix them. From keel to topmast and from stem to stern, everything was carefully examined. It spoke highly both of the shipyard and of the warrant officers, who had made very exacting inspections of everything that fell within their domains, that Giles found no changes to be made or short-comings to be set right that had not already been found by his subordinates. By late afternoon, they were through. Giles ordered his boat brought along side and with all the pomp that saw a captain over the side of his ship, returned to the jetty near Mr. Stewart's office.

"Is everything satisfactory, Sir Richard?" Mr. Stewart queried Giles as he entered his room.

"Yes, indeed. I went over her completely and am very pleased with the workmanship. Your people are completing the few flaws that my men have found. As soon as our guns, provisions and powder and shot are aboard we will sail."

"I understand that the barges bringing the guns will be here tomorrow, and the other supplies the next day. I must say it is unusual for the Admiralty to come to us. Most ships proceed to Portsmouth for taking on board their supplies."

"It may have something to do with the Admiralty not wanting us to be delayed by the maneuvering that usually slows everything in Portsmouth."

"Possibly. I hope you don't need crew. All my workers, and most of the men in the surrounding area have their protections, so a press gang would have very slim pickings."

"Thanks for the warning. We are indeed short of men."

"Well, Captain Giles, I wish you luck. Now I have some very good Madeira and we should drink to *Patroclus* and all who will sail in her."

The two men settled comfortably into arm chairs on either side of the fireplace, to sip their wine and talk about a variety of subjects. The only part of real interest to Giles was when the discussion turned to the new design embodied in *Patroclus*.

"I trust that the decrease in beam will make her a faster ship," Mr. Stewart opined. "The heavier bow chasers should also make her a more dangerous opponent. But I think that twenty-four pounders are all she can take. I would have been happier with long eighteens. I know that the Ordinance Office believes that thirty-four pounders would be still more effective, but I am not sure how she would stand the recoil of the heavier guns. As I said, I am even a bit leery of the twenty-fours. It is a big step up from the long nine's that usually constitute the bow chasers."

"Time will tell, I suppose. I'm sure that the man from the Ordinance board who will be overseeing our armament on our shakedown cruise will have an opinion. I am afraid that I shall simply have to rely on his knowledge. I know how to sail and fight a ship, but less about how to evaluate what strains she can undergo. Now I must get back to *Patroclus*. Thank you for the wine. I am afraid that I shall have to forego dinner."

"There is one thing, Captain. My boy, Daniel. He's fourteen. I wanted him to be apprenticed in the shipyard so he would be fully qualified to take over from me when the time comes, but he is dead set on being a seaman. He even argues that sailing ships would give him more insight into what is required than building them. I suppose I should just put my foot down, but I have a very soft spot for him."

"Yes?"

"Do you have a berth for a midshipman, Captain?"

"I might have. But you do realize, Mr. Stewart, that we are going to war, and even at the best of times, sailing on a frigate is not the safest of occupations. In war, it is much more hazardous."

"I know. It's one of the reasons I would like him here, but he wants to go and see the world. His mother supports him, since that is what he is dying to do. I think she also believes that it is a way for him to become a true gentleman. I can't say no. Do you have a berth for him?"

"Yes, I do, Mr. Stewart. As long as you understand the risks, but he'll have to be quick. I'll need him aboard by tomorrow afternoon."

"Very good, Captain. He has already talked me out of the uniform and a dirk, and his mother has his sea chest all ready. And thank you. Many captains come through here who only want midshipmen with influence, and there are others with whom I would not like to have him sail. You have the reputation of not being concerned about influence, and no captain has a better reputation in guiding young gentlemen."

"It's good of you to say so, Mr. Stewart, though you surprise me. I can imagine no one I would prefer to have on my side than a lad who was involved in the building of my ship."

"My pleasure, Captain. I wish you good luck."

"Thank you, Mr. Stewart. I know you have done all you can to make the odds favorable to us."

As Giles left the works office, he noticed a crowd of men gathered at the end of the jetty. One man, wearing a lieutenant's uniform, seemed to be haranguing the crowd. The lieutenant's uniform seemed to be of the best material and cut, not what one would normally expect a junior officer to be wearing, especially if he were journeying to a shipyard. The lieutenant's hat was also of very good quality and somewhat rakish.

"Stand back, you scum! Stand back, I say! I am a King's officer. Clear the way! Stand clear of the jetty!" The effect of these cries was reduced by the rather high pitched and feeble voice of the officer.

Giles realized that the crowd was not blocking access to the jetty in any way, though some of its members stood on the edge of the approach to it. He also noted that the lieutenant seemed to be accompanied by a laborer holding the handles of a barrow with a large sea-chest in it. Near the far end of the jetty, Carstairs was standing, a look of disbelief on his face.

"What seems to be the trouble, lieutenant?" Giles asked, coming up to the angry man. Giles had come ashore wearing his oldest uniform coat and ragged britches, not wanting to change his clothes before visiting the yard. The clothes were fine enough for a ship's inspection that might well involve crawling around in the bilges or rubbing against tarred lines, but they made Giles look like one of the many still unemployed captains with no influence who often hovered around Royal Navy locations, even though no duty took them there.

"This rabble should not be in a King's boatyard, and certainly not lounging around where naval officers are at work."

"Lieutenant, this is a private yard, and I don't see that these men are doing any harm."

"They have no business here!"

"I don't know about that. What is your name, lieutenant?"

"I am Lieutenant John Foster, first Lieutenant of the frigate *Patroclus*. I am told that she is here."

Giles heart sank at the news that this was his new first lieutenant, but retained his civil manner, "Yes, your frigate is the one anchored out in the stream. One of her boats is at the end of the jetty. I imagine that you must be wanted aboard, Lieutenant Foster."

"Yes, indeed. Some of us have pressing duties to perform. Come along, man," Foster said to the laborer with the barrow, "I must get aboard."

Giles suppressed a smile. Knowing Carstairs, Lieutenant Foster would be cooling his heels until Giles wanted to go aboard, unless Foster could be persuaded that he should pay for a wherry to take him out to the frigate.

Giles turned to the men who had been subjected to Foster's harangue. They seemed mainly to be seamen, many of whom had their dunnage with them. He immediately recognized several faces in the crowd and the more he looked, the more faces he knew. The men he recognized were former shipmates dating back in one instance to when Giles was a midshipman.

"Humphries," he cried to one of the men standing nearest to him and who seemed to be some sort of leader. "It's a long time since I've seen you. And there's Trevelyan, and Jones. And Weston. By all that's holy, you all represent a catalogue of my past. What brings you here?"

"We heard that you had been given a new frigate, sir. We thought that you might need hands, so here we are," Humphries replied.

Giles reflected that the secrecy of the Admiralty had not prevented the latest news being spread wide and far by the network of old tars. In this case the failure of secrecy seemed to have the best possible effect. He was nevertheless amazed that the news had caused these men to come to an out-of-the way place like Butler's Hard. It never occurred to Giles that his own reputation, as a captain, was among the very best, or that seamen would rather serve under him than under any other captain.

"That accounts for those of you who have served with me, but what about the rest."

"Why, sir, some are like my brother, Jed, there, who has heard my tales and wants to go to sea himself. Others gathered that you were a lucky captain as well as a fair one, and they'd do better with you than waiting for the press to take them. The seamen among us were all paid off at the end of the war, and many have had a hard time. We'd all prefer to sail with you than have the press catch us and then dump us in some bleeding ship of the line with hardly any prospect of prize money that doesn't come with half the crew killed. A frigate under a bold captain promises much better rewards."

"Well, you are all welcome, especially since you come willingly. I'll arrange for boats to take you out to *Patroclus* – there she is, anchored out in the stream -- and we'll get you signed in. I'll arrange your money for signing voluntarily. I'm glad to have you all. We are rushing to sail as soon as possible, but I will make sure to take time to reacquaint myself with all who have sailed with me before and to get to know those who don't know me at all."

Giles set off at once for the end of the jetty. John Foster was sitting in the stern sheets of the boat along with Midshipman Correll. From the look on Correll's face, and of the rest of the crew, the introduction to Foster had not gone smoothly.

"Mr. Correll, we have some new shipmates to ferry out to *Patroclus*. We can take a couple now, and you will have to return to the jetty to get others as soon as you can. We'll use the other boats as well. Carstairs, we can take two people right now. Can you get them?"

When they reached *Patroclus*, Giles went up the side first to the twitter of the bosun's call, "Mr. Davis this is Mr. Foster, our first lieutenant – Mr. Foster, Mr. Davis our second. Mr. Correll will show you to your berth. Report to me when you have settled in. Mr. Davis, there are some recruits on the jetty. Send all our boats for them. And I want a meeting of all officers in my cabin at seven bells."

Giles proceeded to his cabin. There was already mounds of paper work to be dealt with. The ship had yet to raise anchor and already all the demands of the Admiralty clerks were threatening to overwhelm him. He badly needed to find a clerk, since the previous one had been one of the men who had been drafted to another ship. He would also need a servant, but for that he would rely first on Carstairs' judgment. Any lieutenant worth his salt would try to foist his most useless seaman on the captain as a servant. He wondered if Foster was such a lieutenant.

That thought alone seemed to produce the announcement by the marine sentry that the First Lieutenant was at the door. Foster had changed his uniform, but the new one, though somewhat worn, was again of the finest quality and most flattering cut. Giles decided to ignore the misunderstanding when they first met.

"Mr. Foster. Welcome aboard! Tell me about yourself."

"I was most recently first lieutenant on *Thunderer*, thirty-two, Captain Pritchard, a fine captain, though his enemies malign him. I expected to sail with him again while waiting for my step, but somehow the Admiralty fouled their anchor in making his appointment and also in appointing me here. I trust that they will clear up the error in short order."

"Be that as it may, you are welcome here. We load our guns tomorrow and our powder and shot the following day, and then we can sail. I want to get to sea as soon as possible.

"You'll find the other officers willing and helpful, though Mr. Miller has only recently been promoted from midshipman. They have been with me in the past. As have the warrant and petty officers. We are getting a new middy tomorrow. He'll be green as grass, so go easy on him to begin with. We probably do not have a full crew, but we'll have to see how many have joined today and whether there are any other eager souls to come along. The surgeon is not here yet. Hopefully, he will arrive before we sail.

"The most urgent task is to make the watch and station bills. Mr. Davis, the second lieutenant can help there, he knows all the crew who were already on board. Carstairs, my cox'un, can also help, he knows many of the new men, I believe."

"I am quite capable of making up the bills myself, sir."

"No doubt, but it never hurts to have help."

"When I am going to be responsible for the results, I like to keep the process to myself."

"Of course, Mr. Foster. You can be held responsible for results. But like all of us, you will have to rely on the strengths of your subordinates. Just as I am ultimately responsible for everything that happens on this ship, including the watch and station bills. An officer is foolish who does not use the capabilities of others to perfect his own endeavors."

"Aye, aye, sir," Foster responded in a rather surly tone. As he left, Giles reflected that it would not be easy to like Foster, but for the sake of the ship he would have to try.

The next day the lighters with the guns and their carriages arrived. The guns would have to be brought aboard one at a time, with the tackles rearranged each time. Davis was in charge, with the gunner and bosun also coordinating the work. Giles saw that the task was proceeding without problem and switched his attention to other matters.

"Mr. Foster, we need to bend on the new sails."

"Aye-aye, sir,"

Giles was distracted by a call from the side announcing a man of some importance coming aboard. He hurried over, before giving Foster any more instructions, but surely any first lieutenant didn't have to be told that the sailmaker and the master would want to examine each sail carefully as it was put in place.

The arrival turned out to be a Mr. Timothy Hughes from the Ordinance Board, a large, rather jolly- seeming, red-faced man, who greeted Giles with gusto, after saluting the quarterdeck.

"Captain Giles. Good to meet you, sir. I apologize for being late. Damn horse lost its shoe. I see that you have started. Excellent! Let me see!"

Hughes bounded over to where the guns were being unloaded, stopping just clear of where the latest one was being lowered gingerly onto its carriage.

"Excellent, Captain Giles. Your men know their work. Excellent! If I might make one small suggestion, the slings for the cannon could be positioned just a little differently so that it would be easier to position the gun and to remove the slings when they are no longer needed. I hope you don't mind my pointing it out to the men."

Presuming Giles acceptance, Hughes promptly went to the bosun and made his suggestions in the most diplomatic and even deferential way, even though everyone knew that this interloper had to be obeyed. The suggestions actually were good ones, and Giles filed away the better way of cradling guns for use in similar circumstances. He had been afraid that Hughes' presence on board would be an irritant, the man himself a self-pretentious busy-body with no knowledge of ship-board problems and procedures. He was pleasantly surprised to find that the expert wanted to use his expertise to help rather than just to impress.

"Very good, Mr. Hughes. If I can be of further assistance be so good as to let me know."

Giles turned back to the other aspects of readying his ship for departure. When he looked aloft, it seemed that Foster was trying to raise every sail on every mast at the same time. There was no sign of either the master or the sailmaker.

"Mr. Foster, what is going on?"

"We are bending the sails to the yards."

"All of them at once?"

"Yes, sir, that was how we did the drill on *Thunderer.*"

"You do realize that these are new sails on a new ship, don't you?"

"Yes, sir."

"Did it not occur to you that the sailmaker and the master would want to examine each sail as it was first unfurled to check its cut?"

"No, sir."

"Well then, you should have considered it. Indeed, you should make sure that you inform the master and the sailmaker about what you are doing, and that the sails are bent on one sail at a time, so that those officers can examine them. We can't have the sails all flapping about and catching gusts of wind while loading the guns"

"Aye, aye, sir. Mr. Miller, you heard the Captain. See too it."

Miller quickly started to issue a string of orders to halt further sails being sent aloft and to furl the ones that were already bent on. The orders came so quickly that Giles suspected that the greenhorn third lieutenant had already been practicing in his mind what orders he would give if he were in charge.

"Mr. Foster," Giles turned back to the first lieutenant, "I asked *you* to get the master and sailmaker here. Please do so, since we can't proceed without them."

"Aye, aye, sir. Mr. Miller, my compliments to the sailmaker and the master. They are to come on deck immediately."

Giles was starting to wonder what was the point of having a first lieutenant if the man simply passed on any orders which he was given without amplifying them or taking any action himself. This reflection was broken when Giles noticed the situation that had developed on the main yard. Among the string of orders which Miller had given was one to clear those yards where the sails had not yet been raised. One such yard was the main yard, and Giles saw that one man was frozen.

"Mr. Foster, I see that you have mixed some landsmen with the seamen on the yards."

"Yes, sir. I thought being at anchor would be a very good time to get them some experience."

"A good thought, Mr. Foster. Did you consult with Mr. Davis or Carstairs as I suggested?"

"No sir, I am quite capable of making up a station list."

"Are you? Look at the mainsail yard, starboard side."

"Yes, sir?"

"What do you see?"

"Four men, apparently idling. Ahoy…"

"Belay that! I am talking to you, Mr. Foster. I asked you, 'What do you see?' I didn't ask you to yell at people. Now, what do you see?"

"Four men idling and disobeying orders."

"Do you? Do they look puzzled to you? As if they do not know what to do?"

"Possibly."

"Do you know who you have up there?"

"Let me check my list…yes there are two landsmen who joined yesterday and one able seaman and one topman."

"What do you know about them?"

"Nothing."

"Nothing. Would it surprise you to know that the seaman has only recently been rated able, at the end of his last voyage? Or that the topman is known for acrophobia?"

"Acrophobia? What is that?"

"Fear of heights, Mr. Foster. Fear of heights. Jenks, for that is the name of the man and I will expect you to learn it soon, Jenks was notorious in *Phoebe* for being one of the best men aloft when there was a blow or a problem. But if he was left with nothing to do on the yard, especially in calm weather, he would freeze up completely in terror. You should have known that. Mr. Foster."

"How could I?"

"Mr. Foster, I told you to consult Mr. Davis or Carstairs in drawing up your bill. I told you to do that because they know the men. The crew are not little pegs that you can plug into little holes. They are men who count on us to keep them as safe as we can. Do you understand? The navy is dangerous as it is, without officers who cannot be trusted to do their best for the crew. I don't want something like this to happen again ever. You are to redo the bills with the aid and…and, yes, the advice of Mr. Davies and Carstairs."

"I'll send them to you in the wardroom as soon as I see to this mess."

Giles turned away. "Harris, Trueblood, help Jenks off the main yard and look after those two new men. Mr. Davis, help Mr. Foster with watch and station lists. I'll take over getting the guns aboard, though Mr. Hughes seems to be doing a more than capable job.

"Mr. Osmond, how is the cut of the mizzen topsail? When you are finished, we can move on to the Mainmast.

"Mr. Brooks, see to hoisting the sails as they are needed and taking down any that need more work."

Giles turned his attention to the loading of the guns. It was going slowly, because Hughes insisted on checking each carriage before the gun could be lowered onto it, getting the carpenter to make any alterations needed. And then he insisted on having the gun run in and out a couple of times before giving the gun his approval and moving on to the next one. Seeing that all was proceeding smoothly, Giles turned his attention to other matters. Glancing ashore to the shipyard, he saw that there was another large group of men who seemed to be waiting for someone to pay attention to them.

"Mr. Foster, send a boat to find out if those men are more recruits and to bring them here if they are."

The boat returned laden with seamen who again were volunteering to serve with Giles. It also brought Dr. Maclean, the Scottish surgeon for whose arrival Giles had been waiting eagerly.

"Dr. Maclean, I was afraid that we might have to sail without you."

"I am glad to be here, though the message only reached me two days ago in Inverness."

"So you did get home. Is everything all right there?"

"Aye. If you can call my father dying while I was away, and news of my sister's husband perishing in Jamaica and her with a child on the way all right. I was busy there, I can tell ye, and just as glad to have a strong reason to leave."

"You are much needed already. We have a large number of volunteers for you to check, and the men from the *Phoebe* have had a good run ashore before coming here, so you may be busy treating them."

Giles was called away from further discussion with the surgeon by Mr. Hughes.

"Captain, before we bring aboard the long twenty-fours that will be the bow chasers, I would like to explore how the bow is made again, so that I can judge the effect of the guns themselves, and also have a standard to compare against after we fire them. I need to take the carpenter with me."

"I'll come too." said Giles, recognizing that later he might have to make similar inspections when they came to fire the bow chasers without the presence of Mr. Hughes. It was not easy to get close to the relevant part of the bow, right at the top under the deck where the bow chasers would go. Mr. Hughes was nodding his head wisely, "She should be able to absorb the effects of firing the bow chasers, which will have a heavier recoil than is usual. But the test will come when we actually fire them."

The carpenter nodded his agreement, and the party crawled out of the cramped space and returned to the deck. Getting the bow-chasers aboard and mounted was accomplished swiftly.

The following day was given over to taking aboard the powder and shot for the guns and some additional stores that had arrived by lighter. They were finally ready to sail and had only to wait for the turn of the tide on the following morning to take *Patroclu*s to sea.

The following day dawned clear and bright with a light breeze from the west-northwest. A small crowd of workers from the shipyard, led by Mr. Stewart and his family, gathered on the bank to wish them well. Giles gave the order to raise the anchor and to unfurl the main topsail and jib. Patroclus gathered way to the cheers of the onlookers which continued until she rounded the first bend. Despite having a pilot on board, Giles had ordered a man into the chains with a lead line, knowing the unusual draft of *Petroclus* might invite grounding if the pilot was unable to fully adjust to her unusual nature. They glided down river, with just enough wind to maintain steerage, hastened by the ebbing tide and the river's current, the crew getting early experience as the trim of the sails had to be altered frequently because of the bends in the river. The countryside consisted of lush meadows and clumps of forest, an idyllic and beautiful setting that seemed at odds with the fact that they were sailing to war.

Chapter V

Bush found that it was most enjoyable to let the Moorhouses dictate the pace of his recovery. His period of inactivity was alleviated by conversation with Mr. Moorhouse, but not so much as to become tiresome, and a library full of volumes in which he could lose himself as he wiled away the time. The enforced inactivity, for Daphne had made sure that all in the household would strive to meet Bush's needs without any use of his leg, meant that the swelling in his stump diminished rapidly so that by Friday morning Mr. Jackson, accompanied again by Jake, declared that a new leg could now be fitted. Bush suggested that the new leg include Carstairs' improvement to make it fit a stirrup.

"That is a grand idea," said Jake. "I was thinking of making the base a bit broader than on the leg you have, sir, and maybe have the blacksmith fashion an iron tip, so it will not wear down soon. I think the blacksmith can incorporate a grove that will fit a stirrup easily. We can certainly try to make it so."

As the two men were leaving, Daphne intercepted them. "When will the new leg be finished?"

Jackson looked at Jake.

"We should be able to bring it here on Monday morning," Jake said confidently.

"You are not going to work on it on Sunday surely?" Daphne sounded horrified.

"No. But we won't get it finished before late on Saturday afternoon."

"Then hurry and bring it over on Saturday when you get it finished," suggested Daphne. "Captain Bush would like to get used to it before he meets his agent on Monday."

"If you are sure it will not interfere with your dinner or evening…"

"Of course, it won't. It is much more important to get Captain Bush's leg to him as soon as possible."

Mr. Jackson and Jake, in fact, returned in the middle of Saturday afternoon, while Daphne was away on some business connected with the manor. The leg was quickly fitted, and needed only slight adjustments with Jake's chisel before Mr. Jackson was satisfied. It had a leather socket lined with wool and Bush immediately found that the new leg was much more comfortable than his previous one had been. Jake had also fashioned a beautiful cane from ash that was a bit longer than Bush's previous one.

"You need to get accustomed to this leg gradually so that the stump can get toughened up steadily. But if you do increase use of the leg steadily, you should find that the leg causes no more problems and soon you can use it as much as you want."

"I can't thank you enough, Mr. Jackson."

"Don't thank me. Thank Miss Moorhouse for taking you under her wing. She is a remarkable young lady."

"You know her well?"

"I suppose I do. I've known her since she was just a small child, and have watched her grow. I know no one more adventurous and courageous and kind-hearted than she is. Let me tell you one story which illustrates why I have such a high regard for her."

Jackson took a seat, pulled out his pipe, lit it and proceeded:

"I was called one day to the house of one of the farm laborers who work for the Moorhouses. He was in a very bad way. There is a small appendage on the intestine that can sometimes become afflicted and fill with poison. When this happens, it is very painful and if the sack containing the poison bursts – and it usually does in severe cases – it is always fatal. Sometimes the condition goes away by itself, but rarely when the pain is acute. The only solution is to operate on the patient in order to remove the sack before it bursts, but the operation in itself is very dangerous and the patient usually dies of infection of the wound. I determined that the poor man had developed this condition and the chances of his surviving without the operation were extremely low.

"I really had no choice but to operate. However, I would need assistance. When I mentioned the need for help in the operation to the poor man's wife she collapsed completely and the only other person there, a man, turned white and almost fainted at the thought of the operation. Luckily for the patient, Miss Moorhouse had come by to express her sympathies, and she insisted that she would help. And help she did! When I mentioned that using clean cloths and instruments seems to reduce the chance of mortification, she insisted that everything be cleaned in boiling water, including the cat gut I would use to tie off the vessels. Then she helped to administer laudanum to keep the patient quieter and helped to hold him down when I began to operate. Whenever I needed something, Miss Moorhouse was quick to pass it to me. As a result of her efforts, the operation went more quickly and smoothly than I could possibly have expected. When I finished, she hastily excused herself, rushed outside to get some fresh air and I could see through the window that she was trembling. It takes real courage for a young lady to steel herself to get through something like that!"

"Was the operation a success?"

"Very much so. We got to the appendix before it ruptured. And there was almost no mortification. Very little was discharged from the drain I left in. I don't know, but I suspect that Miss Moorhouse's insistence that everything be as clean as possible had something to do with the result.

"Now I should be getting on. Use your new leg but stop just as soon as it becomes painful and continue to use the salve."

With that, Jackson and Jake took their leave. Bush was not alone for long. Daphne came rushing into the room a few minutes later saying, "I just saw Mr. Jackson leave. Is that the new leg? How is it?"

"It seems to be a great deal better than the previous one."

"Mr. Jackson told me you should practice with it moderately, but regularly. Would you like to take a short walk in the garden before dinner? It will allow you to try that new cane as well."

Bush was delighted. The inactivity of the past few days was weighing on him and he welcomed the chance for some activity.

They set off immediately. The cane was indeed much more of a help than Bush's previous stick.

"Your Mr. Jackson seems to be a remarkable man. He was telling me how you helped him with an operation."

"He makes far too much of it."

"I was surprised to hear that an apothecary was performing surgeries."

"Mr. Jackson is not your usual apothecary. He was trained as a doctor, but found that he did not believe that much of what doctors do in trying to help their patients actually benefits them at all. Indeed, he strongly believes that bleeding, for example, is almost always the worst thing that can be done to a patient. He found that this and similar views put him into very unpleasant confrontations with those who had summoned him as a doctor and finds it easier to call himself an apothecary. Those who know and respect him call on him for all medical assistance, while those who don't, or want the usual treatments, call in Dr. Verdour, but they seem less apt to recover."

"But that doesn't account for the surgeries surely."

"Well, Mr. Jackson is convinced that there are many cases where surgery is necessary and that few barbers are really equipped to do it well. So he studied with some barber-surgeons and can perform operations usually more effectively and more often successfully than regular surgeons."

"A remarkable man."

"Yes he is. And now I think that you have done quite enough walking for today. Let's go back in and you can argue with my father about Rome or Carthage or something until dinner."

With Daphne's firm and irresistible guidance, Bush made rapid progress in adapting to his new leg. By Monday, he and Daphne felt that he could safely venture to the Inn to see Mr. Edwards and consult about the Dower Cottage. They, of course, took the Moorhouses' carriage and Daphne was very solicitous about getting Bush from the carriage to the parlor of the inn.

There they found a group of men, headed by Mr. Edwards and Lord David Giles. Edwards greeted Bush warmly, who in turn introduced Daphne to both Mr. Edwards and Lord David. Edwards then introduced his various assistants. Lord David and Mr. Clark, who had formally been a bailiff for the Bishop, and had smoothed the transition for Lord David to take up the living of Dipton, departed to see the church warden and inspect the church properties, including the vicarage.

"You must be the young lady that Captain Giles told me about," Mr. Edwards commented to Daphne. "He was most impressed with your knowledge. The drainage project will go ahead as you recommend. But I suspect that, if you are willing, you can give Mr. Chester, my agricultural expert, invaluable advice on how the Dipton Hall estates should be managed. From what Captain Giles said, he is afraid that the estate manager may not have been doing his job at all properly."

"That may be true. I understood that Mr. Gramley would not let Mr. Jenkins – that is the estate manager's name – make any investments, but he did seem to be getting yields poorer than they should have been. I don't really know what has been going on, but I'll be happy to help."

"Maybe Mr. Chester and you might start by looking at the drainage project and then you and he can jointly take it up with this Mr. Jenkins. That, I know, is the first priority with Captain Giles. And I should be quite clear: Captain Giles instructed that, in the case of disagreement, your views should prevail. I hope that is convenient with you."

Daphne was delighted to realize that Giles had developed such a respect for her knowledge of the needs of the land in just a couple of conversations. She had had a struggle to get the farmers of her father's estate to take her seriously and to respect her knowledge. It was gratifying that Mr. Edwards and Mr. Chester seemed to be in accord with Giles' instructions, and were not treating her as some foolish female whose opinions were to be humored and circumvented as quickly as possible.

"I would suggest that you and Mr. Chester begin your examination this morning," continued Edwards. "Then perhaps it would be best if Mr. Chester met with Mr. Jenkins this afternoon to go over the estate records and to get a general feeling for the problems which need to be faced. Afterwards you and Mr. Chester can meet with Mr. Jenkins on the drainage project."

Daphne was about to protest fearing that the schedule was a ploy to allow Mr. Chester and Mr. Jenkins to gang up on her, but she stopped when she realized that Mr. Edwards might be implying that Mr. Chester should see if Mr. Jenkins could be relied on, or if, like other senior staff at Dipton Hall, his performance had been deficient. The possibility did not surprise her. Based on this reflection, she quickly agreed to the suggested proceedings.

"Mr. Davidson, my arranger, and I will have a lot to do at the Hall, but first we should look into Captain Bush's needs. I understand that Captain Giles has offered you the Dower Cottage, Captain Bush."

"Yes. And I have decided to accept his offer."

"Splendid. Then I suggest that you and I and Mr. Davidson go over to the Cottage and see what you will require."

Bush was about to concur entirely when Daphne interrupted. "Captain Bush can only walk on his new leg to a very limited extent, Mr. Edwards. The doctor has expressly forbidden him to make great use of it for a while."

"That's all right, Miss Moorhouse. We can use my carriage to get over there, and we can suspend the examination at any time when it is necessary to allow recovery.

"Now that we all know what we will be doing, let's not waste any more time. Lord David, I suggest that you and Mr. Clark proceed to the church. Miss Moorhead and Mr. Chester can take Miss Moorhouse's carriage to visit the site of the drainage. Mr. Davidson, please ask the innkeeper to have my carriage readied, and then you might go and open up the cottage. Captain Bush and I will wait for the carriage to be ready."

Mr. Edwards quite forcibly bustled everyone else out of the inn parlor and then turned to Bush.

"I am afraid that rush was really a ploy to get you to myself for a few minutes. I wanted to tell you about the prize monies that are coming to you. Unfortunately several of the vessels and cargoes involved are still being valued – and disputed over. However, already you have a tidy sum – a very tidy sum – in your account. I have here the reckoning for the progress so far.

"But the main thing is that it has been decided that you were in command of *Squirrel* when *Phoebe* defeated *Resistance* and that the merchant ships which *Phoebe* recovered can be treated as prizes. How it was managed, I don't know. Captain Giles, I suspect, had a hand in it.

"No, no…" Mr. Edwards stopped Bush's protest, "I know that you were not transferred to *Squirrel* until most of the engagement with *Resistance* was over and you weren't really in command of her. But the lieutenant who was her commander was killed early on and, incidentally, left no heirs. If anyone was hurt by your getting the money, it is probably Captain Giles, and he would certainly not claim it. Indeed, I think he must have had a large hand in making sure that the money comes to you.

"The principal point is that you are in better financial shape than I thought when last we talked. If all goes well – and in these matters, where there are substantial funds involved, there can always be difficulties – you should be very comfortably set up for life."

Bush was most encouraged by Mr. Edwards' words. Mr. Edwards looked out the window.

"The carriage is ready. We had better go to examine the Dower Cottage."

Bush struggled to his feet. "What about the rent?"

"Captain Giles said to set the rent at what I think it is worth, but not to make it too expensive. I will know better when I have seen the place. But you will certainly be able to afford it, and the rent will be much less than you would pay for adequate accommodation elsewhere."

With this assurance, Bush was eager to set off. A very short carriage ride took them to the Dower Cottage. Mr. Davidson had already done a quick survey of the property.

"It's in better shape than I expected, Captain Bush. What is needed is mainly decorating rather than serious reconstruction work. And of course furniture. I think that we can go over how the rooms might be used and then I can give you more specific proposals in a day or two. The main question is whether you want a room which will be *your* room, like a library or something similar. And whether your sisters need space for a piano forte. If they are musical, you may want your room to be as far from the drawing room as possible. I dearly love music, but to hear someone practicing, especially learning a new piece, can be very annoying even if the musician is accomplished."

This was something Bush had never thought about, but he did know that he most certainly found listening to his sisters, who were not very accomplished, struggle with a new piece could grate abominably on his nerves.

Davidson proceeded to ask Bush several other questions about the habits of his family, for many of which Bush had no answers. He felt increasingly that he was out of his depth. But the most alarming revelation of the whole process came when he inquired when the work could be finished.

Davidson considered briefly, "With the best of luck, we'll be through in eight weeks, but we also have to work on the Hall, especially as I understand there is some urgency about getting it ready for Lady Marianne. Realistically, we should allow three months"

Bush's mother really wanted to move by the quarter day, and would have to find other accommodation, at least on a temporary basis, before the Dower Cottage would be ready. He would still have to find her lodgings. That remained the only fly in his ointment.

Bush and Mr. Moorhouse were in animated discussion of what might have happened at the battle of Actium if the Persians had followed a different strategy when Daphne returned home towards the end of the afternoon. She was bubbling with excitement and didn't even seem to notice that the hems of her skirts and petticoats were filthy and really should be changed before she came into the drawing room. Instead, she strode in recounting excitedly how the plans for the drainage were progressing and how Mr. Chester had welcomed and agreed with her designs, only suggesting a few minor and, she admitted, worthwhile amendments.

"We talked and talked about the estates," she continued. "Mr. Chester knows so much, and isn't at all threatened by a female who has opinions of her own. And when we went to see Mr. Jenkins, Mr. Chester realized almost at once that the man had been abusing his position and was very old-fashioned to boot. He fired him on the spot. He had a letter that Mr. Edwards had written, for use if the need arose, to confirm his authority.

"But you'll never guess the best part. No, never."

"Since we cannot guess, my dear, you shall just have to tell us so we don't die of curiosity," Mr. Moorhouse responded kindly. He apparently was quite used to his daughter's bouts of enthusiasm.

"Mr. Chester suggested that I could act as the estate manager for the holdings of Dipton Hall – at least, until Captain Giles can make permanent arrangements. He said that he would recommend that I do so to Mr. Edwards, if it was agreeable to me. And he added that he couldn't imagine Mr. Edwards's not endorsing his recommendation. Oh, I'm so excited!"

"Yes, I can see that, my dear; but you are quite ignoring Captain Bush, who has also had a very busy and challenging day."

"Oh, Captain Bush, where are my manners?" Daphne looked quite distressed realizing that politeness dictated that she should have asked after her guest before recounting her own adventures.

"Everything worked out much better than I expected. Unfortunately, I do have one problem. The Dower Cottage will not be ready for some time, so I will have to find lodgings for my mother and sisters in the interim. I just don't know where to look for the accomodation."

"That's no problem," Daphne responded. "We have lots and lots of unused space here with only my father and me in a house that is supposed to have a large family and frequent guests. Father, won't you invite Captain Bush to stay with us together with his family until the Dower Cottage is ready. No, no, Captain Bush, it would be no trouble to have all for you to stay with us and I am quite looking forward to getting to know your sisters. Don't you agree, Father."

"Yes indeed. You would all be most welcome, Captain Bush. I would like to have the house livelier."

So it was settled. After dinner, Captain Bush wrote to his mother telling her about the plans and enclosing a letter from Daphne Moorhouse extending the invitation. When he went to bed that evening, he reflected on how the mountain of problems that he had faced when Giles left him at Dipton had disappeared. Even the question of his career did not worry him any longer. If he were offered a command, he would consider it, but if he were not, he could quite imagine being content with life as a village gentleman. The problem of winning a wife, which had once been a priority when he was ruminating on his future at the Dipton Arms, had quite slipped his mind.

Chapter VI

Patroclus's journey down river went without incident. They dropped the pilot when they reached the Solent and were soon out into the Channel. The wind had backed into the west and strengthened as *Patroclus* left the land. Giles and the master, Mr. Brooks took delight in trying different combinations of sail and sailing directions in order to study how *Patroclus* behaved and to determine what her best points of sailing were. As this exploration went on, the crew was getting a first-class introduction to all aspects of sail handling. Giles' and the Master's prime concern was how easily *Patroclus* tacked and what tendencies she had to miss stays. Overall they were well pleased with her performance, the ship only missing stays on two occasions. They felt that they could overcome that danger by slightly changing the order with which the sheets were let fly and the yards brought around. By contrast, when they wore ship instead of tacking, the loss from turning downwind usually far exceeded the danger of missing stays. They would of course have to study these problems under different states of the wind and the sea, but for now they were well pleased with the performance of the ship and of the crew.

As these sail-handling exercises were going on, Lieutenant Foster, aided by the other two lieutenants, was exercising the gun crews, practicing loading and running out the guns, and then running them back in again to have a mock swabbing out, so that they were ready to load again. It was good practice, but not really the equivalent of actually firing the guns. In most ships, that was about all the practice that was allowed (the Admiralty clerks being very parsimonious about the amount of powder and shot that could be used in practice.) Many captains, realizing that there was no substitute to actually firing the guns, purchased powder and, in some cases, shot from their own pocket so that practice could be more realistic, though everyone knew that the ultimate test came when the crews were being fired on as well as firing, Giles was prepared to spend a considerable amount on powder and shot although, in this instance, it turned out not to be necessary. At four bells of the afternoon watch, Hughes approached him.

"Captain, I wonder if we shouldn't try the guns fully loaded. I would particularly like to see how the ship's fabric stands up to the recoils of the guns. The Ordinance Board will, of course, pay for the supplies expended."

Giles was only too happy to agree. For the next two hours, the guns fired in sequence and as a broadside, the latter of particular interest to Mr. Hughes since it put the most stress on the ship. The last set of exercises involved the bow chasers, single and double-shotted, singly and in unison. For the last sequence, Hughes again disappeared into the bow of the ship to see how the structure stood up to the pressures being placed on it. He emerged after the guns had fired, looking pleased.

"I think, Captain that the ship can accommodate these bow chasers, and I feel that she might be able to take long thirty-four pounders. But before making that recommendation, I shall await further tests with these ones. The special guns have already been ordered from the foundry."

The exercise was completed just as eight bells rang. Giles felt entirely satisfied with progress so far, but that satisfaction did not last long. Three bells of the first watch had just rung when the Marine sentry announced Giles' coxswain.

"Yes, Carstairs."

"Sir, I am afraid that we may have a problem with Mr. Foster."

"Yes?"

"I noticed Mr. Foster going down to the orlop deck with one of the ship's boys. I got Mr. Hendricks and we went after them. Mr. Foster was very angry at our intrusion, indeed he threatened to have us flogged, despite the fact that we are both petty officers. Mr. Hendricks claimed that we were there by your orders to check the hull again for leaks after all the firing of the guns this afternoon. Mr. Foster then hurried away. I don't think that the lad had come to any harm before we arrived."

"So you think that Mr. Foster is a … a … a boy bugger?"

"Yes, sir, though he may also be a molly-boy."

"Whichever, this is the last thing I need. I wonder now if some of the rumors about Captain Pritchard are true and Foster was his plaything. Anyway, you didn't see any sodomy did you?"

"No sir. Their clothing was a bit disheveled, especially the boy's, but no, nothing directly implying that they had already been up to … well, you know what."

"Thank heavens, especially for the boy. But it poses a dilemma. If I do nothing, Lieutenant Foster may well be caught in a flagrant act, and then I would have no choice but to hold Foster for a court martial and to hang his partner. The court martial would keep us in harbor while our mission is urgent. But what can I do? I suspect that confronting him without proof would simply make him worse, harder to catch, but not stop him. I can't have the Master at Arms watch him all the time.

"Damnation, how I wish I were rid of him.

"Well, Carstairs, thank you for bringing this to my attention. I shall have a word with Mr. Foster, though it may not do much good. And I'll order you and Hendricks to regularly check the more obscure parts of the ship on the excuse of checking the state of the hull. I know it will make me appear to be a mother fuss-budget, but the alternative is worse. Pass the word to the other petty officers to try to protect the ship's boys and to find excuses to be in places where the first lieutenant has got himself where he doesn't really belong. We all know this sort of thing happens, but not between officers and crew, especially not the boys who have no way to defend themselves… I know some of the boys are as bad as any of the crew when it comes to unmanly acts, but that doesn't mean I can completely ignore what they do. Let me think about it."

"Aye, aye, sir. But don't tell Mr. Foster that I told you. He has too many ways to make my life and Mr. Hendricks's miserable if he thinks we ratted on him."

"No. I'll say I heard the rumors elsewhere."

"Thank you, captain."

"Carstairs, pass the word when you leave for the gunner to see me."

In minutes, the gunner was announced by the marine sentry. The gunner was an old salt, gray-haired and a bit stooped, but an absolute genius when it came to his guns. He was also very determined to look after the boys as best he could, in the absence of a matron.

"Mr. Abbott, we may have a problem of buggery, involving your boys."

"Aye sir, Carstairs told me. They are not really my boys, except when the guns are in action when they are my powder monkeys and they carry messages. They are the boatswain's nippers when the anchor is raised. But without a matron, they are rather at a loose end half the time. I do try to keep an eye out for them, but I can't really control them."

"I know. I appreciate your efforts. But the problem is that I know the adult who is responsible – and so do you, I imagine. I am about to confront him, and I was going to say that I learned about it from you, to divert his suspicions from Carstairs."

"Yes, sir. If Mr. Carstairs hadn't said he would be talking to you, I would have come."

"Yes, well, I am going to try to put the fear of God, or rather of the Admiralty, into him. I have ordered that the remote areas of the ship be patrolled. I would like you to mention to the boys the hazards of going off with an adult alone."

"I'll be glad to do that, but you have to realize that they would have a very difficult time refusing a command from an officer."

"I know, but we can only do what we can. I'd rather not have him engage in anything that would require me to hold him for a court martial. And you can tell the boys that if they are caught doing something like that, they would probably hang."

"Aye, aye, sir. It seems so unfair, after you were able to transfer us old *Phoebe*s to *Patroclus* that we should now be saddled with this problem."

"Yes, well Mr. Abbott, carry on. Oh, and tell the First Lieutenant that I want to see him."

"Aye, aye, sir."

Foster appeared in a few minutes, He was dressed in clothes that were very fine both in their fabric and their cut, rather surprising in a lieutenant's working uniform.

"You sent for me. Sir."

"Yes, Mr. Foster. I hear tales that we may have a sodomy problem on board."

"Sir?"

"Yes. Apparently it involves the ship's boys and some adults. Bad business, if its's true. Bad business even if it is not true. Do you know anything about it?"

"No, sir. I hadn't even heard the rumors. Who told you?"

"Mr. Abbott, the gunner. He takes some responsibility for the boys. If true, it could be a very bad business. I suppose that you do know that buggery is a capital offense? I would be very unhappy to have to hang a boy who had been led astray. The man who did that should indeed be hung!"

"What do you suggest we do, sir?"

"I want you to inform the wardroom of the dangers and the seriousness of the offense. And to suggest that everyone keep an eye out for any evidence of who the perpetrator might be. We may not catch him, unfortunately, but these precautions may make him leery of following his disgusting proclivities."

"Yes, sir, I agree. Was there anything else, sir?

"No. Get on with it."

When Foster had left, Giles leaned back in his chair and reflected on what lay ahead. Hopefully he had put enough emphasis on there already being rumors that Foster would think twice before renewing his endeavors with the ship's boys. But it would only be a temporary relief, he suspected. Somehow he had to get rid of Foster, in such a way that his own mission was not delayed.

The day's practices had gone better than he could have hoped for; the ship was rapidly settling into the efficient fighting machine that it should be. While firing the guns, several naval vessels had approached them, attracted by the sound of gunfire. While this had produced some good exercise for the signals midshipman, it had not advanced the war one iota. Mr. Hughes still had some tests he wanted to run on the guns, but the ship was well able to defend herself already. It would be better to see if the sound of their guns could lure a French ship into a battle in the ensuing days.

Giles went on deck to find that Mr. Brooks was there as well as Davis, who was officer of the watch. It was the work of minutes to consult with the Master about the course to set for Cherbourg and to issue the orders. The usual organized chaos erupted until the sails had been adjusted for the new course. Giles remained on deck to chat with Brooks.

"I suppose you have heard about Foster and the boys?"

"Aye, sir. A rotten development. And you won't stop him for long, you know. That sort never do desist."

"I know, and I'm hard put on how to get rid of him."

"Aye. I hope you find some way. I don't relish a long voyage with that bugger."

Giles returned to his cabin now dreading even more the problems he might have with his first lieutenant.

Patroclus raised the coast of France shortly after sunrise on the next day. They renewed their sail handling drills and the practice of loading and running out the guns. Mr. Hughes approached Giles at 3 bells of the forenoon watch.

"Captain, I would like to fire the bow chasers with powder and shot, especially to see exactly where the balls land."

"Very good, carry on"

"It might help if you would float some empty casks to serve as targets."

"I'm not sure we have any. If the cook or the purser have some you are welcome to use them. Mr. Miller, would you help Mr. Hughes, and relay any instructions that he has about altering course and so on."

"Aye, aye, sir."

"Excellent, Captain. Incidentally, I hope you realize the cost will be borne by Ordinance Office, and not by you."

"I hadn't thought of who was paying for it, but I'm glad to hear that you are, even though I was quite prepared to pay for the exercise myself."

Four empty casks were found, the first of them was dropped, and *Patroclus* wore around so that her bow would face the cask. With Giles' permission, Hughes first directed the quartermasters on the best way to steer. He found out that the helmsmen certainly knew what they were doing and rapidly understood that the trick was to adjust the steering as much as possible to allow predictable swings of the bow so that one could anticipate just when it would be pointing at the target.

"Your quartermasters are very well trained and perceptive, Captain Giles."

"The Master, Mr. Brooks, should get credit for that."

"Now if you don't mind, I'll go and see how the bow chasers are doing, and maybe I can give the gun captains some hints."

"Certainly, Mr. Hughes. Possibly, Mr. Davis should attend as well as the midshipman who is assigned to the guns. He will be in immediate charge of the bow chasers when we go into action."

"Very good, Captain."

Giles gave orders to Mr. Foster, who happened to be officer of the watch, on how to maneuver so as to bring the bow into line with the cask and how to proceed when the bow chasers missed it. Luckily, Mr. Brooks was also on deck and they exchanged glances to indicate that Mr. Brooks should intervene only if there was a serious difficulty since it would give Giles a chance to see how Mr. Foster was at ship handling. Giles went forward to see what was happening. He took up a position a bit removed from the group that Hughes had assembled around himself.

Giles was immediately impressed that Mr. Hughes was not giving commands, but instead he pretended to be making suggestions and readily accepted comments from the others.

"You will all appreciate," said Mr. Hughes, "that the ship cannot steer directly to any target, but must yaw back and forth about the line that it is sailing. As a result, I would suggest that, for satisfactory results, you will have to adjust your firing to the time when the bow of our ship is pointing just at your target. It is a little more complicated than it might seem, because from the time you pull the lanyard to the time that the gun actually fires, several seconds pass. How long, depends on the gun. Anyone have any idea of how long that will be?"

"Three seconds, sir, for the larboard gun," announced Graham, the gun captain of the larboard bow chaser.

"Quite correct. And how do you know that …?"

"Graham, sir. I counted it off when we were practicing."

"And how did you count?"

"One thousand, two thousand, three thousand, and so on, sir."

"A very good way to do it. Incidentally, it is best if each of you determines the time by your own count, since that is what you will have to use in reality. Anyone have any idea of how you might use it to improve your aim? ... Yes, Midshipman …?"

"Stewart, sir. Could you choose a point on the bulwark that is in line with the target and then count to see how long it takes the bow to swing so that the gun is pointed towards it after the count is made?"

"A very good suggestion, Mr. Stewart. Especially, since you can then adjust your reckoning until it is about right. Do that before you start to fire since it usually takes a few tries to get it right. There is just one further thing to allow for. What would that be? … Yes, Graham?"

"The motion of the target. If it is a ship, you have to allow for how much it moves from when you pull the lanyard and the gun fires."

"Quite right. You have to use the same method to try to allow for it. The one other thing you have to remember is that you will be getting closer and closer to the target as you keep on firing, so you have to redo the allowance a bit each time. It takes some time to get used to all this, which is why practice is a good idea. I suggest, Mr. Davis, that we start the practice."

While this had been going on, *Patroclus* had come around in a circle so that the bow was now facing towards the cask, several cables ahead. The bow chasers started firing at it, first the larboard and then the starboard. The first shots were quite wide of the mark, and raised a few friendly jeers from other gun-crew members who were off-watch and wanted to see the fun. The next shots were closer, so much so that by the time they ceased fire temporarily so that *Patroclus* could come about to again have the bow pointed towards the cask, mild bets were being laid, some as to whether the cask would be hit at all, and others as to whether the larboard or the starboard gun would score the first hit.

Seeing all was well, Giles returned to the quarter deck. Just before the gun-practice had to be interrupted once again in order to bring the ship around to aim at the cask, a loud shout erupted from the forecastle. The starboard gun had hit the cask! The spirits of the crew rose immediately.

Before Giles could decide whether to float another cask, there was a cry from the masthead, "Sail ho! Three points off the larboard bow"

"Mr. Miller. Take a telescope to the mast-head to see what she is. Mr. Davis, secure the bow chasers."

Miller grabbed a telescope and headed up the ratlines. Once at the masthead, he settled himself firmly and examined the sighting.

"Deck, there. Ship appears to be a frigate, based on her royals and topsails. French cut. She is hard on the larboard tack on a course that might intercept ours. She is too far away to clearly determine her nature or her course."

"Mr. Miller. Stay at the masthead until you can determine better what she is," Giles bellowed. "Mr. Foster. Get both watches to dinner. Then clear for action. Mr. Brooks, what do you make of her?"

"Hard to say, sir. We could expect to meet French ships here, though Cherbourg is not a major naval base. If she is a French frigate, her business may be to round Ushant in order to proceed south or to go into Brest. She could also be trying for the Atlantic. The French coast is close enough that there won't be any other French ships near her, under the horizon. And, of course, she might be one of ours if she has not been in service long enough to have her sails changed."

"True."

The watch below had soon finished their dinners and changed places with the watch on duty. Soon the fire could be doused and other preparations made. In a very short time, Giles was able to give the order to clear for action. A somewhat disordered bustle broke out. It was a drill that Giles had yet to practice and the weakness of Foster's stations bill again became evident. Giles doubted that he had conferred with Davis or Miller about it. He was amused to note that the petty officers were quietly righting some of the worst misallocations without raising a fuss. Luckily, they still had lots of time, but they would have to do better in future.

After the hub-bub of clearing for action, a comparative silence descended on the ship as they waited for the vessels to come up to each other.

"Mr. Miller, is she showing any colors?

"Not yet sir. Just a moment, she is raising a flag. It's the tri-color, sir. She's French."

"Very good. Mr. Correll, raise our colors."

"Sir," said Brooks, "by my reckoning, if both ships hold their course, she will cross our bow in twenty minutes at a distance of a cable and a half."

Giles had noted Brooks with his sextant taking repeated observations of the approaching ship and calling for the log to be cast far more frequently than usual. Unlike Giles, who hated all the calculations which he had been forced to learn as a midshipman, Brooks reveled in them and would take great pride in accurately predicting where they might be in the near future. "Very good, Mr. Brooks. Keep me informed as your calculations get more accurate."

"Mr. Hughes," Giles addressed the gunnery expert who had been standing on the lee side of the quarter-deck, "we shall shortly be going into action. As you are a civilian, I must ask you to proceed to the orlop for your own protection."

"Captain, I would like to stay on deck. I might be able to help with the guns. In any case, I would dearly like to see them in action."

"If you are sure, Mr. Hughes, your assistance will be much appreciated. Could you help direct the bow chasers which are likely to be the first guns in action?"

"Aye, aye, sir." Hughes unconsciously confirmed Giles' suspicion that he had served in the Navy at some time.

Giles then turned his mind fully to what the coming battle might involve, especially in its first stages. Like a chess player he had to anticipate his opponent's initial moves and his responses to them and vice versa. If both ships held their courses, their paths would cross with the enemy ahead. As she crossed, their opponent could fire at least one broadside before *Patroclus*'s main guns could bear. The French frigate could then continue on her course, hoping that its cannon balls had damaged *Patroclus* enough to slow her down, and gambling that

Patroclus's reply, fired at a greater distance would not cripple the French vessel. Alternatively, after the first broadside, she could turn to leeward and engage *Patroclus* in the hope that the first cannonade might have done enough damage that *Patroclus* would not be able to respond effectively. It would also allow the enemy to escape to leeward where *Patroclus*'s ability to sail closer to the wind would not matter and on a point of sailing where she might be slower than the French frigate. It was unlikely that the enemy ship would turn downwind before she met *Patroclus* to exchange broadsides since that would expose her stern to having Patroclus turn to rake her as she passed and possibly get in another broadside unopposed. But, if the opposing frigate wanted to escape down wind, she would have taken the opportunity to do so earlier, knowing that a long stern chase might exhaust the daylight before *Patroclus* could come up with her. The same argument held for the French ship turning down wind after crossing *Patroclus*'s bow, but Giles should watch for any sign that that was what she was doing when the time came. That left the question of what Giles should do. He could come about now. That would open the possibility of the enemy turning down wind to rake *Patroclus* as they sailed along. The same problem applied to tacking before their paths intersected, and as the ships converged, the danger being that, if *Patroclus* should miss stays, she would be vulnerable to devastating broadsides from her opponent. So Giles's best move seemed to be to hold his course until the French frigate had passed ahead of her and then tack in pursuit.

Having settled in his own mind what would be the best course to follow, Giles consulted Brooks, knowing that the master would have been performing similar calculations in his head. Brooks' opinion was the same as Giles's so, with everything ready for the encounter, the whole ship's company had to endure seemingly endless minutes as the two ships converged without anything further to do in preparation.

When there were only a few minutes until the French ship passed ahead of them, Giles ordered, "Mr. Davis, open fire as convenient." He had intended to give the usual order, 'Open fire as you bear', but remembered Hughes saying that it was better to have a few ranging shots first to improve accuracy. Within seconds, the larboard bow-chaser blasted out. Giles observed that the shot fell well short of what he had expected. And the same thing happened with the starboard bow-chaser. He was about to investigate what was wrong, but he noticed that the starboard shot had ricocheted far forward when it skipped off a wave.

Hughes had undoubtedly suggested aiming deliberately low to mislead their opponent of the force of metal she was about to encounter. In moments, he was proven right. Just before the bow of the enemy came in line with *Patroclus's* bowsprit, both bow chasers fired, and this time within moments Giles saw the opponent's forestay part even as a large hole appeared in the jib. In moments, the long twenty-fours fired again, doing serious damage to the enemy's foremast shrouds. The third volley was the one that did the most damage, for it severed the mizzen shrouds and hit the mizzenmast itself. The French frigate was just coming over the top of a wave, and the effect was to snap the unsupported mizzen to windward where it went by the board, swiveling the frigate into the eye of the wind. Her starboard battery was able to fire at *Petroclus* as the wounded ship swung into the wind, but all the shots went wide.

Giles immediately gave the orders: "Starboard you helm. Mr. Foster, back the mainsail. Mr. Miller, fire as you bear." He noted, without it really registering with him, that the second order was in fact repeated and implemented by Mr. Brooks and not by Mr. Foster. "Mr. Correll, keep a sharp eye out for her lowering her colors or doing something equivalent since the flag on her spanker gaff is no more."

"Captain, she has just lowered her ensign from her topmast, and there are some men on the quarter deck waving a flag as if to lower it."

"Belay that order for the guns, Mr. Miller."

"Cease fire," bellowed Miller. "Secure the guns."

Only one gun of the starboard battery fired before the order could be complied with. Giles had just captured a French frigate without having to receive a shot.

"Mr. Shearer, Carstairs, get my barge ready, and the longboat with a dozen marines, the carpenter and his mates, and as many seamen for whom there is room. I'll take possession of the frigate. Mr. Miller come with me. Mr. Foster, you will have the ship in my absence." For the first time, Giles noticed that Foster had been standing behind the mizzen, but for the moment thought nothing of it.

The boats' crews were rapidly assembled and rowed across to the French frigate. There they were met by someone who seemed to be in a lieutenant's uniform offering his sword to Giles. There emerged one serious problem, for it became evident that none of the Frenchmen spoke

English and none of the Englishmen spoke French. Giles silently cursed his father who had not thought it wise to spend money on a French governess or to send Giles to a school where French was on the curriculum, and the ships he had served in as a midshipman had no one capable of teaching the midshipmen French, that most useful of languages for a naval officer. Among *Patroclus*'s officers, the one who was nearest to being a French speaker was Miller, but he had only a smattering of the language, and seemed to be able to extract only small amount of useful information from the French.

"Sir, the ship is the *Quatorze de Juillet* – I think that means the fourteenth of July. Her captain was struck by the ball that hit the mizzenmast and instantly killed. The lieutenant is called Robart. He and the other officers are prepared to give their parole. But, if I understand him right, they have no desire to be exchanged for English officers."

"We'll have no say in that matter, Mr. Miller. Get men to replace the forward rigging that has been destroyed. Mr. Hendricks, you and your mates determine how you can rig some sort of jury mizzen. Falmouth is upwind of us and we will need the prize to go to windward. A sail aft, like the driver, would help that endeavor. Mr. Macaulay, your marines can guard the prisoners. Make sure that they are kept below decks. Do you need more marines?"

"It would help sir, but I can also use some of our seamen, suitably armed to help guard them."

"Very well. Round up the French marines and send them over to *Patroclus*. Mr. Miller, I shall send you more of our seamen and marines, also one of Mr. Brooks's mates with suitable charts to make sure that you can find Falmouth. Mr. Miller, if you have a chance, see if there are any documents or other interesting finds among the captain's possessions which were sent below when she cleared for action. Now, Carstairs, I am ready to return to *Patroclus*. We should take the French officers with us."

"Aye, aye, sir."

When Giles returned to *Patroclus,* his first action was to confer with the Master.

"Mr. Brooks, a word with you in private." Everyone would presume that they were discussing the best course to take, given that they would need to accompany the wounded frigate until at least they were away from any possibility of a French rescue being made, but that was not Giles's concern

"Mr. Brooks, where was Mr. Foster when we were approaching the *Quatorze* – that is the name of the French frigate?"

"Sir, he was on the quarterdeck."

"Mr. Brooks, don't prevaricate. Where on the quarterdeck was he?"

"He was behind the mizzenmast, sir."

"Skulking?"

"I couldn't say, sir."

"And Mr. Brooks, when sail handling orders had to be given, did Mr. Foster give them?'

"No sir. Enough time elapsed from when he should give them that I … I stepped into the breech."

"Thank heavens! No, you don't have to pretend any more even though he is senior to you. So we have a first lieutenant who is not only a poofter, but who also is shy."

"I'm afraid so, sir."

"Damnation, what am I to do? Court-martialing him, for either or both offenses would totally distract us from our mission. And Davis is too inexperienced to be first lieutenant, anyway."

"Yes sir. Though I think that Mr. Davis might surprise you. I know that I would be happier with him as first lieutenant than Mr. Foster. But Mr. Miller is green as grass, and Mr. Carrell is hardly ready to be a lieutenant. "

"Confound it. I have got to get rid of Foster, but not in a way that will delay us. I think I would rather be very short of officers than having one I cannot trust! Well, we'd better get all the other things straightened out so that we can proceed."

By late afternoon, the repairs to the rigging of *Kay-torze* – as the hands had taken to pronouncing the name of their prize – had been finished, and Hendricks had succeeded in fishing a spare spar to the stump of the mizzen to carry a driver. The wind had backed into the south south-west so both ships were capable of laying courses that would easily take them into Falmouth if the wind held. Giles had used the luxury that a full crew gave him to send more men to *Kay-torze* to help in controlling the prisoners and in sailing the ship.

"Mr. Stewart, you seem to be midshipman of the watch. Signal Mr. Davis to take station on our leeward quarter and to proceed with us to Falmouth." Giles knew that it was a bit unfair to expect a midshipman of only a few days' experience to be able to fulfill the order, except he also knew that Brooks would make sure that the new midshipman knew what to   do.
"Captain, sir!" broke in Foster. "It is surely my right to take command of the prize."

"Hardly, Mr. Foster. We may well meet other French vessels and I will need you here when we engage them."

"But, Captain. It is always the custom, so that my experience in command can be noted to speed up my being posted."

"I'm afraid, Mr. Foster, that it is not the custom. And you must realize that in taking the prize, Mr. Davis's contribution was much greater than your own."

"Sir, I protest. I want my protest recorded in the log."

"Very well, Mr. Foster. It will be noted and the circumstances in which your protest was made."

The crossing of the Channel was without further incident, and they raised Falmouth at five bells of the afternoon watch on the next day. There was still plenty of daylight by the time they had anchored, with *Kay-torze* to landward of *Patroclus*. Giles immediately ordered his barge readied to take him ashore. As they passed close to *Kay-torze*, there was a loud splash on the opposite side of the ship.

"Man overboard," came the call, followed by, "It's one of the prisoners trying to escape."

Giles ordered Carstairs to take the barge around the stern of *Kay-torze*, and as they came abreast of the rudder, they spotted a man in the water, apparently trying to swim ashore. Carstairs steered the barge to catch the swimmer and, despite some last minute attempts to get away, the man was snared by Humphries who had been rowing bow oar. It was one of the Frenchmen and even in the barge, he continued to struggle. Giles ordered that he be bound with some of the ropes in the barge, and then turned to Carstairs.

"We'd better get this specimen back on board *Kay-torze* before going to the Admiral. I also ought to make sure that Mr. Davis is not in difficulty."

Giles unexpected return to *Kay-torze* was met by a very hastily assembled welcoming party, with only one bosun's whistle twittering and two marines at attention. While Davis was clearly nervous, Giles's only interest was in the well-being of the ship and crew.

"Thank you for catching that man, sir. I should have had him watched more carefully."

"No harm done, Mr. Davis. How is everything?"

"Very well, sir. We did make one discovery about the ship."

"Yes?"

"It was Mr. Correll, actually. He discovered the Captain's desk, where the French had struck it below, and it contained a locked drawer."

"I don't imagine that stopped you opening it."

"No sir. I did. The drawer seemed to contain the ship's log, the signal book, and the captain's orders. We couldn't understand any of them, of course, but that is what I guess them to be. And I noticed a word that looked like 'Ireland' in the orders."

"I'd better take them to the Admiral directly. Anything else?"

"Yes, sir. The man who tried to escape. He is not an officer, but he does not appear to be a seaman either. I wonder if he could have something to do with the 'Ireland'."

"Quite possibly. Since he is already in my barge, I'll deliver him to the Admiral too. Anything else?"

"No, sir."

Carry on then. I'll urge the Admiral to take charge of *Kay-torze* and the prisoners as soon as possible so you can get back on board *Patroclus*."

Giles was shown straight into the Admiral's room when he got ashore.

The Admiral received Giles' report and put it to one side. "I'll read this later and send it on to London. I was told, Captain Giles, that you were coming. I didn't expect you to come with a prize. In what shape is she? And for that matter, how is your own ship?"

"*Patroclus* suffered no damage, sir. The French ship, the *Kay-torze de Jullet*, lost her mizzenmast and suffered some damage to her rigging. Otherwise, she is in good shape."

"The what?"

Giles repeated his version of the ship's name. The Admiral still looked puzzled, until his aide whispered something to him.

"Ah, *Le Quatorze de Juillet*," the Admiral said, in a perfect French accent. "They do love to give their ships names linked to their Revolution."

"Yes, sir. We found some papers in the Captain's desk. I think they may be the log, the signal book and the Captain's orders. None of my people could read them and I don't know French, I am afraid."

"I gathered that! Where are they?"

"Here sir."

Giles handed over the documents. The Admiral scanned them quickly, concentrating on the orders.

"You are quite right. She was supposed to go to Ireland to land an agent, whether a spy or a provocateur is not clear. I don't expect that you know which prisoner he might be."

"Sir, it is probable that he is the man who tried to escape by jumping overboard."

"Where is he now?"

"In my barge, sir. Under guard."

"Mr. Judge," the Admiral said to his aide, "Be so good as to take him off Captain Giles's hands. We'll send him to London under guard along with these documents. They will probably hang him. And, Mr. Judge, have some copies made of this signal book, for Captain Giles and any other captains who call in here in the near future. It never hurts to be able to read the enemy's signals!

"Not yet, Mr. Judge. There is more to attend to. Captain Giles, I imagine that you would like me to take control of your prize. I have no doubt that the Admiralty will buy her into the service. We never have enough frigates, and the French build good ones. Unfortunately, port admirals do not have the authority to authorize such a purchase on our own. You'll also want your crew back. Now you can see to it all, Mr. Judge."

When the aide had left, the Admiral again turned to Giles. "Your long guns arrived yesterday. You can load them tomorrow, if you still want them. I gather there was some sort of controversy as to whether *Patroclus* could take such heavy armament."

"Yes sir. Mr. Humphries of the Ordinance Board thinks she can."

"And I imagine you are short of powder and shot."

"Yes, sir."

"I'll have them sent out on the following day. Have your first lieutenant tell my people what you need."

"Very good, sir."

"I can't help you with crew, I am afraid, and I suspect that your press gangs won't have much luck. That field has been plowed too often in Falmouth."

"That's all right, sir, I am lucky enough to have a full crew."

"How very fortunate! Well, Captain, I wish you well in getting ready to sail as soon as possible. I hope that you will be able to dine with me tomorrow."

"Thank you, sir. I would be honored."

Giles returned to the jetty to find that the prisoner had indeed been taken in charge by the admiral's men, and he could see a couple of laden barges going towards *Kay-torze*, probably a crew to take over from Davis, and possibly guards to start ferrying the prisoners ashore. He idly wondered what the French frigate would be worth at the Prize Court. Like all naval officers, he warmed to the contemplation of his share. He didn't know how the division worked when he sailed under Admiralty orders or whether some admiral would claim the lion's share of the proceeds for doing nothing, but he suspected he would not see much of that money. The wind was getting up from the west, he noted, but the anchorage was well protected, though if it got stronger by the morrow the task of transferring the guns would be rendered difficult.

The lighter with the guns came along side at two bells of the forenoon watch. Giles had put Foster in charge of getting the guns and their carriages aboard and set up and also of sending down the bow chasers they had been using. He noted that Foster seemed to rely on giving rather vague orders to subordinates and letting them get on with things. They had reached the point when the first of the new gun carriages had been hoisted aboard and was now waiting for its gun to be brought from the lighter. Giles was idly watching the procedure from the quarter deck. He noticed that Humphries was descending the lee shrouds near where the lighter was tied to *Patroclus*.

Foster glanced overboard, and ordered, "Mr. Davis, Haul away."

Davis repeated the order and the group of seaman started to walk away with the fall from the tackle.

"Avast heaving," Humphries bellowed from the shrouds. Giles took one step to the side of the ship and saw the reason for the call. The gun had not been properly fixed in its sling and was starting to twist in such a way that it could come loose at any moment. If it did, even though it was only a few feet above the lighter, it could easily go through the bottom, sinking the lighter along with the other gun and itself going straight to the bottom. Before he could commend Humphries or begin giving the orders to lower the gun delicately into the lighter, a high pitched bellow alerted him to new troubles.

"Who counter-acted my orders? I'll have his hide for that! When I give an order it is to be obeyed! You, there, in the shrouds. Was it you?"

"Yes sir" said Humphries. "The gun…"

"Sergeant at arms, arrest that man. It's mutiny. I will have my orders obeyed. Now, Mr. Davis, haul away." Foster was almost dancing in his anger.

"Belay that," bellowed Giles. "Mr. Davis, ease the gun back into the lighter. Easily, very easily. Try to make no jerks on the line."

Davis gave orders to comply. Foster whirled on the Captain. "Sir, I will not have my orders countermanded. I expect you to support me."

"Mr. Foster, are you telling me that I cannot give orders on my own quarter deck?"

"No, sir. It is that man. He deliberately crossed me, telling the men to halt what I had ordered."

"Do you know, Mr. Foster, why this man gave the order?"

"No sir. It does not matter. I expect you, Captain, to support my authority."

"Do you? I'm supposed to support you and not you support me?"

"Both, sir." Foster was so angry and self-centered that he did not realize the trap Giles was backing him into.

"Humphries, thank you for your prompt action. I am sure that you saved us from very serious troubles."

"Captain, you can't support him in his insubordination. I never heard of anything like it. Captain, I cannot serve in a ship where the Captain does not support me."

"Can't you?"

"No, sir."

"Then, Mr. Foster, I suggest you get your things and go ashore."

"I will. And the Admiral will hear of this. I have influence, sir, I have. And you will rue this day."

"We shall see. Carstairs, please help Mr. Foster to gather his belongings and have my barge take him ashore."

Giles turned his back on his first lieutenant to see how Davis was doing in extricating them from the danger. The end of the gun was just touching the floorboards of the lighter, and the lighter-men had secured a line to the muzzle to guide it fully down.

"Carry on, Mr. Davis. I know I can trust you not to haul away until you know that it is safe to do so. Humphries, I meant what I said. You showed praiseworthy initiative. I am just sorry that the First Lieutenant misinterpreted your action." Since everyone there had heard the altercation between the Captain and the First Lieutenant, they realized that Giles was giving a most improbable interpretation of Foster's behavior.

With everything back to normal, Giles resumed his station on the quarter deck.

"Well done, Captain. Well done."

"I don't know what you are referring to, Mr. Brooks. I hope you realize that we are about to sail with only two lieutenants and both of them very inexperienced."

"Better just them than adding *that* First Lieutenant," Brooks muttered, loudly enough that Giles would hear it and softly enough that he could ignore it.

Giles retreated to his cabin. Mail had caught up with *Patroclus* and there were letters from Edwards, Daphne Moorhouse, and Bush. Giles opened Daphne's first. It was a note in response to the one he had sent her from London, expressing gratitude and delight about the improvements he had authorized. It must have been penned very soon after she had received his missive, for it made no comment on progress made. It did however, mention that Bush had suffered a mishap, was getting a new leg, and was staying with Mr. Moorhouse and herself. Edwards simply confirmed that arrangements were being made and that he would be visiting Dipton shortly. The letters brought on a surge of memories both of Dipton and of its inhabitants, but also of the comforts and interests that he had expected to pursue when ashore. He particularly dwelled on Miss Moorhouse, picturing her in his mind's eye while replaying their conversations. He realized with surprise that he had been so overwhelmed by her lively and direct personality that he had not really appreciated her charms. What a lovely face she had, close to the classic ideal of beauty, saved from mask-like serenity by an up-tilted nose and by a face over which different thoughts and feelings swept like the sunlight on an open landscape when the sky was dappled by fast moving clouds. He had also not really noted in person what he now dwelt on in reminiscence: Her eyes had the blue of a summer sky, though flashing more like the sun shining off ripples on the sea. She had a very neat waist and well curved bust. He even idly speculated what she would look like if she were to adopt the new, loose French fashions. Shaking his head to clear it of unseemly though delightful thoughts, Giles resolved to go into Falmouth before his appointment with the Admiral to see what the small town might offer to relieve the bleakness of his cabin and help Carstairs in finding suitable cabin supplies for the coming voyage.

Dinner with the Admiral turned out to also involve his wife, a cheery, buxom woman, far less austere than her husband, and their granddaughter, a girl of eighteen or nineteen years, pleasant enough in appearance though no great beauty, far longer on blushes than on independent observations. Giles was all too familiar how the availability of a successful frigate captain who happened also to be the son of an earl excited the match-making tendencies of the wives of senior officers and was well accustomed to being polite without becoming entangled. He did think fleetingly how much more he would have enjoyed the occasion had the woman who made up the party been Daphne Moorhouse rather than the insipid granddaughter of the Admiral.

When the ladies had withdrawn and the cloth had been pulled, Giles and the Admiral settled to their port and to talk of naval matters.

"I had your First Lieutenant in my room today, Giles."

"I am sorry if he caused any problem, sir."

"No problem, but rather amusement. You are well rid of that one, and rid of him you most certainly are."

"May I inquire what transpired, sir?"

"Of course. He stormed into my office demanding that I remove you from command and restore him to his rightful place. I did glean from his rantings what may have happened. Did a seaman really countermand his order?"

"Yes sir. The ship, or at least her new guns, were in imminent peril, which the man prevented from being realized when he called, "Avast hauling." I have commended the man, where Foster wanted him flogged. I countermanded Fpster's next order as well, which is when he went berserk."

"Good for your crew member! Anyway, I told your Mr. Foster that as a port admiral I was powerless to change the assignments of officers sailing under Admiralty orders, and that he would have to take his complaints up with the Admiralty in London. I did point out to him that in refusing to serve under you, he was in effect resigning his commission. I sent word to the Admiralty with the same sentiment, and will now reinforce my message with the details you have given me. He won't..." the Admiral laughed, "he won't even be eligible for half pay."

"Why?"

"In resigning his commission, he removes the Admiralty's responsibility for him. I suppose that this leaves you short of lieutenants. I hope the ones you have are experienced and can step into his shoes."

"Not really. They were both given their commissions very recently. And I am short of midshipmen and the ones I have are some ways still from making competent lieutenants."

"I'm afraid that I can't help you there."

"Don't concern yourself, sir. I would rather have the lieutenant whom I have than have Foster as First Lieutenant."

"There were other troubles were there?"

"I'm afraid so."

Giles went on to recount the failings of Mr. Foster that he had observed and the ones he suspected.

"Incompetent," said the Admiral. "A bugger, and shy. His previous birth was with Pritchard, wasn't it?"

"Yes, sir."

"Your Mr. Foster must have powerful people behind him. But this, especially as there are undoubtedly rumors elsewhere, should finish him."

"I would hope so. His being assigned to me might already be an indication that his patrons are losing patience with him."

"Let's hope so.

"Well, Captain, we should join the ladies. But if you feel that you have urgent business to attend to, I'm sure they will understand. Incidentally, you dodged my wife's bullet with more aplomb than any of the others she has tried to snare."

Chapter VII

The gossip which had so enthralled the gentry around Dipton faded away with the departure of Captain Bush and Lord David Giles. The work that was being done at Dipton Hall, the Dower Cottage and the Vicarage, under Edwards' direction, provided some fuel for the fire, but not much since most of the workmen were from elsewhere. It was generally agreed that the young ladies' fathers had been grossly remiss in not visiting the Captains at the Dipton Arms, despite the fact that the short time the targeted officers had stayed in the Inn had rendered such visits impractical.

The eagerness with which the returns of Captain Bush and Lord David were anticipated was somewhat stifled by the unfortunate arithmetic of the situation. Counting people of marriageable age, the new arrivals would add three men and four women: Giles half-nieces and Bush's sisters against the two captains and Lord David. Furthermore, one of the men, the prime catch of all, had the disadvantage that he was much grander than the others and, as Mr. Moorhouse had pointed out to Daphne, it was unlikely that Captain Giles would wed one of the local beauties. The same consideration applied, though possibly to a lesser extent to Lord David. The prospects of the widows of Dipton were also weakened by the coming presence of Captain Bush's mother and of Captain Giles' older half-sister. Lady Marianne was likely to outshine them all. This was, however, considered to be irrelevant since the only widower of any substance or good health in the neighborhood was Mr. Moorhouse. He had succeeded in resisting with ease all the widows' charms.

Daphne Moorhouse was widely considered to have obtained for herself a most unwarranted advantage by having inveigled both Lord David and Captain Bush into staying at Dipton Manor until their own homes were ready. The resentment that these facts produced was hardly lessened by Daphne's oft repeated claim that she had no interest in marriage, though it was somewhat mitigated by the eagerness with which she now was directing work on both her father's and Captain Giles' lands. A woman whose chief interests seemed to be crop yields and mucking about in drainage programs could not possibly rival the matrimonial attraction of more properly behaved young ladies, well-groomed in the art of pleasing conversation and accomplished in music.

The facts that Daphne was at least as accomplished on the piano as three quarters of the would-be brides and that she always seemed to have no lack of men interested in her conversation were comfortably overlooked by those who would diminish her threat in the matrimonial derby.

It can therefore be no surprise that the news that a Yorkshire militia regiment was to be billeted in Ameschester was met with fascination in Dipton and all the surrounding area. Ameschester was a small market town about ten miles from Dipton. Though of modest size, Ameschester was by all odds the nearest town of any consequence to Dipton. Young ladies from Dipton would often walk in groups to Ameschester to explore the offerings in the shops and to take tea in the tea room. With the regiment would come their officers and some of those officers might well be gentlemen of interest to the young ladies of Dipton.

The regiment was one of those that had been raised in '95 in light of the danger of invasion after the Duke of York's expedition had returned with nothing but wounds to show for their expensive sojourn in the Low Countries. The colonel of the militia regiment, who had first raised the regiment and after whom it was named was Lord Mosley, but he had not come south with the regiment which was under the command of their lieutenant colonel, James Craig, a lowland Scot who was a solicitor in Leeds.

The regiment held a dress parade on the cricket pitch at Ameschester on their arrival, and crowds came from all around to welcome the soldiers and to admire their performance. Dipton itself sent no fewer than seven carriages filled with young ladies and their chaperones. Excitement among the ladies was immense. Dipton's supply of eligible young men of quality had been diminished when Ameschester's own, locally-raised, militia had gone on maneuvers to other areas and some of their officers had married ladies whom they had met in those places. It was now Dipton's turn to level the balance. Even ladies who doubted the desirability of marrying someone from the bleak and cold northern county still counted on the arrival of the regiment to enliven their rather limited social scene and provide them with opportunities to display their charms to young gentlemen from the other side of Ameschester.

The parade was a splendid affair as the troops displayed their skills. The officers had striking uniforms, scarlet with bright yellow facings and elaborate needlework in black. Their horses looked like first-rate mounts and rumor had it that many had brought several horses with them, including hunters, so that if the regiment were to stay a while, the Ameschester Hunt would become a much larger event. The only sour notes about the affair were voiced by Captain Morse and Major Dimwhittle who had participated in the Duke of York's expedition and were now retired as a result of gout and the onset of creaky joints.

"They don't really know the drill, do they, Major?" asked Captain Morse.

"No Morse, there isn't that snap of soldiers who have drilled long enough that it becomes mindless," replied Major Dimwhittle.

"I hate to think what would happen if these fellows were in the line when one of Boney's columns advanced."

"They'd wet their trousers. Twice. Once before they ran and once in the channel where they'd drown," chortled the Major disregarding the geographic nonsense of what he suggested in favor of the witticism.

The celebration of the arrival of the Regiment was enhanced when the officers provided light refreshments for the local gentry following the parade. Though there were far more locals than officers and the officers were even outnumbered by the eligible young ladies, the occasion gave several of Dipton's own matrimonial hopefuls the opportunity to meet with young lieutenants and subalterns without bothering about proper introductions. Their mothers, noting this, realized that they had to warn their daughters of the dangers of men whose families they did not know and whose standing in their own communities was uncertain. All the older ladies had heard too many tales from elsewhere of officers who had seduced young ladies, even in some horrifying cases by promising marriage when the 'gentlemen' were already married, and of others who had likewise compromised young ladies before their regiments departed. The same ladies also resolved to remind their female servants of the awful consequences that would ensue should their charges become with child. How effective the talks were with either group is doubtful. The warnings were delivered in too circuitous a manner to give any real idea of what was the source of the danger that young ladies must avoid.

Daphne Moorhouse, while not receiving any warning herself, did instruct her servants and farmworkers of the dangers, even though she suspected that they knew as much of the hazards of associating with soldiers as she did

The soldiers were bivouacked for the time being on Ameschester Common, but their officers were billeted in the inns. The exception was the colonel. Although no one was billeted in private homes, and the Moorhouses would have been in no danger of having unwanted guests in any case, they had invited Colonel Craig and his wife to stay at Dipton Manor while the Lord Mosley's Regiment was in the area. At first, this produced consternation among the young ladies, since they could hardly send their fathers to welcome the Colonel to their neighborhood in the hopes of meeting young officers to whom they could deliver reciprocal invitations to visit. The problem was that it was unlikely that the target officers would be attending their Colonel at the hours when such calls would be made, so the invitations could only include Colonel and Mrs. Craig for a quite purposeless engagement. Some of the more devious realized that this was not in itself a drawback.

"Mr. Butler," said Mrs. William Butler one day, "we must invite Colonel Craig and his wife to dinner to welcome them to the neighborhood."

"Very well, Mrs. Butler," replied Mr. Butler, "but we cannot invite them without also inviting Mr. Moorhouse and Miss Moorhouse. The Craigs are, after all, the guests at Dipton Manor."

"True enough, Mr. Butler, but you know how little Mr. Moorhouse likes to go out. Quite possibly the Moorhouses will refuse the invitation on some excuse or other."

"I am afraid, my dear, that I still do not see how this can advance your schemes for the girls."

"That is the beauty of it, Mr. Butler. When I extend the invitation --- for I can call on Mrs. Craig -- you need not visit the Colonel – I can suggest that the Colonel bring two of his junior officers to make up the numbers. Since Miss Moorhouse is almost certain to be away from home, I can extend the invitation to Mr. Moorhouse himself when I am leaving. I will not be surprised if he refuses it. Even if he does accept, it is only two more people and Miss Moorhouse is no obstacle to our girls meeting the young officers."

Mrs. Butler put her scheme in motion as soon as she could. Miss Moorhouse was indeed not home, but Mrs. Craig was and welcomed the invitation. So, regrettably did Mr. Moorhouse who knew that his daughter enjoyed social evenings even though he himself did not. The evening went surprisingly well. Although previous conversations with the Moorhouses could be presumed to have removed the most obvious subject of conversation – an introduction to the Dipton area – talk flowed easily about other matters. Daphne seemed particularly adept at keeping the conversation going and eliciting a great deal of relevant information from the two lieutenants whom the Craigs had brought along to make up the numbers. They indeed seemed highly eligible young men, each embarking on a professional career whose pursuit had been interrupted by the present needs of the Regiment. Lieutenant Strangway was about to become a doctor, and was praised by Colonel Craig as a very useful addition to the medical resources at his disposal; while Lieutenant Barrows was articling with a solicitor's firm in Bradford. It was only when she overheard Susan quietly arranging for Catherine and Susan to meet the young officers in Ameschester at the tea shop that Mrs. Butler saw the weakness of her strategy. Since the officers had duties in Ameschester that would prevent them making afternoon calls on the gentry of Dipton, girls wanting to further their acquaintance would have to see them in Ameschester, unsupervised by their mothers.

The effectiveness of Mrs. Butler's designs was cast into further doubt by the arrival of Captain Bush's family in Dipton. This had not been expected to occur until work on Dipton Dower Cottage was finished. Neither Mr. Moorhouse nor Daphne had thought it worth mentioning to anyone before the arrival of Captain Bush and his family that they had invited them to lodge at Dipton Manor until the Dower Cottage was ready. Daphne had delayed instructing her housekeeper about the visitors until their arrival was imminent.

There was no problem in accommodating both the Bushes and the Craigs. Dipton Manor was a large rambling house that had grown over the ages by the addition of many rooms. None was excessively large, but the dining room could seat twenty at a pinch and the drawing room a similar number. Daphne and Mr. Moorhouse normally used only the dining room, the drawing room and Mr. Moorhouse's library. The first parlor was easily given over to Colonel and Mrs. Craig, while the second parlor could accommodate the Bush family, so each group had their own space if they did not want to meet with the others.

The change in the attractiveness of the great strategy arose from the additional numbers that would be required of an invitation. Just as the Moorhouses could not be excluded from an invitation to the Craigs, neither could the Bushes. And that invitation would not only have to be extended to Captain and Mrs. Bush, but also to two additional ladies, Bush's sisters, both of the critical age. Admittedly, these additional young ladies would need to be balanced by two more young officers, However, where the original strategy had only required six guests, and two of them the target of the enterprise, the new situation would require another six guests, only two of whom would add to men before whom the charms of the young ladies could be displayed. A dinner with eighteen people would strain the resources of many of the families. The additional guests would actually provide three more eligible bachelors, since Captain Bush himself was eminently eligible, missing limbs or not, but the Misses Bush might present accomplished alternatives to the prizes whose offering was the whole purpose of the social gathering.

In making these calculations, the schemers usually left Daphne Moorhouse out of their matrimonial reckonings, since she seemed so singularly not to exhibit those attributes that were believed to be necessary for a young lady to land a suitor. These charms largely were rooted in the ability to dress in a handsome manner, to engage men in shallow conversation that flattered them and that offered no opinions which might drive the hearers away, and to perform music,with reasonable skill, either on the piano forte or by singing. It seemed to be overlooked in considering the benefits and dangers of the invitations that Miss Moorhouse, though she showed no interest in endless discussions of clothes fashions with other women, was, when visiting, as attractively dressed as any of the others. Furthermore, while simpering was no part of Daphne's repertoire, she seemed to be able to hold conversations with gentlemen, with whom she was not herself bored, a good deal longer than any of the other young ladies. In addition, the belief that she lacked musical ability stemmed from her having no wish to perform in public while others were desirous do to so. When called upon, Daphne performed as well as three-quarters of the others. The failure of the schemers to recognize what a threat Daphne could be arose from their mistaking her doubt about the effectiveness or importance of the required social charms in attaining their purpose for a lack of those attractions herself.

Mrs. Bush was a rather dumpy woman, with a constant put-upon look as her standard demeanor. Only when reacting to some witticism that tickled her fancy did a smile break out that indicated that she had been less sour at an earlier age. She was, however, agreeable enough, her prime social weakness being to compare things, usually unfavorably, with Harwich, a habit particularly annoying since everyone was aware that she had been most impatient to leave Essex. Bush's sisters were rather gawky girls, unsure of themselves, and speaking in what some claimed was an Essex-tinged accent. They did seem to be a pleasant pair, though without many airs or accomplishments. They spoke little, and what they did say was unremarkable. The consensus among the Dipton ladies was that they were no particular threat to their own matrimonial endeavors. Bush himself was regarded as a pleasant young man, certainly a very eligible catch, though rather taciturn and with a most regrettable tendency to talk about most abstruse matters of history with Mr. Moorhouse. Possibly the move to the Dower Cottage would cure him of that tendency. Several ladies went out of their way to cultivate Mrs. Bush and her two daughters in the hope of thereby gaining in time privileged entrée to the Dower Cottage.

Bush himself was quite content to accept the hospitality of the Moorhouses. When he wanted to escape his womenfolk, he was always welcome in Mr. Moorhouse's library where, like Captain Morse and Major Dimwhittle in Ameschester, they would rehash battles, though the battles were separated by millennia from the ones argued over at Dipton and the discussions were based not on personal experience but on accounts found in books. If conversation was not desired by either of them, Mr. Moorhouse's library provided a treasure trove of books that Bush wanted to consume.

Bush's recovery was proceeding apace. He had purchased a gentle horse, chosen on the advice of a friend of Mr. Moorhouse who was said to have a very keen eye for horse-flesh. He had then taken to riding every day. Often these excursions simply took him to Dipton to observe the progress being made on Dipton Hall and the Dower Cottage, but sometimes his outings would take him all the way to Ameschester where he formed an acquaintance with the Major Dimwhittle and Captain Morse. Bush shared the usual, naval contempt for the army where officers bought their commissions, often with no experience commensurate with the rank, but his experiences in Corsica had lessened his prejudice and he was happy to yarn with the two old warhorses and agree with their assessment of the shocking state of the militia.

Bush had also adopted an extension for the missing part of his arm, fashioned by Jake to a design of Mr. Jackson. He was getting used to it and was surprised how many normal tasks could be accomplished with its aid. He had found it invaluable in mounting and dismounting from his horse and had discovered that he could even use it to hold down his fork so that he could cut his meat with his knife, a vast improvement on having to wait for a footman to do the task for him.

Bush's equestrian skills had evolved so far that he could confidently accompany Daphne Moorhouse when she visited parts of the two estates on horseback. He was learning that there was more to living in the country than he, raised in a town before going to sea, had ever realized, and that the rural setting provided more ways to keep himself amused than he had expected.

Daphne now rode far more often than she had when her duties and interests were largely in areas that were easily reached by foot. To the horror of everyone, she rode astride her horse, wearing a pair of very loose trousers that reached her ankles so that when she was not on horseback, it looked like an ordinary skirt. The complete modesty of the garment did not silence the shocked gossipers about how inappropriate such actions were.

Mr. Moorhouse noted the growing friendship between Daphne and Bush with pleasure. Mr. Moorhouse was, of course, well aware of Daphne's claim that one of the reasons that she would not marry was the need to look after her father, a claim in which he saw no merit as he had often told her. Nothing would delight him more than to see her happily married, though he saw no need or advantage to Daphne's marrying just for the sake of conforming to social expectation. He was pleased that she had a new, solid friend in Bush, but he observed that there was none of that frisson of excitement that surrounds couples who are courting, even unconsciously. He had observed it when Daphne and Giles had been together, but he had no illusions that that attraction would lead anywhere, for which he was deeply sorry and hopeful that Daphne would not be hurt by forming unrealistic hopes about a future with Captain Giles. His fears on that score had recently been raised by Daphne's suddenly exhibiting a significantly greater interest in practicing the piano-forte and he wondered what the hidden meaning of this change was.

Neither Mr. Moorhouse, nor Captain Bush, nor Daphne liked to engage in conversation at breakfast while the others who were visiting seemed to think it was the time for lively discourse. Luckily the unsociable ones were usually awake before the others and could enjoy breakfast together in silence. One morning, early in the Bush family's stay at Dipton Manor, mail had arrived for both Bush and Daphne. As soon as tea was poured and food assembled, each took up their letters. Bush was the first to comment on the content of his, though almost at the same time Daphne had given a little squeak of astonishment.

"Captain Giles has taken a frigate."

"Oh?" queried Mr. Moorhouse, looking up from his newspaper.

"Yes, with almost no damage to either vessel. A French 32. Crippled with *Patroclus*'s bow chasers. That will be a handy bit of prize money!"

"My package is from Captain Giles, too," said Daphne. "He sent me some sonatas by Herr Mozart which he saw in Falmouth thinking that I might like them. They are for piano-forte and violin, but he says that he thinks that the piano-forte part can be played by itself"

That is not quite what Giles had written. His words had been, 'I stopped by a shop in Falmouth that had some music. There were some sonatas for piano-forte and violin by Herr Mozart. I noticed that you had some sonatas by Mozart lying on your piano-forte. There were two copies of the sonatas, so I have kept the other one. I hope to learn the violin part of at least the first sonata on this voyage. Then, perhaps, we can play it together when I am again in Dipton. Looking over the works, I believe that the piano-forte part can, if necessary, stand on its own."

It was after this episode that Daphne had shown renewed interest in the piano-forte and it was quite evident that she was working on a new piece. Mr. Moorhouse doubted that it was simply the fascination of a new piece that had Daphne working so hard. Daphne enjoyed playing, but was easily bored by the tedium of getting a piece as perfect as possible and was usually content to take her pieces to the stage where playing them gave her satisfaction, even though the performance might still be sprinkled with wrong notes and dubious emphasis. She seemed to be trying to get the new piece beyond that stage.

The manifest difficulties of the Dipton schemes to get access to the officers of the militia regiment left but few options to participate in the matrimonial sweepstakes. The most obvious one was led by the Misses Butler and was adopted by several other young ladies from the Ameschester side of Dipton. This was to walk as a group to Ameschester and hope to meet the officers that way. The Misses Butler took the lead because they had been introduced properly to Lieutenants Strangway and Barrows. Their first foray to Ameschester accompanied by the Trusly sisters had been a success in that they had met in the street, by chance, the two lieutenants. These lieutenants in turn introduced two of their brethren and the now very proper party of eight descended on the tea shop. The lack of chaperoning worried the young ladies much less than it would have bothered their mothers, had they known what was afoot. Other young ladies soon joined their outings. Since the Butler sisters had been in the habit of walking to Ameschester at least once a week before the arrival of Lord Mosley's Regiment and since it was not unusual for some of their friends to join them, it was not appreciated by their parents that there was now a new and dangerous attraction in the usually sleepy town of Ameschester.

The only other options that seemed to be available for the young ladies to meet the officers were the balls. These were held in Ameschester and in nearby places quite frequently, sometimes in private houses, but more usually in halls that were attached to inns for just that purpose. Dipton, unfortunately, was ill served in possibilities to host a ball. The Dipton Arms had no rooms anywhere near the size needed for any but the most modest of dancing parties. Dipton Manor was blessed with a very large number of rooms, but none was very large nor were any of them connected in such a way that dancing could be held in several rooms at once. Dipton Manor also lacked any room larger than the dining room to accommodate the supper and the gatherings of older men and women which were such a feature of balls.

That left only the option of going to as many balls elsewhere in the area as possible. Some were held too far from Dipton, on the Horsmarsh side of Ameschester to be feasible. Otherwise, any ball near Ameschester could expect a larger continent to come from Dipton than was usual. No return calls were made on the ladies of Dipton as a result of these efforts, but some of the officers – and even of the country gentry – asked some of the ladies for places on their cards more frequently than would indicate simple politeness, but, all in all, the balls did not produce any successes or even any hint that success could be expected.

One ball, which was particularly memorable for the people living at Dipton Manor, came soon after Bush had received and mastered the device for the end of his arm. The party from Dipton manor consisted of the Craigs, the Bushes and Daphne Moorhouse. Mr. Moorhouse was glad to beg off, with Captain Bush and Colonel Craig able to see to the safety of the ladies. The gentlemen rode their horses, Bush now having enough confidence even to attempt the feat of riding to Ameschester in the dark.

Daphne was among the five women crowding into the carriage. She loved dancing for itself and she was a very good dancer. She also enjoyed mingling with people from a wider area than just Dipton. At the previous ball which the group had attended, Bush had not yet acquired his arm extension, and had claimed that a one-legged man with an empty sleeve could not possibly dance. This time would be different.

Daphne approached Bush just before the third dance. "I see, Captain Bush that your name is on my card for the next dance."

"It cannot be, Miss Moorhouse. You know that I cannot dance."

"I know of no such thing, Captain. You are now very steady on your feet and where a left hand is required in the dance, the addition to your arm will serve very well. The next dance is a slow, indeed stately, one. I am sure that you can manage it with aplomb."

Daphne was quite correct. By the end of the dance, Bush was dancing with some pleasure, the activity being itself a welcome change from the conversation with the idle men in which he would otherwise be engaged, and Daphne herself led him in such an unobtrusive way that the mysteries of the dance were soon mastered. A second dance with Daphne got Bush very comfortable with participating in the activity.

"Now, Captain Bush, you must ask one of the ladies to dance."

"But I do not know any."

"Let me introduce you to some."

The Butler girls were sitting alone with their mother and another older lady. Daphne steered Bush to them.

"Mrs. Butler, Misses Butler, let me introduce Captain Bush, the guest who is staying at Dipton Manor for a while. Captain Bush, Mrs. Butler, Miss Butler and Miss Susan Butler."

Bush bowed, acceptably if not elegantly, despite his lack of limbs. Daphne had made it quite clear that she expected him to ask one of the Butler sisters to dance and the danger of arousing her disappointment quite overcame Bush's shyness with women. He chose Susan, as being the less intimidating of the two sisters.

The dance proceeded without incident. Susan was a rather shy girl, not overly eager to make conversation nor to demand it, and Bush had too much to attend to in negotiating the dance to want to make conversation. Nevertheless, Susan appeared to enjoy the dance and Bush discovered that it was not nearly as dire an endeavor as he had expected.

Daphne was a popular dancer and well occupied during the ball so Bush realized that only modest efforts on his part would keep her from insisting that he dance with new partners. Just to show that he was participating in the dancing, he invited Susan Butler again and one final time before the evening ended. He had found her an agreeable partner and he had no desire to seek other introductions to dancing partners, even though many of the men wanted to talk with him about the war and he could have easily asked them to introduce him to more ladies. It never occurred to him that his attentions devoted simply to Miss Susan Butler might be misinterpreted by many of the onlookers.

Daphne's interpretation of Bush's action was indeed far from the mark. She was not above the match-making that so enthralled others. She liked Bush herself, and she would like him to have stronger reasons to stay in the neighborhood since he was one of the few men whose company her father enjoyed. Bush's singular interest in Susan Butler, especially noteworthy because he had not asked her sister to dance, struck Daphne as the beginning of a romance, one that she must endeavor to encourage.

Daphne had spent the beginning of the ball introducing the Craigs and the Bush family to many of her neighbors. That should provide Mrs. Bush and Mrs. Craig with a circle of people to talk with while the dancing proceeded, and possibly introduce Mrs. Bush to women who would become her friends as she continued to reside in Dipton. The introductions also provided companions for the Bush sisters to chat with as they awaited invitations to dance. Several men had indeed asked the sisters to dance and both ladies were, as a result, quite pleased with the ball.

Other balls followed, but while they were enjoyable, they produced no progress on the matrimonial needs of the families of Dipton. Mrs. Butler was one of the most desperate of the mothers. Mr. Butler was a second son and his progress toward a profession had been interrupted by marriage to Mrs. Butler, whose dowry he fancied would allow them sufficient funds that he need not pursue the learning necessary for a professional career, which he found tedious. This expectation had been based on frugality and despite Mrs. Butler's attempt to limit the housekeeping expenses, Mr. Butler had not been able to limit his own expenditures by a large enough measure to avoid eroding the capital Mrs. Butler had brought to the marriage. It was doubtful that there would be enough for Mrs. Butler to look after herself comfortably when Mr. Butler died. She had absolutely no desire to have to reside with her brother-in-law, who in any case might die first.

The Butlers could provide only very modest dowries for their daughters, and it was Mrs. Butler's hope that not only would the girls cease to be a burden on her own finances, but that they would provide a home for her when it was needed. She had stressed to her daughters that it was not enough to marry, but they must marry into a secure income, preferably from land, but otherwise from the practice of a profession, in the latter case with the revenues already well established before the nuptials could be approved. In her heart, she knew that this would be difficult, especially with only the small dowries with which Mr. Butler could provide their daughters. Mrs. Butler had little hope for Susan's finding the necessary suitor, but surely Catherine's vivacious, even flirtatiousn, manner, her striking figure, narrow at the waist and full in the bosom, and her sparkling eyes must attract someone with the minimum requirements. It had been disappointing that no match had been found in the previous three and a half years. Mrs. Butler was becoming increasingly anxious as the window of opportunity closed for Catherine.

This may have accounted for Mrs. Butler's lack of concern about her daughters' walking to Ameschester at least twice each week. They were, after all, accompanied by others from the area, and Mrs. Butler believed that she could count on the steadiness and sense of Susan to restrain any imprudent behavior by her sister. Though rumors had been circulating about the noisy gathering of the officers and young ladies in the tea room at Ameschester, surely the public nature of the meetings would provide safety and it could be hoped that Catherine's vivacity would soon induce some young man to visit Mr. Butler.

It came as a complete mystery to the family when it was discovered one morning that Susan had disappeared. The first intimations of trouble came at breakfast when Susan did not appear. A maid sent to see if she were ill, returned to say that she was not in her room, though her bed appeared to have been occupied. Catherine, who had a room separate from Susan's, suggested that her younger sister had probably risen early and gone for a walk. Since that frequently happened, though Susan had in the past always returned in time for breakfast, little concern was expressed until eleven o'clock. A search of the neighborhood was then undertaken, arising from the fear that Susan had somehow injured herself in such a way as to prevent her returning. The search was fruitless. More pointed questioning of Catherine revealed that Susan and Lieutenant Barrows had talked about eloping to Gretna Green to get married. The couple knew that they would not get Mr. Butler's permission, since Lieutenant Barrows' career in Bradford had yet to start, and his pay in the militia was of uncertain duration, though it would be enough to support a wife. They felt urgency to wed since Lord Moseley's Regiment was expected to move into barracks nearer the coast imminently. The two young people had spent their time together in Ameschester in conversations that excluded others and in taking walks while the other young people were enjoying themselves as a group in the tea shop.

Mrs. Butler was beside herself with anxiety for her daughter and worry about her own future. Mr. Butler was away from Dipton and could not be relied on to find a solution to the problem. Susan was clearly ruined and would have to be shunned in future by her family. Even if the couple did indeed get to Gretna Green, there would be deep shame attached to the marriage, and Mrs. Butler in her panic presumed that Susan would simply be abandoned by her seducer.

The immediate consequence of the news spreading of Susan's terrible action was that all the other young ladies who had walked to Ameschester were prohibited from going there again, and in some cases from going anywhere at all. Catherine Butler found this prohibition particularly galling since she had arranged with a Captain Crockett to take a pic-nick basket to the banks of the River Amesnott, unaccompanied by those they described as the shallow denizens of the tea room. Captain Crockett, also of Lord Moseley's Regiment, was a most dashing and entertaining officer who had paid much attention to Catherine. It only increased his allure that no one in their group knew Captain Crockett well, even his standing in Yorkshire seemed unknown. Her sister's irresponsible action had prevented Catherine from enjoying what promised to be a very exciting rendezvous with a worldly, older man.

The crisis ended the next day when Mr. Butler returned accompanied by a rather woebegone Susan and a subdued Lieutenant Barrows. The eloping couple had got as far as the posting inn on the Great North Road where Mr. Butler happened to be staying on his way back to Dipton. He immediately took the situation in hand, separated Susan from Lieutenant Barrows, and insisted that Lieutenant Barrows return to Dipton with him, using the threat that he would have him drummed out of the Regiment and have his name blackened in Yorkshire where he had hoped to practice law.

In the interview that followed their return to Dipton, Mr. Butler very firmly stated that the Lieutenant must marry Susan. Lieutenant Barrows was more than happy to oblige and when Mr. Butler found out that the Lieutenant was not without hope of an inheritance from a well-off uncle, he even took the step of halving Susan's dowry, thinking that the other half could well be applied to his own needs. Mr. Butler's only regret was that Mrs. Butler's panic when she learned that Susan had eloped meant that the news was widespread, while had Mrs. Butler remained silent the whole incident could be ignored with no damage to their reputations.

Among those who were least shocked by Susan Butler's fall was Daphne Moorhouse. She had had no doubt that the liberal ways of Mr. and Mrs. Butler could be leading to disaster, but she would have put her wager on Catherine being the one to bring shame on her family rather than Susan. What Daphne felt most strongly about the affair was chagrin at how far from the mark had been her understanding of the situation. She had believed that there was a budding romance with Captain Bush, but now Daphne suspected that Susan had been inspiring that belief in order to hide her infatuation with Lieutenant Barrows.

Chapter VIII

Patroclus sailed from Falmouth as soon as her supplies were on board. Sailing with her was her tender, H.M. Schooner *Swan*, which had arrived in Falmouth that morning. The Admiralty had seen fit to assign her to Giles for this venture claiming that he might need a vessel to carry dispatches to Falmouth about news that he had obtained in searching for the French marauder. Giles suspected that *Swan* had been assigned to him so that a report would be made if *Patroclus* met the fate of other British frigates which had tangled with the French threat. Whatever the reason for her assignment, Giles was happy to have her, even though her fighting abilities might be minimal. *Swan* was a gaff rigged schooner, mounting only ten nine-pounder pop-guns. She would be hard put to take even a small merchant vessel, and would be no match for almost any privateer. But her value lay in her speed, especially to windward where she could sail far closer to the wind and more speedily than any square-rigged vessel.

Swan's captain came aboard *Patroclus* right after she had dropped anchor. His name was James Duncan, and he was a Master and Commander, which was normally the rank to which lieutenants rose on the way to becoming captains and was often the end of a promising career for officers without influence and who had not been lucky enough to be prominent in a notable and bloody action. Such probably was the case for Captain Duncan who was Giles' age and then some. His officers consisted of one lieutenant and one midshipmen, with a contingent of warrant officers between him and the crew. Though habitually stooped from being in berths with inadequate headroom, Captain Duncan was a cheerful man, apparently quite happy to be sailing under Admiralty orders on tasks that offered little glory.

Giles outlined the nature of their mission. He pointed out that initially their most likely task while patrolling in the approaches to the Channel was to speak other vessels in order to seek for information on the French raider. They would take prizes only if doing so did not interfere with their primary mission and Giles made it clear that they should be convinced that such activity was not being pursued at expense of concentrating on their primary mission before it could be approved by him or by the Admiralty.

Giles had decided that the search for the French frigate must take precedence over trying to discover what had happened to the missing ships, but he did inform Captain Duncan of the need to discover where the missing vessels might be and he also intimated that the time might come when Duncan would be called upon to pursue that objective while *Patroclus* concentrated on the first.

Giles found that he liked the man. His questions were few and those he did ask were valid points of clarification or elaboration. He quickly understood what Giles wanted and showed no resentment at a man who had clearly advanced farther and faster in the Navy than he had.

"Captain Duncan," said Giles when the business part of their conversation had ended, "I hope you will join me for a glass of wine."

"With the greatest pleasure, Captain."

"I obtained several cases of claret in Falmouth yesterday. I'd like your opinion on them."

"I expect that if they came to Cornwall in the usual way, they must be excellent."

Both officers knew that the wine might well have been imported by smugglers, but neither would announce that belief explicitly.

The wine was indeed excellent and served to make unofficial conversation flow freely. Duncan had had a variety of commands of minor vessels. He was delighted that *Swan* had come his way for he had been on half pay during the peace and had feared he would not again find employment.

"I was tempted to go with the revenue-ers just before this war started," Duncan confided to Giles, "for they needed men who could speak French for their cutters."

"So, do you speak French fluently, Captain Duncan?"

"Och aye, Captain, as we say in Scotland, I learned it from my sister's governess who was a French lady."

"Pity you couldn't join us earlier. We could have used you in the last week... No, no, Captain Duncan, I did not mean to imply that you have come late in any way. It is just that we took a French frigate, and it would have helped if anyone on *Patroclus* had been able to speak French properly."

Nothing would do other than Captain Giles's recounting in detail the story of the capture of the French frigate.

"I noticed your bow chasers, Captain Giles, as I came aboard. They look a formidable weapon if they don't take the bow right out of your own ship."

"Well, they have served me well so far."

"Let's hope they do again."

Patroclus and *Swan* patrolled the approaches to the Channel from roughly ten leagues west of Ushant to at least ten leagues west of Land's End, and extended their search farther out into the Atlantic. Giles stationed *Swan* to leeward of *Patroclus*, almost on the horizon so that their search area could be maximized while *Swan* would be on her best point of sailing to join with *Patroclus* if threatened. In terms of their main mission, this cruising proved fruitless for many days. They did indeed see large numbers of friendly vessels and they were not idle in seeking information. Giles realized that they must talk with almost every ship sailing alone and with every convoy to investigate whether there was news of their quarry. So far that had proved fruitless. None had seen any French frigate or privateer, though a couple had found flotsam recently which might have been the result of damage occurring when a ship was taken. The evidence was so slight and the time that lapsed since the sightings was so long that there was no point in Giles's deviating from his pattern to seek the source of the flotsam.

Two merchant ships that *Patroclus* and *Swan* approached for news turned out to be French. In both cases, when *Patroclus* came up with the target ship, she surrendered as soon as it was clear that she could not out sail the frigate. Both were from Martinique, trying to sneak past the British blockade by passing through waters where British shipping was common and usually not bothered by warships. These ships also had heard nothing of the sought-after French frigate. They did provide valuable prizes which Giles sent into to Falmouth with *Swan*. The escort was ordered not for protection of the prizes, since *Swan*'s ability to save them from a French privateer was minimal, but to get news and to make sure that Giles' prize-crew would return promptly.

Finally one morning, first light revealed a frigate to windward of *Patroclus* about four leagues distant under all sails to the royals, close-hauled on the starboard tack, sailing east into the south-south-east wind. *Patroclus* had been reaching to the north under all plain canvas and Giles had been about to wear to larboard when the other vessel was spotted. Instead, he turned to starboard and ordered *Patroclus* to spread all canvas that could be carried as *Patroclus* herself came onto the starboard tack. Giles was fairly certain that they had encountered a French vessel by the course she was steering and the press of canvas she carried, but he would have to be sure before attacking her. There were too many French frigates of the same class that had been captured and bought into the Royal Navy to be certain that *Patroclus* had encountered an enemy. The fact that, when *Patroclus* hoisted her British colors, the other ship did likewise indicated nothing. It was within the well-established conventions of war to sail under false colors until a hostile act was made. That the frigate to windward signified that it belonged to the Royal Navy, with the blue ensign indicating that she sailed under the orders of an admiral of the blue, was no more to be relied upon than if *Patroclus* had hoisted the French tricolor in the hope of attracting the other vessel to her side.

By the next turn of the glass, it was evident that *Patroclus* was going through the water faster than her rival and sailing a bit closer to the wind. The elaborate calculations that Mr. Brooks performed as a result of very careful use of his sextant indicated that, if the wind held and each ship maintained her present course, their courses would intersect at three bells of the afternoon watch, and that *Patroclus* would be in a position to engage the enemy substantially before that time. Unfortunately the wind weakened so that by the next turn of the glass, the calculated meeting time was postponed until six bells of the afternoon watch. If it fell much more, the meeting would be postponed into the dog watches or even until after the sun had set, in which case the rival might well get away. The wind continued to weaken and turned a bit fluky, so that now one vessel would have a stronger puff and get ahead in their race only to find that soon her rival would be the favored one. By six bells of the forenoon watch, they had got close enough that Giles could order the hoisting of the private signal which should tell them directly if the vessel they were pursuing was French. The response of the other ship was to haul down her British colors and hoist instead the French tricolor. However, the state of the wind was such that they could have no confidence in closing with the enemy until long after dark. Since the moon was waning, there would then be any number of ruses by which the French ship could slip away.

The possibilities of the two vessels meeting in a short time had faded to the point where Giles felt confident in ordering the galley fire rekindled and a hot dinner provided to the crew. He himself stayed on deck with only a hunk of ship's bread and a slice of cold beef for sustenance. The tender meat was a reward for his having sent *Swan* into Falmouth with their previous captures; otherwise he would have had to try to eat salt pork straight out of the barrel. He ordered the wardroom officers to have their dinners before the ship came up to the enemy and hoped that they also had some fresh supplies.

By one bell of the afternoon watch, the wind began to fill in, still from the south east to Mr. Brooks' surprise. Before long both vessels were bowling along and studding sails had to be taken in and then Royals. By five bells the ships were close enough that Giles had to think more seriously about his tactics. His position now was such that if he shortened sail or just spilled the wind, *l'Hercule*, for so the French frigate was named, would have to come up to him with less than a quarter of a cable separating the ships. A bit closer might be desirable, but that distance would be entirely satisfactory for them to exchange broadsides. If his rival wanted to avoid that confrontation he could tack, leaving himself vulnerable if *Patroclus* also tacked with him. Anyway, if he was going to take that step, he should have done it earlier, since then the consequence of missing stays would be less disastrous and he could equally hope that *Patroclus* would not come about smoothly. He could wear to cross *Patroclus*'s wake, possibly hoping to rake *Patroclus* as he passed. But *Patroclus* would wear as well and would arrive at as favorable a position, possibly even a better one, than if the French ship had maintained her course.

The next subject that Giles needed to resolve was how to conduct the battle when he had the French ship in range. The usual procedure would be to exchange broadsides in the hope that the damage done by the guns would open up an advantage. Since British gunnery was usually faster than French, and more accurate, this tactic often yielded an advantage to the British combatant. In this case, Giles was skeptical. His adversary looked to have been at sea for some time, judging by the weather-beaten appearance of her sails and by the clearly foul nature of her bottom which Giles had glimpsed as she had crested waves. Her crew might well be as trained as his own, though he doubted that she had had much practice firing loaded and shotted guns.

However, if several broadsides were exchanged, it was quite likely that *l'Hercule* could do very serious damage to *Patroclus*'s rigging. This might well give the Frenchman a chance to escape if her own rigging was not also seriously damaged. Furthermore, serious damage to *Patroclus*, even if she still was able to defeat *l'Hercule*, could quite possibly leave her unfit to meet the ship whose destruction was the purpose of her present cruise. In addition, if *l'Hercule* was coming from the West Indies, as Giles suspected, it was unlikely that she had a full complement of sailors. That was a luxury unusual in any ship, and a ship that had been in Martinique or Guadeloupe was likely to have suffered serious attrition through illness. Giles' good fortune in having a full crew would give him an advantage if the fighting came to close quarters.

In view of these considerations, Giles resolved to fire only an introductory broadside as the ships approached each other and then to pinch up to board *l'Hercule*. He ordered the guns to be double-shotted with cannon balls for the first broadside and immediately to be reloaded with grapeshot and canister. He instructed that the guns be aimed to sweep the Frenchman's deck. Giles also told Mr. Brooks, who would have tactical control of *Patroclus*'s course, to close with the enemy for boarding as soon as the first salvo had fired. These orders given, he instructed his officers to be ready to board as soon as the ships could be grappled together, and then hid a fair portion of his boarding parties from view of the Frenchman, both to protect them from the initial French broadsides and to disguise as much as he could what were his intentions.

The rails of the two ships should be at just about the same height so his boarders would be able to cross without trouble at midship as soon as the ships touched. Giles commanded Lieutenant Macauley to take his marines to secure the forecastle. Lieutenant Davis would try to secure the waist, while Giles himself would lead the attack on the quarterdeck. Only a minimal crew would be left on board *Patroclus*. Parties were chosen to grapple the two ships together as they met. Giles had the seamen crouch behind the hammock nettings for their own protection and in the hope that they might be overlooked as the ships approached each other.

When these arrangements had been made, and the boarding parties armed suitably, there was nothing Giles could do but wait. *Patroclus* was maintaining little more than steerage way, most of her sails brailed up. The two ships slowly approached their meeting. Giles had done all he could in preparation. Now he could only walk calmly about the quarter deck trying to show no fear even as he was all too aware that he would be the prime target of the marksmen *l'Hercule* would have stationed in her fighting tops. Time crawled agonizingly for everyone as they waited in silence, interrupted only by muttered prayers from some of the men awaiting action.

The angle of approach of the two ships meant that *Patroclus's* guns came to bear on her opponent first, but Giles held his fire until the broadside would cover most of *l'Hercule*. By contrast, the later started firing the moment her foremost gun bore, and her rippling broadside sent cannon balls towards the stern third of *Patroclus*. As was standard for French ships, her broadside was aimed high, intending to shred *Patroclus'* rigging and so render her helpless. While the guns caused few casualties directly, it did considerable damage aloft and blocks rained down into the nets spread to catch them. More seriously, one ball glanced off *Patroclus* mizzenmast, taking a large chunk from it and spreading lethal splinters everywhere.

Just after the mizzenmast was damaged, Giles bellowed the order to open fire. Now *Patroclus*'s broadside roared out, aimed at *L'Hercule's* bulwarks. As soon as the guns had recoiled, their crews worked feverishly to reload them and haul them out. The loads of grapeshot and canister that followed swept the decks just as the ships met and the grapnels were thrown. *L'Hercule's* second broadside roared out moments after *Patroclus*'s, but again it was high, though the closeness of the range meant that it did much more damage than had the previous one. *Patroclus*'s grapnels were heaved, the ships pulled together, and Giles' order of "Away Boarders" sent a hoard of vengeful fighters onto *l'Hercule's* deck, all screaming like unoiled hinges as they released the tensions that had built up while they waited. Their onslaught would have done their Viking ancestors proud.

Giles did not lead the hoard; his need to keep the quarter deck until the last minute prevented that, but he was close behind, unsheathed sword in hand. He was quickly at the front of the attackers, joining the other in his yells, while trying to make sure that his contingent fought their way toward the quarterdeck ladders. Time seemed now to stand still as each separate step of the fight froze in his memory. He countered a slash from a cutlass and then stabbed the man holding it in the belly. A twist of his wrist, and his sword was free, just as he had to duck a roundhouse swing of a club by a giant Frenchman. His opponent's miss had swung the attacker around and Giles dispatched him with a thrust in his neck and a boot in his behind to clear the way. A man filling the gap left by the giant had his wrist severed by a slash from Humphry's sabre while Giles completed the destruction by landing the pommel of his sword on the man's head. Kicking the body aside, he perceived a path had opened up to the ladder to the quarter deck and pushed ahead, his flanks luckily being guarded by Humphries on his left and someone to his right whom Giles had not had time to recognize in the heat of the struggle. An opponent trying to hold the ladder with slashes of a cutlass, striking down viciously at Giles whose own momentum was halted by the need to parry the slashes and the thrusts from above, suddenly toppled forward with a thrown knife lodged in his throat. Only a desperate step to his left saved Giles from going down under the man, and the bulk of Humphries to his left kept him from being toppled over.

Giles sprang up the ladder and a thrust and a slash from his sword carried him to the top. He was confronted by a group of officers with drawn swords. Seeing Giles emerge and hearing the bloodthirsty shouts of the men following him, the leading French officer stepped back, lowered his blade and bellowed some order that Giles did not understand. But the substance of the order was clear as the other officers lowered their weapons and bellowed to their crewmen.

"We surrender. We surrender." Shouted a junior officer at the rear of the group of French officers. "We 'aul down hour couleurs."

Giles in turn shouted to his men that the French had yielded and that they should cease fighting. He stood leaning on his sword breathing heavily as the hub-bub died down. Then he stepped forward to accept the sword of the man whose uniform, more elaborate that the other ones, marked him as the enemy captain. Giles reversed the sword and gave it back to the captain with the words, "You fought well, Captain. I will be happy to accept your parole and those of your officers so that you need not suffer the indignity of being bound until we can straighten things out." The French officer with a smattering of English translated the remarks

Lieutenant Macauley showed up at this point, followed by Mr. Davies. They were instructed to secure the ship and its crew and did so with the aid of translations by the French officer who understood English. With the enemy ship secured, Giles went down the ladder from the quarter deck. He was horrified by the number of dead bodies littering the deck, some the result of *Patroclus*'s second broadside, others of the hand-to-hand combat. Crossing to *Patroclus*, there were few dead bodies, the ones that were lying on the deck probably the result of the splinters that showered the decks when *l'Hercule*'s second broadside fired. Mr. Brooks already had men aloft splicing rigging that had been severed in the fight. The carpenter and boatswain with their mates were examining the mizzenmast. Giles went to them.

"How does it look?"

"It's badly weakened, sir. Almost broken. We can fish timber around it, probably using some of our spare yards, but it will not be able to carry a full set of sails in any type of a blow. Setting the rigging up tighter and doubling it would help, but she still will not be able to take the full load, nor will she bear much tension coming from the mainmast."

"Do the best you can, Mr. Hendricks."

"Aye, aye, sir. I've had a quick look at *l'Hercule*, sir. Her larboard side will need to be rebuilt, but she can sail as she is, pretty much. But what we can do out here will not avoid the need for a shipyard."

"Can she make it to Falmouth the way she is?"

"Certainly sir. And fight, sir, if she had to. I just would be cautious about anything that might swamp the larboard side."

"Carry on, then. I hope to get both ships under way before dark."

Dr. Maclean was waiting to get Giles's attention.

"Have you been across to *l'Hercule*, Doctor?"

"Aye, sir."

"What's the butcher's bill?"

"We lost ten, sir. Three on board here and seven on the other ship. There are another fifteen injured. Two of them may not make it. The French lost far more. Their doctor is looking after their wounded, but since I am finished here, I will go back and help him."

"We'll bury our dead as soon as we've made the most urgent repairs. Can you tell Mr. Davies that the French can give their dead a proper burial if they wish and not just throw the corpses overboard?"

"Aye, aye, Captain, but you yourself are bleeding. Your left arm."

Giles looked at his arm. He had been feeling some discomfort from it, but had just presumed that it had been bruised. Now he saw that his sleeve had been slashed above the elbow and that blood was oozing out of the hole in the cloth.

"I'll have it looked to when everything else is complete."

"No, you won't, sir. That is the way the putrification sets in. Take off your coat and shirt, please."

Giles complied, finding that the pain increased markedly when he had to pull his sleeve away from the wound.

"Just as I thought," said the Doctor. "I'll clean it and sew it up and you'll be right as rain."

Dr. Maclean was none too gentle as he cleaned the wound, making sure that no foreign matter still remained in it. He finished by pouring rum onto the injury. His sewing needle felt as if it was in need of sharpening. When the doctor completed his procedure by having Giles raise his arm so that more rum could be poured over the wound before bandaging it, Giles felt much more injured than when Dr. Maclean's ministrations had started. He realized again the high price that even those who were mildly wounded paid as a result of his decision to chase and engage the enemy.

By three bells of the first dog watch, the ships had both been readied to sail again. Giles had held a service for the burial of those whom *Patroclus* had lost and he had allowed the French officers to attend a similar service on board *l'Hercule,* a service that was closely overseen by *Patroclus*'s marines and many of her crew members also heavily armed. He had decided to send *l'Hercule* into Falmouth accompanied by *Swan*, but with one important difference. Commander Stevens would act as captain of *l'Hercule* while his own lieutenant would assume temporary command of *Swan*. The arrangement had been made to prevent Davis from being absent from *Patroclus* since Giles was so short of lieutenants. Another reason for the appointment was the hope that it might help Stevens to be posted. The man had already done handsomely in prize money from his voyage with *Patroclus*, but his role would have done little to advance his career. Even temporary command of a frigate might catch the eye of someone involved in raising commanders to captains.

Giles had decided to keep *Patroclus* on station. His ability to chase enemy ships had been compromised by the damage to the mizzenmast. However, *Patroclus* was still a swift ship. Except in very rough weather, she could outrun any French 64. The vessel he sought had in the past clearly not shied away from British frigates. If *Patroclus* could find her, Giles was confident that she would be as keen as he was to engage.

The only difficulty in executing Giles' plan was that *Patroclus* was still unable to find the enemy ship. Five days passed without sighting anything hopeful. *Swan* returned with *Patroclus*'s prize crew. She also brought a dozen more volunteers who had approached Commander Stevens, indicating that they would volunteer for the navy, but only if they were to serve with Giles. When Stevens came aboard, he was full of amazement at Giles's ability to attract crew. Such a quality was unheard of.

At Dawn on the sixth morning after the capture of *l'Hercule* a call from the masthead announced that four sails were in sight one point off the larboard bow, with just topsails showing so far. *Patroclus* was scudding along on a broad reach driven by a northwest wind. She was carrying all plain sail to the topsails, with the exception that the mizzen topsail was furled to ease the strain on the weakened mast. Giles knew that *Patroclus* could safely carry more sail, and ordered the main and foremast royals unfurled. They appeared to be catching up with the group when the ship closest to them, which had been recognized as a frigate, tacked and headed toward *Patroclus*. She was certainly French built, and she looked surprisingly like *Patroclus*.

Giles ordered a change of course that should bring *Patroclus* as directly as possible to the distant group. Minutes later, the distant frigate came onto a course heading to intercept *Patroclus*. Each ship was on a reach and they were closing rapidly. Giles gave the command to clear for action and ordered *Swan* to come within hailing distance so that he could order her to stay clear of the approaching enemy, and to try to determine where the other vessels were going. *Swan* shook out a couple of reefs that had held her off *Patroclus*'s quarter and surged well to windward of the approaching frigate. With the two vessels so equal, each making the same leeway, it appeared that they were destined to crash into each other, bow to bow. The powerful bow chasers that each mounted meant that if either flinched, the other could pound her with cannon fire that could not be returned immediately. That would also happen if either ship's bow chasers damaged the other's rigging in such a way that the victim slewed aside. If that didn't happen, a battle of broadsides might ensue, to be continued until one ship or the other was unable to continue or until both were reduced to helpless hulks. The alternative to engaging in this battle, if the exchanges of broadsides had still not given one or the other an overwhelming advantage, was to grapple and take one's chances boarding. Giles could not presume that his opponent was short of crew members. If she were a privateer rather than a naval vessel, she might indeed have a larger crew than *Patroclus*. If it came to hand-to hand combat, should *Patroclus* actually board the enemy, or should she play the defensive role? Taking into account his damaged foremast, Giles decided that the grappling objective must be pursued, and he felt that the violence, more suitable to berserkers than to ordinary sailors, which his crew had shown in taking *l'Hercule,* warranted his taking the attacker's role.

Giles went about the ship telling each of his officers what he expected and what their role would be. Since speed now would be of little advantage, he ordered sails shortened and the foremast main sail to be furled. His opponent also shortened sail before the bow-chaser duel could commence. With all his preparations made, Giles returned to the foredeck to watch the coming confrontation.

Giles had left the ports for the bow guns closed, in the hope that his opponent would not realize what weapons she faced. The enemy opened fire while they were still some distance apart, the ball skipping off the water before harmlessly sinking well in front of *Patroclus*. Giles suspected that she might be using Mr. Hughes's tactic of lulling an opponent into thinking that the threat was less than it was. Giles had been tempted to use it himself, but felt that his enemy might well not know what sort of guns he faced and that it would be better for Giles to have his first shot be one that had been loaded and aimed at leisure. He ordered the ports raised and the guns fired. The result was satisfactory. One ball whistled over the bow and what damage it may have done as it passed down the ship could not be seen. The other one smashed into the bow almost directly below where the enemy's larboard bow chaser was being run out. It must have done some damage, for only the opponent's starboard gun fired immediately, but soon the larboard one was back in action. The duel continued with only minor damage to either vessel, though the cumulative effects might soon prove to be significant. Neither vessel was forced off course as the distance narrowed. The two ships had almost reached the point where one or other must flinch or their bowsprits would crash into each other.

Giles had been concentrating on the activity on the other ship around where *Patroclus*'s ball had struck when he noticed a powder monkey racing towards the gun with another cartridge for the gun. The cartridge was clearly leaking a thin stream of powder as he ran. *Patroclus*'s guns fired at that time and one of the balls must have hit some iron for a shower of sparks erupted from where it struck. Giles, in that superior vision that extreme danger can produce, saw a spark ignite the powder trail and flames race in both directions from where it had first ignited the powder. In moments, the cartridge the lad was carrying burst violently into flames. The other trail of fire had disappeared, probably stamped out by someone or stopping where there was a break in the powder trail. Giles thought no more about it, until a ball of fire seemed to erupt from the center of his opponent. A moment later the shock wave hammered into *Patroclus*, carrying a miscellaneous assortment of missiles that wreaked havoc to *Patroclus*'s rigging. The enemy had blown up!

Giles was thrown backward by the shock wave, landing up against the foremast. He was dazed, but confusedly was trying to get to his feet when he heard the unmistakable crack of a large timber breaking. The mizzenmast had gone by the board. The accompanying lurch of the ship again knocked Giles off his feet, and he was clearly both dazed and confused as he struggled to rise. As his head cleared, he stared ahead. Through a gap in the tangle of ropes about the bowsprit he could see that there was no ship ahead. Slowly he realized that the opposing frigate had exploded, leaving only a dense litter of flotsam behind.

Giles turned towards the quarter deck to bellow an order, but saw that the boats were already in the water searching for survivors. Other seamen had been ordered to start cutting away critical rigging that might otherwise spread the disaster stemming from the collapse of the mizzenmast. Giles in fact had little to do until the reports on damage and injuries started coming in. He was immensely tired. He would make his way to the quarter deck and if there was nothing pressing he would go to his cabin.

His journey, and it felt like a journey even though it was only a few yards, was interrupted by the surgeon, "Four dead, Captain, seven wounded. The worst are a couple of broken legs, but I should be able to save them. Twenty men were blown overboard, but have been rescued. Six are still missing. The boats are searching for them. So far, they have only found French corpses, no one alive."

"Very good. We'll bury the dead later in the afternoon."

"Captain, you are not steady on your legs. Let me look...Turn your head...Lord, I should have seen this immediately. You have given your head a monstrous blow on your right side. I'll take you to your cabin and clean the wounds and dress them. But you must stay immobile for a while. Bad knocks on the head do strange things to one, and can have funny effects on one's thinking. I should tell you not to make any important decisions for the next few days, but I expect that would be pointless in your case. But get some rest right now. I insist."

Dr. Maclean guided Giles to his cabin. The captain's cabin was one of the first areas attended to when the ship was restored from action, so the Doctor was able to ease Giles into an armchair, before examining his wound. The wound itself, though nasty looking, was not too serious. It would only require bandaging. Dr. Maclean was more worried about the effects that the crack on Giles's head might have on his mind.

When the doctor looked into Giles eyes, the signs were not good. The Captain might be incapacitated for many days, he might never regain his full powers, or not for a very long time. He might even die. All Dr. Maclean could prescribe was rest. He was a firm opponent of the standard procedure of bleeding patients. In his experience bleeding did more harm than good. Disagreement with others on this subject had led to heated discussions with other practitioners. More importantly, Dr. Maclean's income had suffered. Disputes with patients who expected to be bled whenever they felt ill, led to their seeking other doctors who would give them the long-approved treatment. The bickering and the loss of patients was one of the major reasons Dr. Maclean had come to sea. Only time would tell when or if Captain Giles would be able to resume his duties effectively.

Chapter IX

The furor over Susan Butler's elopement died down quickly, though it was generally agreed that her reputation was permanently ruined around Dipton, but that it might be restored when she began to live in Bradford. Mrs. Butler, while wishing that the marriage had followed a more conventional route, was pleased to have one of her daughters off her hands.

The happy outcome of Mrs. Butler's younger daughter's forays to Ameschester resulted in all her qualms about Catherine's walks to the town evaporating. If Susan could make such a good match, surely her more vivacious, older sister could too. Since other stratagems to acquire husbands from the ranks of the militia had been a complete failure for the mothers of Dipton, it would be nonsensical to abandon the successful one. After all, Lord Mosely's Regiment was officered by the very best class of men. Mrs. Butler would now most graciously allow Catherine to find healthy exercise in the walk to Ameschester, quite forgetting the grounds for the earlier prohibition on any such activity. Other mothers could see the same logic, and soon the meeting of the young ladies with officers of the Regiment resumed in the tea room of Ameschester.

"You see, Catherine, there was merit in my allowing you girls to visit Ameschester to see the officers there. Susan is getting married in the most romantic way. You can't let Susan get far in front of you. You must renew your walks to Ameschester. I'm sure that you can find romance and marriage there." Miss Butler's riverside picnic had only been postponed, not cancelled.

Mr. Butler was less clearly delighted with the outcome. He couldn't help remembering that Lieutenant Barrows seemed to be a man with no fortune and no income other than his militia pay, a most uncertain and probably most inadequate basis to set up married life, and his ability to rise in his chosen profession had yet to be tested. Mr. Butler had visions of the newly married couple having to live with the Butlers, putting an extra strain on his own precious finances.

Other news quickly took the place of Susan Butler's misdemeanors. The work on Dipton Hall had been proceeding apace and the end was in sight. With its completion would come the return of Lord David Giles, who would, in any case, be taking up his duties as Vicar of

Dipton shortly. His half-sister, Lady Marianne Crockett, and her daughters, Miss Catherine Crockett and Miss Lydia Crockett, would be arriving with him to take up residence in the Hall.

Speculation about the new arrivals ran rampant, despite not being fueled by any new information. The social structure of Dipton would be changed radically. Lady Marianne would take precedence over all the other ladies of Dipton. It was less clear where Miss Crockett and Miss Agatha Crockett would fit into the hierarchy. They would clearly be ahead of any of the other unmarried young ladies including, the nastier among the gossiping ladies would remark gleefully, Miss Moorhouse, who had been giving herself such airs stemming from her closeness to Captain Giles. But would the daughters outrank the wives of prominent land-owners? That was a question suitable for endless debate, since none of the ladies had access to a volume of precedent and etiquette that could settle the issue.

On the male side, things were much clearer. Even though he was only a fourth son and a country vicar, Lord David would take precedence over everyone else until his even more exalted brother returned. Where Captain Bush should be ranked was a bit more difficult, since he had no lands and his income or wealth were unknown, as yet. That his standing was unclear made things very difficult because where his mother and sisters should be slotted in depended so much on his own status.

The approaching completion of the works being undertaken on Captain Giles's behalf gave rise to innumerable complaints. Many people were interested to see what changes were being made. Indeed, few had seen much of the inside of Dipton Hall or the Dower Cottage, and the improvements that were rumored to be taking place in the Vicarage were the subject of much addional speculation. All visits of inquiry were turned aside, politely but firmly, by the workmen, or in more persistent cases by their foreman or one of those whose designs were being implemented. Protest was met with the response that this was on the orders of Mr. Edwards, who was in charge of all the work on behalf of the Captain. Application to Mr. Edwards was met with refusal. Curiosity would have to be left to be satisfied after the work was completed.

This was all very galling for two reasons. The main one was that Captain Bush had access to all three properties. It was reasonable that he should be able to inspect progress on the Dower Cottage, for he would be living there and, as the prospective tenant, he should be in a position to select some aspects of the work which was being done. It was even reasonable that he should be able to take his mother and his sister on these expeditions. Indeed, from the start, Captain Bush had in effect been overseeing the work on the Dower Cottage. It was not so reasonable that he should be given free access to the other two projects. He might be Captain Giles's good friend, and it might be the case as Mr. Edwards had indicated, when complaints had been made to him, that implicit permission had been given by Captain Giles when he had asked Captain Bush to keep an eye on his interests in Dipton. That this permission had referred rather explicitly to the antics that might accompany Lady Marianne's arrival in Dipton was not mentioned by Mr. Edwards. Worse still, Captain Bush was frequently accompanied by Miss Moorhouse, and there was great doubt that Captain Giles's foolish encouragement in matters of drainage and farm management should extend to the house itself. Especially annoying was that Miss Moorhouse was said to have commented on the disgraceful state of the gardens at Dipton Hall to Mr. Edwards himself. Apparently, Mr. Edwards had forgotten that bringing the gardens into their best state should be part of his commission. When the state of the plantings, the lawns and the beds was pointed out to him, Mr. Edwards had recruited Miss Moorhouse to plan and oversee the work needed to bring the gardens into first rate condition. This may have been based on Captain Giles' remarkable faith in her agricultural talents, but it was outrageous to engage her in the much more delicate matter of planning and making gardens which surely should have required a true professional to be engaged. Just who did Miss Moorhouse think she was? One could only hope that Captain Giles would soon return from his voyage to put the hussy in her place.

It was known that Captain Giles had engaged some very superior servants from his father's London house and that they were now engaged in recruiting other servants in preparation for the arrival of Lady Marianne and Lord David. Little was known about the details, but the numbers of servants were soon exaggerated, so that more and more the talk turned on how rich would be the welcome in Dipton Hall when the neighbors came to visit.

As time passed, the most important subject of conversation moved from the work being done on Dipton Hall to the imminent arrival of its residents. It became widely known that Lord David had gone north to bring back his sister and nieces. Excitement reached almost fever pitch when it was learned that the party had rested at Ameschester for a night before coming on to Dipton Hall.

The anticipated group did indeed move on to Dipton Hall the next day. There was considerable discussion about when it would be appropriate to call. The consensus was that a week should be allowed for Lady Marianne and her daughters to settle in, though each lady who agreed with her friends that this was the suitable length of time, did not dream that the period should apply to herself; she would call much sooner.

No one was surprised that Captain Bush was at Dipton Hall to receive Lady Marianne and her daughters. He, after all, was Captain Giles's special friend and had had a major role in readying the Hall for its new, elevated residents. But that he should have invited Mr. Moorhouse and Miss Moorhouse to accompany him passed belief. That they should receive special treatment because of Miss Moorhouse's underhand ways of getting Captain Bush to stay at Dipton Manor was intolerable.

The coterie who so carefully analyzed all the activities that occurred in the Dipton area might have been astounded as well as insulted had they witnessed the scene of greeting that marked Lady Marianne's first encounter with her neighbors at Dipton Hall. She first railed at the fact that Mr. Edwards had refused to accommodate changes to features of the Hall which she considered essential to her wellbeing. She believed that Captain Bush should have countermanded all of Mr. Edwards's orders that displeased her, quite ignoring the fact that Captain Giles had made it perfectly clear that Mr. Edwards had full authority on such matters. Captain Bush was the height of civility, without actually promising any changes. He certainly wasn't going to state that, in some of the matters that so exercised Lady Marianne, Mr. Edwards had in fact consulted with Captain Bush and that it was often at Bush's firm recommendation that the desired changes had not been made. All he would say now was that he was sure that when Captain Giles returned all the problems would be resolved, carefully avoiding pointing out that he was sure that his friend would undoubtedly uphold all the decisions that Mr. Edwards and he had had to make.

Lady Marianne then began to complain about how her father had starved her of funds and how her brother had been positively miserly. What sort of family members would leave her in penury? Her father had ceased to advance her money and she had had to cut her spending to the bone after Captain Giles had visited. Captain Bush would have to see that Captain Giles was more generous. Bush's sympathies to this line of cajoling were less than they would have been had Lord David not informed him in an aside that he had had to find more than £350 to settle the bills that Lady Marianne had run up since Captain Giles had visited even though Giles had left her with a generous amount of money to pay for her needs until she could move.

Amazement would have been even stronger had the local gentry been able to see what happened next. Lady Marianne had gone to the tall windows to look out on the garden. It might have been taken for a gesture dismissing her visitors, but before they could comply, Lady Marianne again started unfavorable comment. Why was there a garden bed here which clearly obstructed a much better view? Who in the world thought that rhododendrons should be planted in front of the tall holly bushes? Why was there no rose-garden immediately next to the perennial beds? And so on and on, not noticing that many of her later suggestions, delivered in the form of hectoring questions, were contradictory to earlier ones or were quite impossible to carry out given the lay of the land.

Lady Marianne had been startled and horrified when the young chit of a girl who had accompanied Captain Bush, a Miss Morecatch, or Moorland or some such name, had the temerity to start explaining in patient tones the answers to her questions. Worse still, when Lady Marianne asked who this young woman thought she was, she was told by that same young woman that she had been engaged to restore and improve the gardens and that was what she was doing. The young woman went on to explain, in detail, why Lady Marianne's complaints made absolutely no sense given how God had chosen to lay out this part of the countryside. Well! Lady Marianne would have to have a word with Mr. Edwards about that! Even this threat seemed to leave the hussy unconcerned. It would never have occurred to Lady Marianne that Mr. Edwards would almost certainly know that Captain Giles would side with Miss Moorhouse over Lady Marianne on any subject, let alone on one where Miss Moorhouse had made herself expert.

The Moorhouses realized that poor Lord David must have been enduring this sort of haranguing all the way down to Dipton. Daphne, after getting a nod from her father, invited him to accompany them and Captain Bush for luncheon at Dipton Manor. Lord David accepted the invitation with alacrity, and enjoyed the first meal with pleasant company that he had experienced in some time.

At the end of the meal, Mr. Moorhouse surprised everyone by saying, "Vicar, if you would like to stay at Dipton Manor until the vicarage is ready, we would be happy to have you as our guest. I am afraid that the atmosphere at Dipton Hall may not be conducive to writing sermons. We have no end of space here. While the Bushes are staying with us now, and so are Colonel and Mrs. Craig, you can be on your own as much as you like. You are welcome to use my library and I am sure that Miss Moorhouse can arrange for you to have a sitting room to yourself in which to compose your thoughts.

Lord David attempted to refuse using the excuse that his brother had entrusted him to try to keep some control over his half- sister. That met with a rather unsympathetic comment from Captain Bush, "I'm afraid, my lord, that your chances of reining in your sister are negligible. You saw how she evaded Captain Giles's financial strictures and I doubt that you can stand up to her. I also doubt that I could. Mr. Edwards, however, partly because he is rarely here, is made of sterner stuff. Steves, I am sure, has orders to follow Mr. Edwards's commands and not Lady Marianne's if they clash. From what I've seen of your sister, you can do no good there, and you will be a lot happier here."

Lord David required no more persuading. He very much wanted to have as little to do with his half-sister as he could. For the first time in a very long while, he felt some sympathy for his father, who had earlier been confronted with this harridan. He was very glad that a house of his own came with his living. He could see himself being very content with friends like Mr. Moorhouse and Captain Bush in the district, especially if he could avoid having much contact with his half-sister. That that would have to mean not seeing his brother very often did not bother Lord David. He was in fact rather intimidated by his confident brother.

News of these developments had not reached Mrs. Butler when she called on Lady Marianne at 10:30 the following morning. The agreed-on one week hiatus in paying visits did not, of course, apply to her! She was greeted not warmly but regally by Lady Marianne. Her ladyship had spent too many years known primarily as the wife of a captain in a minor regiment, an officer whose main abilities were drinking and gambling, both to excess. She thought she had to immediately establish her status as the daughter of an Earl in her new location, rather than as a nuisance dependent of her younger brother. Unfortunately, she did not realize that to assume this role of a grand lady, she would need to show interest in and sympathy for her visitors, rather than contempt at being again forced to associate with her inferiors.

Lady Marianne spend the whole visit lecturing Mrs. Butler on how evil the Earl had been to cut her off and abandon her and how unfair was his son in keeping her penniless in this house. Lady Marianne furthermore did nothing to praise her own daughters' accomplishments or to make the visitor warm to them. Mrs. Butler was nonplussed to find that her intended words of welcome and warm invitation to take tea with her in the near future could not even be uttered as the stream of complaint was unleashed. As to singing the praises of Dipton and its residents, Lady Marianne trumped Mrs. Butler's attempts by complaining bitterly about how her brother was forcing her to live in an area with no refinement or worthwhile society. Mrs. Butler rather felt, as she took her leave, that she had been blown from the house by a full gale from the north.

Mrs. Butler noticed that the next carriage to be visiting, also rather jumping the gun, was that of Mrs. Sandforth of Deepling Hill who was accompanied by her daughter. Mrs. Butler wondered if Mrs. Sandforth would receive the same welcome as she had. She resolved to call on Mrs. Sandforth that afternoon to find out. The two ladies agreed that they had received the same welcome and joined in expressing shock that Lady Marianne had heaped such invective on her benefactor, Captain Giles, and such contempt for the community in which she would now be living. Their daughters agreed that the Misses Crockett seemed to be without refinement or graces, and were both ugly and uncouth, even speaking with a pronounced Northumbrian accent, like some navies. All were agreed that in future they would have no dealings with Lady Marianne or her daughters, and concurred on the proposition that noble birth did not always produce noble character.

Much the same results were obtained by the string of ladies who visited Dipton Hall in the next few days. By the end of the week, all visits ceased and the consensus among the gentry of Dipton was that the situation at the Hall was now much worse than it had been even in Mr. Gramley's time.

The reception which they had received at Dipton Hall also put a spoke into the plans that the mothers and daughters of Dipton had been formulating to deal with the militia problem. The balls were all held in locations in Ameschester or in locations which were not on the road to Dipton. Even if the young ladies of Dipton met gentlemen or officers at the balls, the lack of familiarity with the roads were believed to cause the gentlemen not to pursue any young ladies from Dipton whom they had found attractive. It was reported that one or two ladies from the other side of Ameschester had successfully caught the eye of eminently suitable young men, while Dipton's only success had been Miss Susan Butler. It was believed that if Dipton could mount their own ball then their own young ladies would have the advantage that in the past had gone to others.

The problem with implementing this scheme was that Dipton had only one place to hold a proper ball. The Dipton Arms only had small public rooms, not well connected, that could not be used to mount a the lavish festivities that were being envisaged. Dipton Manor, though having enough space in total, had no room that could remotely be considered to be a ballroom. Only Dipton Hall had the facilities, and, with the recently completed improvements, must surely offer space that was more elegant than anything in the whole area. A ball held there would undoubtedly astound all who attended and its magical aura could be expected to rub off on the young ladies who were associated with the village where this wonder was to be found. It had been hoped that when Lady Marianne took up her residence in the Hall, she could be persuaded to host a ball. It was expected that Captain Bush, who clearly liked to dance, could be relied upon to smooth any objections that Mr. Edwards might have. Those hopes seemed to be totally dashed by the reception that Dipton's ladies had received when they visited Dipton Hall.

The usual peace-maker in Dipton, Daphne Moorhouse, was not available to try to smooth over matters so that a ball might be arranged. Daphne had already had one encounter with Lady Marianne, but it was nothing compared to their subsequent meeting. Daphne had been going about her business as the planner of the gardens at Dipton Hall, a task she was most comfortable in performing when she was actually on the grounds and could direct the workman in exactly where various plants should be located, and even in which direction they should face. She was engaged in this endeavor when Lady Marianne noticed what she was doing through the parlor windows. Lady Marianne was still smarting from her previous encounter with Miss Moorhouse, and the sight of her calmly making decisions, in her garden, without a parasol, in a skirt with dirt on its edges and with her own hands begrimed in soil, clearly indicated that Miss Moorhouse was no better than a tenant's wife and had no business even being in Dipton Hall let alone lecturing its occupant on what was appropriate. How she could possibly be arranging the garden was beyond all understanding. Lady Marianne stormed out of the French doors to confront this presumptuous commoner who had even presumed to instruct Lady Marianne in garden arrangement.

Daphne Moorhouse was usually a friendly, helpful mild-mannered person, always prepared to give others the benefit of the doubt. She was, however, well known for speaking her mind without cloaking unwelcome comments in a froth of apologies and circumlocutions designed to avoid offence. And when her patience had been overly tried, she was capable of the most intimidating of angers and the most devastating of insults. It happened rarely, but when Miss Moorhouse lost her temper, what happened was the stuff of legend repeated endlessly in the drawing rooms and alehouses of Dipton.

Lady Marianne came storming out of the Hall demanding at the top of her voice to know what Daphne was doing, why she was installing plants without consulting Lady Marianne herself, and who did she think she was. Lady Marianne got so carried away that she ordered Daphne to depart at once, and stated that she would make sure that Daphne would be dismissed without a reference.

Daphne tried to explain that she was doing only and exactly what Mr. Edwards had requested that she do, implying a bit ingenuously that the commission had come from Captain Giles, that the plant being installed at the moment would hide some rather ugly storm damage evident farther away, and that it was a plant that would in fact improve the beauty of the garden all by itself. This reply further enraged Lady Marianne and it was at that point that Daphne Moorhouse lost her temper. She pointed out that Lady Marianne was only a guest in Captain Giles's house, that Lady Marianne had no right or permission to make any decisions about the garden and furthermore was demonstrating total incompetence on the subject. Having dealt with Lady Marianne's interfering in the gardening, Miss Moorhouse went on to declare that she knew that Lady Marianne had been rescued from a rather squalid existence as the widow of an undistinguished captain of a regiment of no account by Captain Giles. That Lady Marianne's own father had abandoned her, and that it was only through the pleading of the Countess with Captain Giles that Lady Marianne and her daughters had been invited to reside at Dipton Hall – and that this was the same Countess whom Lady Marianne had reviled and denigrated in conversation with the ladies of Dipton who had been good enough to try to welcome Lady Marianne and her daughters. That if Lady Marianne continued to act this way, Captain Giles would throw her out of Dipton Hall to fend on her own—and Miss Moorhouse would rejoice in his action. Daphne went on about these matters at more length and detail until Lady Marianne fled the scene to retreat into the house and to lick her wounds in a room that did not overlook that part of the garden. All this was gleefully reported and spread abroad by a parlor maid who had witnessed it all and who, like other servants in the Hall, had put up with so much abuse and condescension from Lady Marianne that she felt no compunction about gossiping about what happened at the Hall.

This tale was retold with keen satisfaction by the ladies who had been driven away on their visits to Lady Marianne with their tails between their legs. The incident, so gleefully reported, did have the implication that Miss Moorhouse could hardly be expected to approach Lady Marianne to hold a ball in the very house where Lady Marianne resided. Daphne was not convinced that the ball could not be held at Dipton Hall unless Lady Marianne gave permission, though it would be awkward if Lady Marianne were not engaged in the preparations for the event. Better than most in Dipton, Daphne knew how restricted was Lady Marianne's authority over what happened at Dipton Hall, and that if push came to shove, Mr. Edwards and Captain Bush could authorize the holding of the ball. But the rage of Lady Marianne if the ball were held over her adamant objections would likely doom the event itself to failure,

Daphne, having vented her anger to her own great satisfaction, realized that the state of antagonism that now existed between the ladies of Dipton, including herself, and Lady Marianne might have dire consequences for the extent to which Captain Giles would join the community and continue to show interest in his own estate. He might just wash his hands of Dipton and spend his time ashore elsewhere, among his many friends in the Navy and in the fashionable society of London. After all, it would be difficult for Captain Giles to entertain if his hostess was reviled by his guests. It would also be difficult for others to invite Captain Giles to social events in which they would have to include Lady Marianne and presumably put up with her tongue.

Daphne was eager to have Captain Giles present in Dipton as much as possible just so that, Daphne told herself, they could jointly improve the conditions of their properties. When Daphne raised these concerns with her father, Mr. Moorhouse was amused by the reason she gave for wanting Captain Giles to enjoy residing in Dipton. Mr. Moorhouse thought that Daphne was deluding herself in claiming that she wanted the Captain only for his agricultural interests. Daphne wanted Captain Giles's presence for himself quite apart from his ability to further her own schemes.

Daphne was fully aware of her own inability to serve as the peace-maker after her outburst at Dipton Hall. She also was not at all surprised when Mr. Moorhouse refused decisively to serve in that role. She was surprised when her father suggested that the only person who was likely to succeed was Captain Bush. Daphne pictured Bush as a pleasant young man, given to doing his duty, but far from being the sort of forceful but diplomatic individual needed for the task. Until her father pointed it out to her, she had not realized that men without influence did not rise to being post captains in the His Majesty's Navy, especially not at a young age, without the ability to take decisive action in tricky situations. Nor had she recognized that Bush's determination to overcome his handicaps indicated a character that would not shy away from difficult tasks if he thought them necessary. If Daphne could persuade Captain Bush that he must try to change Lady Marianne's behavior, he would be determined to effect that change and would pursue that outcome relentlessly.

Somewhat to Daphne's surprise, Bush agreed to undertake the task after only a little pleading on her part. Bush, too, had his reasons to want Giles to spend as much time in Dipton as he could, and he, too, recognized that having a harridan in residence in Dipton Hall would make it likely that Giles would decide to spend most of his time elsewhere. He also was in the best position to persuade Lady Marianne that she should remember her own tenuous situation at Dipton Hall, and that she should do as much as she could to seem an agreeable hostess who could enliven Captain Giles's life at Dipton with well-chosen dinner parties and other entertainments. He would also remind Lady Marianne that her daughters' situation was even more precarious than her own, and that they would benefit from having their mother a welcome and welcoming part of the community.

Lady Marianne for her part had begun to reflect on her position after she had recovered from her consternation and anger at the blunt way in which Miss Moorhouse had confronted her with her situation. She was stuck in Dipton Hall, like it or not, and she would undoubtedly find it less unpleasant if she were on good terms with the local gentry, inferior to her though they might be. What she couldn't see was how to undo the harm that she realized that she must have already done. Miss Moorhouse could have been a conduit into the society of Dipton. Lady Marianne's dispute with her – no matter how justified her position was in Lady Marianne's own eyes – must have made that impossible. As a result of Lady Marianne's reflection, Captain Bush's visit went a great deal more smoothly than he had anticipated.

Bush's approach to Lady Marianne lacked subtlety.

"My lady, I am sure that you are aware that Captain Giles only agreed to provide you with a place to live at his mother's urging and that, if you didn't have a home here, you would not have one anywhere. Also, you must know that you are going to be here for the foreseeable future, and for that to be tolerable either to you or to your brother, you need to be on good terms with your neighbors. Furthermore, your daughters need to find husbands and they will not do so if you anger everyone by disparaging them and their neighborhood. Right now the gentry of Dipton are ready to leave you to your own devices, neither invited elsewhere nor called upon."

Lady Marianne was startled to be talked to in this manner. However, she did not fly into a rage as she was inclined to do for two reasons. First, Captain Bush was only saying what she had already concluded, and secondly she presumed that Captain Bush must be from an elevated strata of society, for he was the close friend of her brother who was both the son of an earl and had a knighthood in his own right. Surely her brother would only associate with men of his own rank. When she had suppressed her immediate reaction to Captain Bush's remarks, which was to dismiss him without further hearing his opinions, she decided that seeming to agree with him, rather than flying into another satisfying rage, might be beneficial to her interests.

"I realize Captain Bush that I did not greet the ladies who were kind enough to call on me when I arrived in a proper manner. I was tired and out of sorts as a result of the long journey, and I believe I said some things about Dipton that I now regret. How do you suggest that I rectify the situation?"

"Let's see. You might invite those you think you insulted to visit again, saying that you were unwell when they first came. You might yourself visit various houses, just to return the call they made on you. I don't believe that you would be refused entry, even if that might be the first inclination of some of them. You might invite some of your neighbors to dinner."

'Do you think that Captain Giles would allow the expense of entertaining? He doesn't allow me free rein to spend as I think fit. Do any of these families have young men to make up the numbers?"

"I'm sure Captain Giles would approve. As to young men, I don't know. I suggest that you consult Miss Moorhouse."

"You cannot expect me to have anything to do with that…that … that wanton! She has treated me abominably. I have never been talked to in the way that she has."

"I don't know about the treatment," said Bush in an amused tone, "but I can well believe that no one has ever been so direct with you. However, right now, I think she is the only one who might be considered your friend. I know she wishes you well, even though you seem to have insulted her more deeply than any of the others. If you don't make friends with her, you will find it very difficult to make friends with others. If I were you, I would invite her to visit you here. Calling at Dipton Manor unannounced would not do, since she is frequently away from home, and you might find Mr. Moorhouse most unwelcoming. And if you called on Miss Moorhouse, you would also be calling on my mother and sisters and it would be more difficult to have a useful discussion with her."

"I'll consider doing so, though I do not relish groveling to Miss Moorhouse. Do you have any other suggestions?"

"There is a widespread desire to host a ball in Dipton where Dipton Hall has the only ballroom in the village, and it would be a splendid way to show off the improvements Captain Giles has made. We have no idea when he may return, so it might be all right to have a ball here even in his absence. I would talk to Mr. Edwards about it, and to Miss Moorhouse about how it might be arranged."

"Balls cost money and I don't have any."

"I would talk to Miss Moorhouse about that also. I believe that Mr. Moorhouse would be happy to cover the expenses."

"You really do want me to meet with your Miss Moorhouse, don't you, Captain Bush?"

"She is not my 'Miss Moorhouse'. She is very much her own person. And if she were anyone's 'Miss Moorhouse', it would be your brother's"

Bush soon after took his leave. He didn't know if Lady Marianne would follow any of his advice, but he could hope that she would and reconcile himself if she did not by being assured that he had at least tried.

Lady Marianne did take Captain Bush's advice. Her first step was to send a note to Dipton Manor asking Miss Moorhouse to visit at her convenience. Daphne was happy to comply. She was delighted to learn that Lady Marianne was somewhat in favor of the ball, seemed anxious to undo some of the damage she had done earlier to her chances of having pleasant social interactions with her neighbors and was seeking her advice on young men who might make up the numbers at a dinner party. Maybe they could get along tolerably, at least if Lady Marianne did not try to tell her how to improve the garden.

Daphne left Dipton Hall well content with the result of Captain Bush's intervention. She thought that she would probably never like Lady Marianne, but at least the Ball would be forthcoming and perhaps the social turmoil caused by Lady Marianne's arrival would now die away.

Chapter X

Captain Giles awoke in the late afternoon with a splitting headache. The ship was swaying easily, with the main sail backed, in a light wind. Sunlight streamed through the cabin windows. His mind felt fuzzy and he seemed to have trouble focusing on the details of his cabin. He felt a terrible sense of urgency, but could think of no action he should be taking. He remembered that his ship had been going into action with her rival and a vision of a spark setting off the powder trail came to his mind. But nothing further could he remember. He had no idea how he came to be lying in his hanging berth, but clearly he must be needed on deck.

Giles struggled to get out of bed. His movements roused Carstairs who had been sitting in the armchair in shadow where Giles had not seen him.

"Easy, Captain, easy. You should stay where you are until you get your bearings."

"I must get on deck. What happened to the French frigate?"

"She blew up, Captain. Don't you remember?"

"She blew up? Were there survivors?"

"None, Captain."

"And *Patroclus*? Was she damaged?"

"Some, Captain. The mizzenmast went by the board and the bowsprit was damaged. Mr. Davies and Mr. Hendricks have almost finished their repairs."

"I must get on deck. Help me up, Carstairs."

"Is that wise, sir?"

"Damn your insolence, Carstairs. Help me up!"

Carstairs helped Giles to the deck where he stood swaying, supported by Carstairs. Carstairs half carried him over to the armchair into which his captain collapsed. Giles felt so tired, but he must fulfill his duties to the ship.

"Carstairs, pass the word for Mr. Foster ... I mean Mr. Davis ... and Mr. Brooks."

When the two officers appeared, they were glad to see their Captain awake, but they were shocked by how weak he seemed to be, and how disoriented. This was evident from the moment they laid eyes on him.

"There you are," muttered the Captain. "Tell me, did we win the battle this morning?"

"Captain," said Mr. Davies, quietly, "you have been unconscious for two days."

"Well, did we win?"

"Yes, sir. The other ship blew up."

"Oh, yes. Yes, Carstairs did tell me. And the damage?"

"The mizzenmast broke where it had been injured previously. We were able to retrieve all the top hamper. Mr. Hendricks and Mr. Shearer have been able to pull out the stump of the mizzenmast and stepped the remaining part of the mast. She can only carry a much reefed driver, of course. The sail master has almost finished re-cutting the sail. *Patroclus* will be able to sail as well as before, maybe better than we could after the mizzen was damaged by *l'Hercule*."

Even as this report was being made Giles's attention seemed to wander.

"I am so tired. I must lie down again. Mr. Foster, we must find the French frigate and sink her. Crack on sail. We cannot be idle. Carstairs, help me into bed."

It was a very disturbed pair of officers that saw Carstairs half carry Giles to his bed. His Majesty's Navy had well established procedures for junior officers to take when their captain was killed or rendered unconscious. Nevertheless, a captain who was injured in such a way that his mind was affected, or even one who developed madness during a voyage, presented a problem that was fraught with danger for them. If they obeyed crazy orders that put the ship or her crew into needless danger, they could be blamed if the outcome were disastrous. If they failed to obey, they stood the danger of the captain regaining his senses and having them court martialed for disobeying orders. Giles' final orders had clearly made no sense. They would ignore them and fail to log them. However, if Giles's condition continued, there were decisions to be made which were the Captain's responsibility and the officers could only hope that the orders were such that they could obey them in good conscience.

Giles didn't awake again until the following morning. He felt considerably refreshed and even his headache had diminished. When Carstairs helped him from his bed, he was a good deal steadier and he felt that he could get dressed without Carstairs' help. Dressing did tire him and he was glad to sit while Carstairs arranged for coffee and breakfast. He was tempted to continue sitting in his cabin after breakfast, and maybe summon his officers later for their reports, but he knew that his duty lay in going on deck and being seen by the crew, even in his weakened state.

When he stood, Giles realized that he could go nowhere unassisted. In fact, when he stood, his head spun wildly and he had to grab the back of his chair to avoid collapsing onto the deck. He again engaged Carstairs's help and the two of them made their way past the marine sentry and up the ladder to the quarter deck without incident. Giles sank gratefully into the chair that Carstairs had arranged to be placed for him abaft the mizzenmast. The brief exertion had tired him unreasonably. His officers left him alone, except for the routine report about the weather and the ship's course and sails. There was, in fact, almost no wind, and the bright sunshine warmed both Giles's body and his spirits.

"Mr. Davies," Giles called when he had somewhat recovered, "Any news of *Swan*?"

"No sir. We are hoping to rendezvous with her here, but so far she has not appeared."

"Here?"

"Yes, sir. You remember that you signaled her to return to where we were engaging the French frigate. That is where we are now."

"It's been three days since the fight?"

"Yes sir."

"Then isn't she overdue? Mr. Brooks, how far way is the French coast?"

"About 100 miles, Captain. About 120 miles on the course that the ships were steering when last we saw them. But the wind has been very light and fickle since the engagement. I would not be surprised if *Swan* is delayed simply by the lack of wind."

"Yes, it is only three days. We'll give her another three. Now, Mr. Davies, have we tested the new rig?"

"No, sir."

"Everything is finished, is it not?"

"Yes, sir"

"Then we should set all plain sail to the topsails and see how she performs. I would like to see how she does in this light wind, especially going to windward and whether she will miss stays when we tack"

"Aye, aye, sir."

The maneuvers were carried for the rest of the morning. *Patroclus* could not go to windward quite as well as she had before, largely because the injured bowsprit could not take as much pressure, but, on the whole, the jury rig stood up well. Downwind she did as well as Giles expected her to, though noticeably slower. After two hours of concentrating on the performance of his ship and the set of the recut sails, he was exhausted. Leaving word to carry on, without any clear meaning attached to that catch-all phrase, he went below with Carstairs's help and soon was sound asleep in his bed.

The following morning brought with it a fresher wind and a fresher Giles. He was able to dress and mount the quarter deck by himself, though only by steadying himself at numerous stages along the way. He sank into his chair with relief, but soon he was taking a more active interest in the doings of the ship. He was about to order the resumption of gunnery exercise when there was a call from the masthead that a ship was in sight to the east. Minutes later it was reported that the ship was a schooner-rigged sloop on a converging course with *Patroclus's*. Then the ship was recognized as *Swan*.

When Captain Stevens came aboard, his report quite restored Giles, who had again been fading as his time on deck was extended.

Swan had trailed the little convoy of vessels to the French coast, despite the attempts of the brig to drive her away. *Swan* was always able to avoid these sallies while keeping the group of other ships in sight. In the end, these ships disappeared into what appeared to be the mouth of a river in the low swampy land that marked that part of the coast. The brig blocked *Swan's* access to the coast, so at the time Stevens had only a vague idea as to where the ships had gone. When the others had disappeared, *Swan* followed the brig of war to the coast where she too entered the same waterway.

Commander Stevens had then been in a quandary. Should he return to *Patroclus* with the information he had acquired or should he follow the brig into the coast? He knew that the information of where the ships had vanished was critical, but his report would be more valuable if he could say something about the entrance he had found. He doubted that he could use *Swan* for any further exploration. She was too vulnerable to being trapped against a hostile shore if she ventured into the creek or whatever the opening might be and the nature of the surrounding marshy countryside made it all too likely that she might go aground without any pilot to guide her.

Despite the temptation to undertake a bold stroke that might solve the mystery of the missing ships, Commander Stevens decided to seek out *Patroclus* before taking any further action to determine what might have happened to the missing ships. It had been frustrating that the lack of wind prevented him making a speedy passage.

Giles' reaction to Stevens's report was immediate. As soon as Commander Stevens had consulted with Mr. Brooks to mark the location of the channel entrance on the master's chart, the schooner was ordered to lead *Patroclus* to the site. The wind continued light and foul for the rest of the day and into the night, so the two ships did not arrive off the coast until noon on the following day. The coast here was a rather featureless stretch of swampy reeds and grasses, without a proper beach but instead with drying beds of grass and other water plants. A hundred yards or so back from the shore low shrubs appeared and behind them stunted trees. The passage inland could hardly be detected from seaward and would easily be missed if one did not know there was a waterway leading inland.

Giles was surprised how close *Patroclus* could come to the shore before she reached a depth where it would be comfortable to anchor. He ordered Davies to drop the hook and signaled *Swan* to do the same. The lookouts aloft were doubled in order to assure him of an early warning should any other ship approach. It was a clear day, and with the land breeze blowing, he would have plenty of time to raise the anchor and get under way should the need arise.

Giles would have to send a boat up the channel to get any more information. A meeting with his officers left two of them very disappointed. *Swan* was ordered to return to Falmouth to deliver Giles's reports about the destruction of the French raider and of the discovery of where the French captures seemed to be hidden. Commander Stevens had hoped to lead the expedition inland to find out more, but he recognized that *Swan's* proper role was to carry news. Davies thought it his right as first lieutenant to lead the exploration and to get credit for what was discovered. Giles recognized the validity of his claim, though he most certainly did not tell the lieutenant that he did, but his officer was very young and inexperienced and Giles doubted that Davies would fully appreciate what he might see. Giles also knew that, however accurate and complete might be his subordinate's report, his own nature would require him to verify the finding for himself. While Giles knew that this was a failing on his part, he still wanted to be the one to collect the information on which he would evaluate the situation.

Giles' orders were crisp and definite. He would take the long boat with Carstairs and Midshipman Correll. The oarsmen were to be carefully selected so that the crew consisted of those who could row most quietly. Lieutenant Davies would command *Patroclus* while Giles was gone. An hour before sunset the lieutenant was to raise the anchor and head off shore. In the morning he was to return to await Giles's return. If Giles did not return during the next day, the procedure was to be repeated for the next two days, after which *Patroclus* should head for Falmouth. If an enemy vessel of small size appeared, Davies was to try to capture it without being pulled too far off station. If the vessel were a frigate or ship of the line, Davies should avoid battle if he could, but could use his discretion if he believed that victory was likely. As he issued these orders, Giles wondered to himself why he didn't just let Davies command the expedition into the mystery passage. Giles's head again hurt abominably and he was once more feeling waves of tiredness wash over him. Nevertheless, his own duty came first.

The boat entered the channel rowing slowly with the lead going in the bow to establish the depth of the channel. There was enough water to allow quite large ships to pass. *Patroclus* would have had three feet below her keel and the tide had only just turned to the flood. The width of the channel was about one hundred feet before the bottom started to rise to the shore. It would be tricky for ships as big as *Patroclus* to be brought up the channel. Before they had proceeded very far inland, the channel entered a sharp S-curve. Near where the turn began a white painted stake had been driven into the bottom. Giles sounded all around the stake and discovered that it marked the starboard side of the passage and that the deep channel was narrowing as it entered the curve. A series of stakes continued to mark the starboard side of the channel as it rounded the curves. Giles did not trust that the stakes necessarily indicated the starboard side of the passage; if he himself were marking a hidden route, he might vary the positioning in the hope of lulling any vessel unfamiliar with the channel to go aground. As a result of this consideration, Giles ordered that they should take soundings all around each stake. So far there was no sign of trickery.

They continued inland. The afternoon was advancing and the work of checking each marker was tedious. Giles fell asleep. He didn't mean to; he just did. He was woken by Carstairs gently shaking his knee and whispering to him to be silent. The afternoon was now well advanced and the boat had just rounded another bend. Ahead they saw the end of a ship possibly moored to a dock where the channel next curved. No one was in sight, but they could be discovered at any moment.

When Giles had gotten his bearings, he ordered the boat to back gently out of sight of the landing where the ship was moored and then to tie up in an indentation of the bank across the stream from the landing. Pulling the boat into some bull rushes meant that they were hidden. Telling Midshipman Correll to make sure that everyone kept quiet and to keep a good lookout, Giles went ashore together with Carstairs. Each had a cutlass and a pistol and Giles had his small telescope. They worked their way upstream, following animal paths that seemed to be leading in the right direction. When Giles judged that they had proceeded far enough upstream, they worked their way back to the bank of the river. It was a somewhat scratched as well a mosquito-bitten pair who finally were able to part some branches to look across the river.

The sight that greeted them already answered many of the questions which were at the heart of their remaining mission. Across from them were three frigates. As Giles studied them through his telescope, he concluded that they were British because he detected many small features that tended to be different in the French Navy from the British. Two of the frigates also showed signs of recent battle, which appeared to have been patched though not as well as a naval dockyard would fix them. Giles recognized the middle frigate as HMS *Artemis*, which he had seen once at Spithead. The others were unknown to him and to Carstairs, but that was not surprising since they neither of them had ever seen the other missing frigates. The Admiralty had provided Giles with descriptions of the missing frigates and these ones did fit those descriptions. There was no sign of the fourth missing frigate, so maybe it had perished at sea.

Ahead of the frigates was the brig of war that *Petroclus* had seen in company with the frigate which they had destroyed. Ahead of the brig were moored three merchantmen. The commercial vessels seemed to be low in the water suggesting that they had not been unloaded. No one was visible on any of the ships.

Behind the ships was a number of structures. Several appeared to be warehouses. Then came a large building with many windows which might have been a barracks. It looked to be of recent construction. The final edifice was a long, low building with few windows, but a large door at one end. It might be a stables or possibly some sort of cattle shed. Right now, there was no sign of life to show for what it might be used, but three guards with muskets lounged in front of it. No one else was in sight.

Giles whispered to Carstairs asking whether he had any idea of what kind of a building would warrant guards, even such lackadaisical ones. Carstairs was just as mystified as Giles and answered with a shrug.

A bit back from the waterfront there was a village of ten or twelve small, red-roofed houses with some farm sheds and a small church. The church had no steeple or tower, just a low belfry, which accounted to it's not being visible from sea. No one could be seen moving about the village

Just as the two observers were about to leave, their curiosity was partially satisfied by the appearance of a column of men from a path that led off into the woods at the end of the mystery building. The column was preceded by two men carrying muskets. What was remarkable about the column was that the men were all chained together. One long chain was riveted on to shackles on their left ankles. They were also wearing iron neck collars that were joined by chains locked to the collars so that each man was joined to the man ahead and the man behind. Giles had seen coffles of black slaves similarly shackled in the West Indies, a practice that he abhorred. Now the same restraints were being used on white men here in France. From the tattered clothes which the men were wearing, Giles could recognize them as seamen, seamen now enslaved. Within moments a second coffle appeared. Giles counted a total of forty-three seamen who were enslaved. The light was now fading quickly so Giles and Carstairs eased away from the bank and retraced their steps to *Patroclus*'s long boat.

The moon would be up in a couple of hours. Giles wanted to wait for it before trying to get closer to the dock in the long boat. Moonlight would also be helpful when they made their way back to the mouth of the river. In the interim, he allowed everyone to sleep except Midshipman Correll and Carstairs who were designated to keep watch. Giles himself gladly sank into oblivion. For the past hour his ability to give his full attention to the situation had seemed to be coming in and out.

He was wakened by a light touch on his thigh. Carstairs whispered, "Quiet sir, there is someone out there." Other members of the crew were also being roused quietly. Everyone waited tensely for more indication of strangers. It was not long in coming.

"Englishman, you are surrounded and we are armed." A low voice spoke from the darkness in a thick French accent. "We are not your enemies. We wish to talk, but quietly."

"Who are you?" Giles replied, in little more than a whisper. He knew that sound would carry over the still water to any guards posted at the frigates and the slave pen.

"We are peaceful men, but enemies of the pirates who hold those ships and of the general who has seized our country. We would wish to talk to you, but not so close to the river."

"That doesn't tell me who you are."

"I am Jean de Beauboeuf, Sieur de Gorgrasse, though my status is not recognized by the present government. Come, you are surrounded and outnumbered. Listen, if you don't believe me." A low whistle came from the direction of the speaker and promptly rustling in the bushes was heard, starting on the downstream bank near where their boat was moored and going in a semicircle to the bank upstream from them. "I imagine that you are interested in the British warships across the river. I can help you."

Giles wondered if he could trust the man who had trapped them. He had an aristocratic name. If his intention had been to capture or destroy Giles's party, he could have done so easily without warning them. Giles decided to take the chance.

"I will come with you, bringing one of my men." Giles whispered orders to Mr. Correll that if he wasn't back in half an hour, the boat should be pushed from shore without them and they should take their chances on getting back to *Patroclus*. Then signaling to Carstairs to come with him, Giles stepped from the boat. Strange hands took his elbows and guided him into the bushes for a few feet. The shutter on a lantern was then opened to reveal a stocky man of about fifty years of age with several more men in the shadows around him.

"Captain Richard Giles, commander of HMS *Patroclus*," Giles introduced himself. He reckoned it would be best to forget his aristocratic titles in France. "Are you Monsieur de Beauboeuf?"

"Oui, mon capitaine. Please come this way, where we can talk." They proceeded down a narrow path until they emerged into a small clearing. A fire was burning in the middle of the glade and Beauboeuf indicated that the two British sailors sit near the fire with him and a henchman.

"Let me tell you something of myself and the ships you have seen and then I'll answer your questions."

Monsieur de Beauboeuf had been of the lowest level of the aristocracy before the Revolution. He had been nothing more than a farmer, a fairly prosperous farmer. Any feudal dues owed to his family had long since disappeared. When the old order was overturned, he and his neighbors in their largely forgotten corner of the country had had little to do with it. Their lives continued as they always had until the rampages of the Committee fueled the flames of old grudges. Monsieur de Beauboeuf had been denounced as an aristo and a gang from the nearest town had come looking for him and his family to use the popular method of settling old grudges, the guillotine. Luckily his neighbors were little in sympathy with the revolutionary thugs who had replaced the principled, if naïve, first adherents of the Revolution. They warned de Beauboeuf of the force that was coming for him and helped to spirit himself, his family and some of his animals into the wilderness that bordered his farm. Others of his neighbors were denounced, mainly as enemies of the people who had helped the aristocracy to escape their fate, and they too had to join de Beauboeuf in the wilderness. When the fever of the Terror had passed, they returned to their farms and rebuilt where necessary, but they kept a weather eye open for a return of the thugs with their easy way of gaining land by denouncing the owners, and they maintained the refuge to which they had resorted when the need had been great, making sure that its paths were known only to them and made inaccessible to others.

Their neighbors across the river had had a rather different history. The major landowners there were of a somewhat more noble family than de Beauboeuf's and gave themselves still greater airs. They had not abandoned all of their old rights, and indeed in the years preceding the Revolution had tried to revive old exactions, especially the ones requiring peasants' labor. When the new regime took over, they were among the first to be denounced, their home and buildings burned and the members of the prominent family guillotined. There was, however, a third son, who had taken the name Jean Leclerc. He had moved from the family estates to Bordeaux before the Revolution and had embraced the Republican cause from the beginning. He had been a sailor, rising to being a ship's captain and then a merchant and ship owner. Following the Revolution, he had taken up piracy, though calling it privateering, and sailing with forged letters of marque. This enterprise was successful, and he made a fortune in a very short time taking vessels – both English and French -- and selling the cargoes and the ships in Santander with no questions asked. He had selected his crew largely from men who were from this part of the country and had no particular love for the Revolution or for government authorities.

With the rise of the Directory, and the start of the Terror, Leclerc had been worried about denunciation both by those who despised his aristocratic roots and also by any of the many people who were aware of his piracy and who and been affected by it. He had offered his services to the navy and with his record, and now again loudly proclaiming the Republican cause, he quickly rose to command a frigate. Somehow he managed to keep with him as officers his mates from his privateering days, and most of his crew. His other officers and crew members were as keen on lining their own pockets as were the ones he brought with him, and when a lieutenant was appointed to his ship who was not prepared to enjoy the proceeds of piracy, a false denunciation led to that lieutenant's losing his head before he could counter the accusation. As a frigate captain, Leclerc showed himself adept at escaping British blockades and acting as a commerce raider. This activity further enriched both Leclerc and his crew and also his superiors. That some of the captures found their way to Santander and disappeared from the frigate's logs was either not known or overlooked, for a price, by Leclerc's superiors.

Not surprisingly, when a new type of frigate came off the ways, those same superiors arranged for Leclerc to be given the command along with his most useful officers and crew. A most unfortunate change in command, from Leclerc's point of view, occurred at this point, and the new admiral felt that Leclerc's new ship could better be used as a scout and courier for the fleet rather than as an independent raider. In this role, Leclerc did indeed make himself useful, and in one encounter off Brest, he captured a British frigate. The French Navy bought the capture in at what Leclerc considered a very good price and the bounty for the sailors captured was worthwhile.

Unfortunately for Leclerc, word of his shady dealings was spreading and the regime was looking more closely at the dodgy behavior of its officers. Added to his aristocratic origins, he was becoming a very ripe target for the Guillotine. When an informant, who was in his pay in the local government offices, sent word that preparations were being made for his arrest, Leclerc decided that a return to piracy was in order and sailed without orders in his frigate. He needed a base, well hidden, from which to carry out further raids. Santander as a market for captures might still be available, but it would be asking for trouble to base a stolen French frigate there. Leclerc remembered the river where he had grown up and realized that it would be a perfect base from which to operate.

His piratical ventures were again successful, and Leclerc found that with his unexpectedly heavy bow chasers, he could even cripple frigates of the Royal Navy in such a way that they could not bring their broadside to bear, and so he could capture them. Remembering how lucrative had been his capture while still in the navy, he had brought the captured frigates to his base. He had, however, not yet succeeded in finding a way to both sell the frigates and their crews to the authorities and keep his head on his shoulders, which accounted for the three frigates still being at his dock. He kept the crews of the frigates hoping to sell them too, just as he implicitly had with the frigate he had captured. He separated the officers and petty officers from the rest possibly, Monsieur de Beauboeuf thought, because Leclerc realized that his prisoners might escape, but without officers they would be unable to take their ships away. He had taken the officers on his last voyage, to where de Beauboeuf did not know.

De Beauboeuf reported that the brig of war had accompanied Leclerc's latest captures to the base. It had reported that Leclerc was engaging another frigate and that when they were almost out of sight the enemy frigate had blown up. It was presumed that Leclerc had gone on to Santander and then would resume his cruising and was not expected back for several weeks.

When Giles asked about the seamen in chains, de Beauboeuf said that he understood that they were being used to do agricultural work on Leclerc's holdings and those of his neighbors. Providing labor would keep the beneficiaries quiet about what was happening. A lot of what the prisoners were doing was clearing ground that had once been fields but had reverted to scrub. There were three other captured gangs of captives who were also treated as slaves and who were housed in buildings several miles away. One of Leclerc's early captures had been an American slaver engaged in the triangular trade who had as part of her cargo the slave fetters. They were now being used by Leclerc to control his captives.

Giles was astonished by how much information de Beauboeuf had been able to give him. When Giles asked how he came to be so knowledgeable, the Frenchman laughed and explained that several of his own men periodically crossed the river and went for some wine to a tavern where Leclerc's people also imbibed. They had picked up the information on their drinking trips.

Giles recognized that, with the force under his command, he could neither retake the frigates nor free the prisoners. If he brought *Patroclus* up the river, he could possibly recapture the frigates and set the prisoners free, though it would be a close thing. But without officers, he could not sail the frigates away and he did not have the boats to ferry the prisoners to *Patroclus*. Certainly, he could not release those who were kept farther away. As he explained to Monsieur de Beauboeuf, he would have to return to England. The knowledge that Leclerc was not expected to return for several weeks gave him the hope that he could return to England and then come back to France with a force that could clear out this pirate's nest before it became evident that Leclerc himself would not be returning. He hoped that de Beauboeuf would be able to help whoever might come by providing them with more up-to-date information, a task that de Beauboeuf readily agreed to perform.

Giles and Carstairs were guided back to their boat. The moon was up, but Giles abandoned his plan to explore the moored ships more closely from the water. He thought he now had so much information that it would be foolish to row the boat closer to the landing place and risk warning the enemy that they had been discovered. Instead, he ordered the boat to be rowed downstream. They emerged into the ocean just after dawn. The land breeze was still blowing, and they could just make out *Patroclus's* topsails beating towards them. Giles ordered the men to keep rowing for he was impatient to get to *Patroclus* in order to speed up the rescue process as much as possible.

Patroclus arrived in Falmouth late the next day. Even before she could drop anchor, a boat sent by the port admiral met them. It carried orders to take *Patroclus* back to Butler's Hard for repairs immediately. Giles's report for the port admiral, which was to be forwarded to the Admiralty, was exchanged for the orders from the admiral. *Patroclus* turned to the east without dropping anchor. They arrived at the mouth of the Sloth River late the next day and had to wait overnight for the flood tide to carry them inland. At Butler's Hard, *Patroclus* anchored and Giles took his barge ashore with a proud Midshipman Stewart at the tiller.

Mr. Stewart had already received his orders to repair *Patroclus* as quickly as possible. He had been paying very close attention to any news of *Patroclus's* doings and was bursting with pride that his son had been part of such a successful cruise. He insisted on accompanying Giles and his foreman to see what the damage was. When they stepped into the barge, he had trouble concealing his pride as he shook his embarrassed son's hand, before Midshipman Steward resumed his duties of commanding the boat.

The two men from the shipyard wasted no time evaluating what had to be done to replace the mizzenmast and to repair the damage done to the side of the ship and the bowsprit. They then disappeared to assess what strains may have been made evident by the firing of the bow chasers. Mr. Stewart emerged shaking his head.

"I still think that the thirty-four pounders are too big for her," he told Giles when he emerged. There are some places which we can reinforce, but she will tear her bow to pieces if those guns are fired repeatedly."

"How long will the repairs take?" Giles demanded.

Mr. Steward took a few moments to consider the question. "We have several timbers that will serve to replace the mizzenmast, and the replacement of some staves that have been damaged and other carpentry work should be straight forward. We'll have to shape the mast, of course, but a couple of days, say three at the most, will have you ready for sea. Now let me go ashore again to get it all started."

Midshipman Stewart again commanded the boat that took his father ashore. It was unclear who was more bursting with pride: the midshipman showing off his newly acquired skills or the father admiring how confident his son was in his chosen role.

The boat came back carrying orders for Giles that had arrived while the damage was being examined. They were simple. Giles was to make sure that all arrangements had been made for the rapid repair of his vessel. Then he should go to Dipton to await further orders from the Admiralty.

Giles instructed Davies in what he should do while waiting for the return of the Captain. The main one was that each watch was to be given a day's run ashore. Giles had no worry that he would lose his crew if they were at liberty, though he could see that Davies had his own doubts on that score. It was tempting to career *Patroclus*, in the good ways that the shipyard had, so that they could clean her bottom. Davies was ordered to see to that with Mr. Stewart's concurrence. It was evident from Giles's orders allowing him to proceed to Dipton that *Patroclus* was not going to sea in the next few days.

It was too late in the day for Giles to leave Butler's Hard. He sent Carstairs ashore to arrange horses for them at the crack of dawn the next day, and then retired to his cabin to play his violin. His playing of the Mozart sonata could still use a lot of improvement.

Chapter XI

Clara, Countess of Camshire, Giles's mother, had learned patience over the years. She had very much wanted to see the estate that her older son had bought and the vicarage he had provided for her younger son. She also wanted to see her step-daughter and her two step-granddaughters. She had never seen the girls, for she had not seen Lady Marianne since her step-daughter's disastrous elopement with Captain Crocker and her subsequent banishment from the world of the Earl of Camshire. But the Countess had delayed visiting Dipton until they were settled there.

The Countess's life with the Earl had been a disappointment. The dashing, confident nobleman, full of grace and good bearing whom she had thought she was marrying turned out to be an erasable and tight-fisted bully. He had met the problem of his overspending by engaging in highly speculative ventures that had turned out not to be the vehicles for rescuing the Camshire fortunes. He became sour as this continued from one fiasco to another and his political ventures, usually no better founded than his financial ones, were frustrated by narrow-minded politicians who had no vision or realization of their brilliance. Lady Camshire had devoted herself to helping the tenants of their estate, maintaining as best as she could the standards of a great house when the finances were precarious, and bringing up her two sons. That latter task had now become minimal as her older son had long-ago gone to sea and had quarreled with his father on so many issues that he rarely visited Ashbury Abbey. Richard was only rarely in town during the Season, when the Earl and Countess were in residence at Compton Square. She remembered with sadness the pimply faced young man who had left for his duties as a midshipman when he had really wanted to be a barrister with time to spend on music and literature. That he had been an astounding success as a sailor had not surprised her, but she knew that he still would have preferred a different life. By contrast, her son David had desperately wanted to follow his brother, who was his hero from the time David was a little boy. Instead, David had been designated for the church, partly at Lady Camshire's insistence that one of her sons should be properly educated, especially as he was in no way suited for other professions. She knew that her sons' inheritances would be minimal, and that the Earl would leave nothing to his daughter. It was with great satisfaction that she realized that Richard's success would enable here son to make up for his father's failings in maintaining the estate and she felt only mild regret that his other sons, by his first wife, would find that noble blood had little value when not accompanied by noble estates or noble character.

Lady Camshire had waited for the news from Lord David that Dipton Hall and the vicarage were ready and that Lady Marianne had been fetched from the North. She had then delayed her visit for a suitable period in which Lady Marianne could settle into her new quarters. Now the Countess would visit. The excuse for the visit was Lord David's first sermon at Dipton, not the gala occasion with the Bishop in attendance, but the more modest one where first the parishioners of Dipton would get to experience what they could henceforth expect as their Sunday fare. Of course, Lord David might hire a curate to take on his duties, but his flock would still hear the occasional sermon from him.

Lady Camshire's interest in Dipton had been particularly piqued by reference in letters by both of her sons and by Lady Marianne to a Miss Moorhouse, who seemed to play an inordinately large role not only in the lives of Dipton generally, but also in those of her own family. Most intriguing had been that Richard had mentioned her on several occasions, though he had only spent a very short time in Dipton. She was also interested to meet Captain Bush, who had been Richard's first lieutenant and as such had occupied a good few pages in Richard's letters of the time.

Lady Camshire picked the time of her arrival in Dipton with care. While the journey from Ashbury Abbey could be completed in one day, she preferred not to arrive at a late hour. In consequence, she broke her journey in Ameschester so that she could arrive at 10:30 in the morning. She had informed Lady Marianne of her coming and also Steves, the butler who had formerly played that role in her London house.

The passage through Dipton and up the drive to Dipton Hall of a coach and four with a coat of arms on the door caused quite a stir in the village. The Countess was greeted by Steves and a footman who opened the coach door and supplied a step to ease her way to the ground. She swept into the Hall with all the aplomb of someone who was there by right and was guided by Steves into the morning room where Lady Marianne and her two daughters awaited her.

Lady Marianne had never got over the bitterness that she had felt when the Earl had married the young Lady St. John eliminating Lady Marianne's hopes of becoming the suzerain of Ashbury Abbey and of winning the affections of her father which had never in the past come her way. That resentment had in fact been at the heart of Lady Marianne's scandalous behavior which had required Lieutenant Crocker to marry her and for the Earl to purchase a captaincy for Lady Marianne's new husband, though the commission was in an unfashionable regiment. Even that action only occurred because of forceful pleading by the Countess; the Earl would have disowned Lady Marianne entirely to save the expense.

When Lady Camshire and Lady Marianne were seated in the morning room, they proceeded to have a prickly conversation about the Countess's trip to Dipton, their health, and the weather. Soon, however, Lady Marianne let loose with a string of complaints about her treatment, especially her inability to make substantial changes to Dipton Hall at her own fancy and how that churl Edwards limited her expenditure on clothing and other necessities. Lady Camshire, who had been informed by Mr. Edwards, on Captain Giles's instruction, of how generous was the allowance and of how hard Lady Marianne had tried to get around its strictures, was not sympathetic to her step-daughter's complaints and did not hesitate to make her own views known. With conversation at an impasse after that discussion, Lady Camshire tried to talk with her step-granddaughters, but she found that was an uphill effort, her questions and comments being answered by rather sullen, one-word replies.

Only when the subject of balls was somehow introduced did the girls show any enthusiasm. The news tumbled out that Dipton Hall would be the site of a splendid ball in the very near future. Their mother was helping to arrange it with Miss Moorhouse. Mr. Edwards had authorized a special allowance for ball dresses for all three of them. Steves knew all about how these events should be carried out. Even Captain Bush, who only had one leg and one arm, could be counted on to dance. The ball would draw young men from all over the county, not just from Ameschester and not just the militia officers. The Dipton Arms was swamped with people wanting to stay there, and the good houses for miles around were going to have visitors who were coming only for the ball. One could expect a large number of young, unmarried men.

Lady Camshire loved balls. The excitement of anticipation and the actual event with crowds of people in brightly lit rooms, strains of music vying with the chatter of the onlookers, the constant observation of whose dance card was filled and whose was not, and whose romance might be flourishing or wilting. She had never been happier than when she was the hostess at the magnificent balls which she herself had held, better even than attending the other ones in the Season. She missed them now that she was not holding balls anymore and the Earl was not celebrating the Season as he formerly did. She resolved immediately to stay at Dipton until after the ball was held on the Wednesday following her son's first sermon. After all, her presence could not help but add luster to the first ball held in her son's revitalized Hall. Otherwise, as far as she could make out, the guests would lack anyone of real quality – except, of course, her son David. She would send her groom immediately to Ashbury Abbey to return with a suitable ball gown for herself.

Lady Camshire was surprised that Lady Marianne's flood of complaint and criticism had not included the holding of the ball. Instead, Lady Marianne announced herself to be very much in favor of the ball; in fact, she was helping to organize it. From her own description of her role, however, Lady Camshire deduced that Lady Marianne's part was very small and that the true organizing talent must lie with Miss Moorhouse. Lady Marianne had indeed adopted an enthusiastic and somewhat meek attitude toward the ball and this even extended to not complaining at the inconvenience which having a major event at Dipton Hall was bound to cause her or that it was being planned by the lowly Miss Moorhouse,. This strange behavior led Lady Camshire to believe that at last Lady Marianne had realized the need to show off her two daughters in the hopes that they would find a suitable mate despite the rather remote prospect that they would receive dowries from their uncle. They certainly would receive none from their grandfather. What Lady Camshire had yet to realize was that Lady Marianne had hopes that her own, far from faded, charms might attract a well-off and mature gentleman who would take her away from the necessity of eating at her half-brother's board and sleeping in a bed he provided. That Miss Moorhouse was indeed arranging a good showcase for those charms, and that Miss Moorhouse's father might be the one to succumb to them, was what allowed Lady Marianne not to complain about the rude and uppity behavior of Miss Moorhouse in arranging the ball.

Lady Camshire was becoming very impatient to meet Daphne, who seemed to be taking on far too large a role at Dipton Hall, "I want to meet this Miss Moorhouse," she announced imperiously.

"That's easy," replied Lady Marianne, a bit pettishly. "I see that she has just arrived outside. I'll ask Steves to request that she come in."

Lady Camshire followed Lady Marianne's gaze out the window. In the drive she saw a young lady riding a horse who was just coming to a stop at the portico. To her horror, she realized from the draping of her skirt that the lady must be riding astride though there was no bunching of the material at the pommel as one might expect. No sooner had Lady Camshire observed this strange behavior than the young lady swung her leg over the horse's back to dismount, not waiting for the aid of a footman. Surprisingly, when she was on the ground, her skirt appeared to be perfectly normal. It was also made of very high quality cloth.

A moment later Steves announced, "Miss Moorhouse," as the lady in question strode into the room.

Lady Marianne promptly said. "Lady Camshire, may I introduce Miss Moorhouse. Miss Moorhouse has been organizing the ball about which we were talking."

Lady Camshire couldn't resist trying to take the wind out of Miss Moorhouse's sails. "I am surprised you are arranging such an elaborate ball for my son when he isn't even here. It must be costing him a fortune."

"We are using Dipton Hall; that is true, though only with Lady Marianne's enthusiastic participation and we consulted with Mr. Edwards and Captain Bush about having it here before making any definite plans. Lady Marianne is, after all, a resident in Dipton Hall. The ball is being held to welcome Lady Marianne and her daughters and Lord David and Captain Bush and his mother and his sisters to Dipton. You have no idea how their arrival has changed our social scene. We had thought of waiting until Captain Giles could be here too, but Captain Bush informed me that, in time of war, there was danger that Captain Giles would be gone for years, or that if he could come to Dipton sooner, it might only be for a couple of days at very short notice. Furthermore, Captain Giles is not paying for the ball; my father is."

"Why would he do that?"

"It would hardly do to have Captain Giles pay for his own welcoming party, especially since he isn't likely to be here. My father has always wanted to have a ball in Dipton, but neither Dipton Manor, which is his estate, nor the Dipton Arms have suitable rooms, so he jumped at the very generous offer of Dipton Hall." Daphne was well aware that she was stretching the truth.

"What exactly are you planning, Miss Moorhouse?" asked Miss Lydia Crocker eagerly.

"Oh, I'm hoping for a very elegant ball. The dancing will begin at six. It will start with an hour and a half of minuets. Then the musicians will switch to country dances. At nine, we'll have supper, after which there will be another two hours of dancing. The ball will end at half past eleven o'clock.

"There will be a card room, in the drawing room, actually, and a separate room for those who just want to talk, away from the dancing. And of course, lots of chairs around the dance floor."

"Will there be a master of ceremonies?" Lady Marianne asked.

"Yes, Mr. Jackson has agreed to serve in that capacity. He knows everyone around here and can get the name of anyone he doesn't know. Since the point of the evening is to introduce new people to the community, it wouldn't make sense to have any problem with introducing people who don't know each other to one another."

"I am most interested in the ball you have been planning, Miss Moorhouse," announced Lady Camshire. "It sounds as elegant as the balls we used to have in London and at Ashbury Abbey. Indeed, more so, in that we did not have minuets and, especially towards the end, we just had tea rather than supper."

"It may be a trifle overdone for a country ball," conceded Daphne, "but my father did want to put on a very memorable one. It is more elaborate than any of the balls that are held in the great houses around here. Indeed, it will be more formal than the ones at the Assembly Rooms in Ameschester. Of course, for those one has to have a subscription ticket. I've never known them to dance the minuet. My father wanted something at least as fine as the balls we attended in Bath."

"You have been to Bath, Miss Moorhouse?"

"Yes, two winters ago my father hurt his back and Dr. Verdour prescribed a course of the waters to cure it. We spent a couple of months in Bath and that is where I got my ideas about how to make a ball more special than the ones we usually have here."

"I hope that the stay in Bath was good for your father's ailment."

"Not really. It was still as painful when we returned as when we left Dipton."

"Does it still bother him?" asked Lady Marianne

"No. Mr. Jackson said that the cure at Bath was nonsense for my father's ailment, and he prescribed a good course of exercise. I have persuaded my father to go riding for at least an hour every morning and now his back does not trouble him and he has more of the sparkle that he used to have."

Lady Camshire reflected that she wished the Earl was as biddable a man. She also realized that she would have to be more direct with this young woman if she wished to make any progress on her main task.

"I hope that you are not starting to think that you would want to be permanently in charge of Dipton Hall, Miss Moorhouse," the Countess declared.

"Heavens, no! Captain Giles will be perfectly able to manage his residence, and I'm sure his wife, when he marries, will be more than capable of maintaining and decorating the Hall and ensuring the Captain's comfort."

Lady Camshire was most relieved to hear that implicitly Miss Moorhouse had no designs on her son. After some more conversation about the ball and about Lord David's coming sermon, Miss Moorhouse took her leave so that she could carry out some tasks related to the garden, a role that the Countess felt confirmed her opinion about Miss Moorhouse's eccentricity.

Sunday came and Lord David's sermon was deemed a success. Since almost all the congregation, including his own relatives, were in the habit of not listening to anything after the text was stated until the closing hymn was announced, the success of the sermon was a foregone conclusion and indicated only that Lord David had a voice whose tone was pleasant and that he did not preach too long.

The only dissenting opinion was held by Mr. Moorhouse who actually had listened to the learned discourse on a heresy concerning transubstantiation. He felt that the discussion was too dense for the parishioners of Dipton, and thought the heresy of little interest or relevance to any of the congregation. After the service, Mr. Moorhouse was introduced to the Countess, who was surprised to find an urbane and unpretentious gentleman not much older than herself who was the father of the most unconventional Miss Moorhouse. After the introduction, the Countess thought that she could better understand Lady Marianne's unexpected enthusiasm for Miss Moorhouse. Mr. Moorhouse appeared to be an eminently suitable target for Lady Marianne's wiles.

The day of the ball arrived with perfect weather. By five o'clock, all the preparations had been made. The coaches started to arrive and by six o'clock there was a large crowd gathered as Mr. Moorhouse led Lady Marianne out onto the dance floor, and Captain Bush led Miss Moorhouse for the first minuet. They were soon joined by other dancers and the ball was well under way. For the second minuet, Mr. Moorhouse asked Lady Camshire. After she got over the shock of being asked by a man so much her social inferior, Lady Camshire found that she quite enjoyed the dance, and when other men summoned up their courage to invite her, she found that dancing with men who were quite awed to be dancing with a countess entirely to her liking. Mr. Jackson made sure that Lady Marianne, the Crocker sisters and the Bush sisters were asked frequently, while he also made sure that Mrs. Bush, who declined to dance, was introduced to a stream of other people who did not want to dance. Daphne was never without a partner, though she never allowed her card to be filled for more than the next one or two dances in case there were some last-minute crisis that she would have to resolve.

A crisis did occur just after everyone had gone in for supper. The sound of a very loud voice erupted in the entrance way. Hurrying there, Daphne found a tired-looking and very angry Captain Giles shouting at Steves who was trying to calm him,

"Captain Giles! How wonderful to see you tonight," declared Daphne.

Giles turned to her. "What is going on? Why is my house full of people?"

"We are having a ball."

"What? Whose idea was that?"

"Mine. And I have Lady Marianne's permission, and Mr. Edwards's and Captain Bush's."

"I don't like it. I told Steves that he should clear the house right now."

"Captain! You can't do that! We had no way of knowing that you would be arriving. Come into the library. You look exhausted."

Giles and Carstairs had indeed had a long journey from Butler's Hard. The distance was not great, but there was no way to get from Butler's Hard directly by coach, so that they had followed a circuitous route, with delays at various points. It was late in the day before they arrived in Ameschester, only to find that the only mounts available were a pair of worn-out nags which no amount of encouragement would get to go faster than a slow walk. Something about a ball at Dipton having taken all the decent horses. They arrived in Dipton with Giles' head aching and his vision occasionally blurring so badly that he had wondered if he would be able to stay in the saddle until they arrived. There he had found his house filled with people and noise, just what he had not been wanting on his arrival.

Daphne whispered to Steves to bring some food and some wine – and to ignore the Captain's order to clear the house. She led Captain Giles into the library and had him sit in a chair at one of the tables.

"I'm sorry that you are upset to find the Hall in use. We didn't know you were coming."

"I shouldn't have to warn people that I am coming to my own home! I was too rushed to get here even to let Steves know I was coming. We only turned *Patroclus* over to the shipyard yesterday. Tell me, what is going on!"

"As I told you, we are holding a ball. It is to introduce your half-sister, Lady Marianne, and your two half-nieces to the community. And your brother, Lord David, and Captain Bush, and his mother and his sisters. Your Hall is the only place in Dipton to hold a ball. It was to be for you, too, but Captain Bush told us that we could not count on you being here on any particular day. It is a happy coincidence that you have arrived to be part of it."

"And who is the 'we' you are talking about."

"My father and I. But most of the better people of Dipton wanted to have a ball in Dipton so we are holding it here. Everyone has come; even your mother. The Countess decided to stay for the ball."

"My mother is here? And just who is paying for this?"

"My father is."

"That is very generous of him. I see that I can't very well shut your ball down."

Steves appeared at this point accompanied by a footmen bearing a tray with cold mutton, some chutney and some crusty white bread. The footman spread a table cloth, and laid places. Steves poured glasses of wine from a decanter for Captain Giles and Daphne.

"Steves, please pass the word for my cox'un"

Daphne, who was missing the supper upstairs, was both hungry and glad for a break from making sure that everything was going properly. With the problem of continuation of the ball resolved, she and Giles fell into easy conversation, though she noted that he steered the conversation away from his doings onto what had been happening in the fields of Dipton. Carstairs appeared a few minutes after Steves had left.

"Carstairs," ordered Giles. "Make sure my sea chest is in my bedroom – I suppose that I do have a bedroom, Miss Moorhouse?"

"Of course. I imagine that it is all ready for you."

"Then Carstairs, look out my best clothes. I will be along in a few minutes to put them on."

"Aye, aye, sir."

"Are you going to attend the ball, Captain?"

"Yes, Miss Moorhouse. I can't very well miss a ball in my own house. I am still angry with you, but since it is you who has arranged it, I insist that my first dance must be with you."

It happened just as Giles had specified. Daphne found that he was a very good dancer. She only wished that he had been there to dance a minuet with her. But she insisted that he should ask his mother for the next dance. The following one she did reserve for him, but she told him she wouldn't dance with him again until he had taken each of his step-nieces out on the floor. That task over, Giles again danced with Daphne. Afterwards, he found that he was a bit disoriented and not really able to participate in this activity much longer. He was experiencing one of the waves of blurriness that still followed his having been knocked unconscious.

"I believe that that is enough dancing for you, Captain Giles," said Daphne, rather bossily as she saw that he was fading even if she didn't know the reason. "I think that we should repair to the library again."

Daphne noticed that when she touched his arm to steady him, he winced. As she steered him subtly toward the library, she whispered to Steves to see if Mr. Jackson was free.

In the library, Daphne maneuvered Giles into a chair and poured him a glass of wine.

"What is the matter with your arm?" she demanded.

"Nothing."

"No, it is not 'nothing'. I saw your reaction when I touched you."

"It's just a wound that is still healing."

"I will get Mr. Jackson to look at it."

"It's nothing."

"No, I don't think it is. I will have it looked at by someone who knows what to do."

Giles demurred, but found out that, when Daphne was concerned about someone's welfare, she would not be put off. Soon Mr. Jackson appeared. Once Daphne had left the room, Jackson had Giles's coat and shirt off so that the angry-looking wound that he had suffered in the taking of *l'Hercule* was exposed It was far from healing properly. Mr. Jackson took one look at Giles's wound and called for his bag, a basin of hot water, some towels and a bottle of rum. Giles couldn't help wondering what sort of a physician Daphne had summoned whose first need was a bottle of spirits.

Mr. Jackson washed his hands thoroughly and poured a bit of the rum over them. He examined Giles's wound more carefully, and then started to remove the stitches, so that he could open the wound and clean it using the rum. It must have hurt like blazes, but Giles emitted only a couple of groans. Mr. Jackson then rubbed some gray salve on the wound. When Giles was dressed again, Jackson indicated to Steves that Daphne could return.

"There, Captain, that should do for now. Make sure to change the dressing twice a day and use the salve each time."

"What is in the salve?" asked Daphne.

"It contains some mold and bark of willow. The mold seems to help prevent putrification."

"Mr. Jackson, Captain Giles seems to be suffering from some dizziness," Daphne said as Mr. Jackson was packing up his bag.

"I'm not," said Giles just as Mr. Jackson asked, "How long has this been going on?"

"Since the French frigate blew up," said Carstairs even as Giles again tried to protest that nothing was wrong.

The story emerged from Carstairs, even as Giles continued to protest that his being knocked unconscious was nothing.

"It can take a long time to recover from that sort of injury," said Jackson. "There is nothing I can do to help. Just get plenty of sleep and when you feel disoriented, try to rest."

By now, the ball guests had all left. Daphne and Carstairs saw a somewhat unsteady Giles to his room. Mr. Moorhouse had waited for his daughter, who was pensive on the trip home. Seeing Giles wounded and dizzy as a result of his battles brought home to her the seriousness and personal danger of the fighting that was so often pictured as gallant and brave.

Chapter XII

Giles was just finishing breakfast the next morning when Steves announced, "Miss Moorhouse."

Daphne strode in, "I'm so glad to see that you are feeling better, Captain."

Giles felt that he couldn't complain about his headache, which was indeed a bit better than it had been, but it still hurt badly. He was also feeling very grumpy, "Good morning, Miss Moorhouse. What brings you here so early?"

"I just wanted to make sure that there was nothing left over from last night that I had to attend to. It's a gorgeous day, would you like to see the garden? or maybe you haven't seen how Mr. Edwards has renewed the Hall yet. But did you have your wound's dressing changed?"

"No. It didn't seem necessary."

Steves was just bringing in some fresh tea for Daphne. "Steves, get me some bandages and fetch the ointment that Mr. Jackson left last night. And some warm water."

"Oh, Miss Moorhouse. Really, would that be proper? I know that your attending to the bandage would greatly upset the Countess if she heard about it."

"Oh, all right. Get Carstairs. But Captain Giles, you must make sure that Carstairs uses the ointment generously."

Steves, getting an unobtrusive nod from Giles, hastened to summon Carstairs.

"Now, Miss Moorhouse, you must tell me all about how our farms are doing," said Giles.

Daphne launched into a detailed account of the progress that had been made and the present state of her various endeavors, but she did not get very far before Steves returned.

"I have had to have Carstairs woken so that he can attend to your wound, Captain." The butler said in a most disapproving voice. Steves had classed Carstairs as being Giles nautical equivalent of a valet, and so Carstairs should not be asleep when his master was awake.

"Don't be upset, Steves. There is no urgency in getting the dressing changed."

Giles and Daphne continued their discussion until Carstairs appeared looking rather annoyed at having been woken and being required to dress in a rush.

"Carstairs, please change the dressing on the wound on Captain Giles's arm. And use this special salve. I will wait outside the door. Tell me when you have finished."

Carstairs complied, even though he and Steves exchanged a look that indicated that they did not appreciate being ordered around by some woman who was not the mistress of the house. When the bandage had been renewed, Carstairs informed Miss Moorhouse.

"How is the wound, Carstairs?" asked Daphne.

"It looks much better than it did yesterday, Miss, when I was rather worried about it. That salve must be doing some good."

Giles and Daphne resumed their discussion as if there was nothing remarkable about a guest breaking off a conversation to deal with a wound and then continuing to discuss their chosen subject. But they soon realized that to appreciate fully what had already been accomplished and the items that had yet to be done would require their presence at the sites they were discussing.

Nothing felt more natural than to mount their horses and start a tour of the estates. Giles was amazed at how Daphne had all the details of the operations at her finger tips and could point out what had been done and what still needed to be done. It didn't occur to him to compare it with his own knowledge of any ship which he commanded, even though the same type of complete knowledge was required. Giles also noticed that all the men whom they encountered who were involved in the operations respected Daphne and readily took orders from her. As a man used to commanding other men, he could easily appreciate how successful and how unusual was her ability to get ready cooperation. He rather vaguely realized that what he was observing was leadership that did not rely on the threat of the cat to accomplish its end; he still could not comprehend that it was no more surprising that an intelligent woman could display leadership than that a naval captain should; certainly he could not picture any woman, even Daphne Moorhouse, commanding a ship of war.

All too soon Giles's headache and slight disorientation returned. They happened to be closer to Dipton Manor than to Dipton Hall at that moment, so Daphne led them to her home. With Giles ensconced in an armchair in the parlor with a cup of tea at hand, Daphne confronted him: "Tell me how you got your concussion."

"I got hit on the head."

"I guessed that. How did you get hit on the head?"

Slowly. Daphne dragged the whole story out of Giles, at least as much as he could remember. She was fascinated by the strategy he was outlining as well as with the firing of guns and the explosion that ended the encounter. She was about to pry from Giles the story of how he had received the wound in his arm when her father entered the room.

"Good morning, Captain Giles. I am glad that you were able to participate in the ball last evening even though, I confess, you looked exhausted. And I suppose that my daughter has been tiring you all over again with her agricultural pursuits.

"I have just been seeing Captain Bush. What a wonderful addition to our community he is! And, of course, his mother and sisters. His understanding of ancient warfare is amazing!"

"I'm glad to hear it. I don't really know his mother and sisters. I met them for the first time yesterday evening."

"Fine people, fine people! I'm sure that you will enjoy their company, now that they are here.

"Daphne, it is almost time for luncheon. I hope that you have invited Captain Giles to have it with us."

"Oh dear, I have quite lost track of time. You must have lunch with us, Captain Giles!"

Giles agreed readily. Mr. Moorhouse expertly turned the talk away from agriculture whenever it was about to swamp the conversation, finding out from Giles more about naval life and also steering the conversation towards the society of Dipton, a subject where Daphne could contribute as well as her father. When it emerged, after talk reverted to naval life, that Giles was expecting a summons to the Admiralty any day, Mr. Moorhouse suggested that Daphne and he should invite Captain Giles and Captain Bush to dinner with them, along with Mrs. Bush of course, so that Captain Giles could dine with his friend and meet Mrs. Bush. When Giles protested that he could easily see Captain Bush and his family that afternoon, he ran into firm opposition from Daphne who asserted that he must rest that afternoon, citing the orders of Mr. Jackson. Giles was again feeling very tired, and thought that it would be very pleasant to lie down for a while. Mr. Moorhouse surprised everyone by suggesting that Daphne should invite the Countess to dinner as well.

"Oh, she'll never come," protested Daphne. "She will think it is very presumptuous of us to even think of inviting her."

"Well, let her think what she wants," replied Mr. Moorhouse. "We should have another woman to balance the party. After all, the Countess was willing to dance with me last night; indeed, we danced together on four occasions. What do you think, Captain Giles?"

"I think it is a good idea. My mother does love being the Countess of Camshire; there is no denying that. But I know that she also finds it limits her contact with people, especially since my father has limited the range of people they can easily see. I think it would be worth finding out where she stands now on her status by inviting her. The worst that can happen is that she will refuse the invitation."

The invitations were duly delivered, and accepted, somewhat to Giles's surprise in the case of his mother. The dinner itself was a great success. While they were awaiting the announcement of the meal, Mr. Moorhouse succeeded in drawing out the Countess by talking of the relative charms of Dipton compared with those of Ashbury, where Ashbury Abbey was situated. He had never seen it, of course, but his questioning quite broke the social barriers as Lady Camshire described the gently rolling country in which the Earl's estate was located. She was so used to people listening, not to herself but to her title that she found it a welcome relief when Mr. Moorhouse politely quizzed her opinions and even disagreed on occasion about which sort of vista most conformed to the romantic notion of a lovely countryside. This was a pleasant change from her usually stilted conversations and one that made her enjoy the gathering more than any she had attended in a long time.

Captain Giles was equally adept at putting Mrs. Bush at ease. She had never even seen a countess before the ball, and could not imagine how one could converse with such a being. But her son's former commander, who had been equally terrifying in anticipation, easily got her talking about Harwich, which he had never visited but about which he had heard much. He wasn't interested in the important society of Harwich, but rather what life had been like in the parish she knew so well. His questions showed no sense of superiority, but simply curiosity about various situations that the person with whom he was conversing might have experienced. He wouldn't hear a word of gratitude to himself about letting the Dower Cottage to Captain Bush, but did inquire most solicitously on how she found the cottage. Dinner carried on easily with the same gentlemen adept at keeping the conversation going smoothly.

The only difficulty came when Captain Bush turned to Lady Camshire. He was intimidated by talking with a genuine countess. Luckily, Lady Camshire took the matter in hand, and asked Captain Bush about how he lost his hand and his leg. That released Bush's tongue. Before long, he was using the salt cellar and other table implements to demonstrate how the fight had gone. The subject soon engrossed all the table as Mr. Moorhouse began asking questions and Captain Giles was called upon to elaborate on some points that Bush was not sure about. When Bush's account faltered, Lady Camshire would restart it with a pertinent question about the next step. Mrs. Bush was fascinated for she had had only the vaguest notions of what a sea battle entailed. Lady Camshire, who had heard many a sea captain recount battle tales, was nevertheless fascinated to hear how her son had conducted a battle. Only Daphne seemed concerned, even overwhelmed, by the account.

"How many were injured besides Captain Bush?" she asked when the tale was finished.

"There were forty on *Phoebe*, of which twenty-one are permanently disabled. We also lost thirty-five dead, either in the battle or who died as a result of the wounds they suffered. *Squirrel* lost fifteen dead and twelve wounded. I don't know how many were lost on *Semiramide*. But it must have been many more. At one point they were simply throwing the dead overboard," Giles replied.

"How awful!" breathed Daphne, silencing those who were more likely just to cheer the butcher's bill. After a few moments, she stood and led the ladies from the room.

In the drawing room, the Countess finally got a chance to talk to Daphne when Mrs. Bush absented herself for a few moments. She plunged straight into what she was worried about.

"Are you engaged, Miss Moorhouse?"

Though Daphne was startled by Lady Camshire's directness, she was not intimidated by it. "No, my lady. I am quite content looking after my father. And in any case, there is no one who has asked for my hand."

"I am astounded to hear it. You seem to be a lady of very varied talents."

"I do enjoy managing my father's estate, and helping with Captain Giles's. That is true, my lady."

"And children? Do you not want children?"

"That requires a husband, my lady. Dreaming of having children before one has found the right husband would be putting the cart before the horse."

This was not at all what the Countess wanted to hear, though it seemed clear that, at least so far, Miss Moorhouse was not considering her son a marriage prospect. To make matters worse, she had no idea of how to interest Captain Giles in any of the young ladies who would make a more suitable match than Miss Moorhouse. Daphne, for her part, realized that the Countess was seriously considering the possibility that her son would ask for Daphne's hand. She had herself never considered the possibility except as a silly fantasy since she could see the merits of her father's warning that Giles's status was far too elevated for him to consider her. That is not to say that she had not had daydreams about the subject even though her reason told her that they were ridiculous. Could they have any reality? Maybe they could if the Countess was worried about it.

The separate reveries of the two ladies were interrupted by Mrs. Bush returning and turning the conversation back to the account of the battle that they had just heard. Both mothers were inordinately proud of the roles of their sons in the battle. Daphne could only rejoice that she had lost neither of her new friends before she had even met them. She knew that they had to do their duty, but she could take no delight in the horrors that doing so would entail.

The men did not sit long over their port, and when they joined the ladies, Giles persuaded Daphne to play for them, but only after she had received a promise that he would visit her the following afternoon with his violin. She played with elegance and feeling, even if sometimes the notes were not quite right and some passage work was smeared. When she had played a few pieces and insisted that she knew no more, Captain Bush persuaded his mother to play, and she turned out to be a skilled musician who was a great pleasure to hear.

"I didn't know you played, Mrs. Bush," said Daphne. "I didn't realize that you had a piano- forte at the Dower Cottage."

"I am afraid that I do not," Mrs. Bush replied. "I had to leave my instrument in Harwich, since it was part of the vicarage furniture. Captain Bush has ordered one for me, through the good offices of Mr. Edwards, but it is not likely to arrive for some time."

"Then you must come and use this one whenever you like. I am away much of the day on one task or another and it just sits idle most of the time."

"But wouldn't it disturb Mr. Moorhouse?"

"Not in the least," replied the object of the inquiry. "I should be delighted to have you come. Do your daughters also play?"

"Yes, after a fashion."

"Then they must feel free to come also," said Mr. Moorhouse. "I know of no occupation which can give so much satisfaction both to the performer and the audience."

Giles was yet again fading. When Daphne noticed it, she immediately, but unobtrusively, arranged for the party to break up, with Giles and his mother returning to Dipton Hall in the Countess's carriage, while Mr. Moorhouse prevailed on the Bushes to accept the use of his own vehicle.

The next day was in some ways a continuation of the preceding one. In the morning, Daphne again appeared early at Dipton Hall, ostensibly about matters concerning the garden. She and Giles happily wandered about the garden and if their conversation veered away from the plants and planting, and even from important subjects such as proper drainage, neither seemed averse to the widening of their discussions.

Captain Bush accompanied his mother and sisters to Dipton Manor where he and Mr. Moorhouse were soon happily ensconced in armchairs discussing the merits and weaknesses of the Greek and Persian generals. Bush did divert the conversation to practical matters for he had realized that his family would need a carriage. Mr. Moorhouse had many helpful suggestions on the type of vehicle to get, where the best carriage makers were, and how to find horses that could be relied on. He might also be able to put Bush in touch with a good coachman.

Daphne accepted an invitation to luncheon, where she proceeded to draw out both Lady Marianne and her two daughters on their interests. It emerged that both the young ladies enjoyed music and playing the piano-forte, but there was no instrument at Dipton Hall as yet. Daphne immediately suggested that they would be welcome to visit Dipton Manor to use her one.

Daphne urged Giles to lie down for an hour after luncheon, and to his surprise he complied with her suggestion, even though he was feeling much better than he had in the recent past. When he had rested for a short time, he went to Dipton Manor with his violin and music case. After a couple of false starts, he and Daphne played the first movement of the Mozart sonata with gusto, and then worked on the dynamics of the piece and on the best shading and blending of the two instruments in various segments of the work. Before they could get to the second movement, it was time for tea where they were joined by Mr. Moorhouse. As Giles was leaving, Daphne said to him,

"I think you should get a piano-forte for Dipton Hall. Your sister and your nieces need one."

"Did Mr. Edwards not get one when he was furnishing the house?"

"No."

"Then I must tell him to purchase one. I hope he can count on your assistance in choosing it."

"He can. But he should also consult with Lady Marianne, who will be playing the instrument."

"I suppose he should. But I very much hope that you will be using it as well."

The next morning brought a courier from the Admiralty. Captain Sir Richard Giles was to present himself at ten o'clock to meet with the Second Secretary two days hence. If possible, he should be accompanied by Captain Tobias Bush.

Giles's first reaction was deep annoyance. He had just started to get settled into life in Dipton Hall and now he was called away again. And he felt he had no choice but to comply. He did wonder why Bush was summoned as well as himself and whether Bush would feel up to accepting a command.

Giles immediately walked over to the Dower Cottage to confirm that Bush had received similar orders and to arrange their journey to London. Next he decided to walk to Dipton Manor instead of returning home. All the way, he was debating with himself:

It was ridiculous to even think of marrying a young lady whom he hardly knew. One could count the number of times he had talked with her on the fingers of his two hands, and have some fingers left over; but most marriages were contracted with the partners having spent less time with each other and usually only in vapid conversation.

She couldn't marry – she had to look after her father; but she would still be living in Dipton and she could continue to look after him; and Mr. Moorhouse seemed perfectly able to take care of himself.

She had shown no interest in getting married, quite the contrary; but that could be because she had no prospect of finding a husband who would be worthy of her; anyway, that was her decision to make, not his.

He came from a more elevated tier of society than she did, and he was now a member of the aristocracy in his own right; she might find the social manners required of his wife to be foreign to her and be embarrassed when she made a faux pas; but he knew no one more ready to make necessary accommodations and anyway, he didn't give a fig for the social proprieties and she had the ability to charm anyone: look how she had won over his mother, whom he was sure had come partly to forestall any possibility of marriage and how she had bridged the gap between herself and his half-sister. And he really didn't care about rank and protocol, so why should it matter to him if Miss Moorhouse was not conversant with the details of precedence and deference? Her lack of concern was a breath of fresh air.

She, alone of the company at dinner, had been alarmed and disturbed, indeed horrified, when Captain Bush had detailed what it was like to be aboard a ship in battle; but any sensible person should be horrified; it was only justified because it was necessary for the purpose of the nation; having a proper understanding of the risks he would run was necessary; anyway, it was a decision that was hers to make whether she would want him when going into battle was part of his life, not his place to make it for her.

Round and round the arguments went in Giles's head, even though he knew, deep down, why he was going to Dipton Manor and what he would do when he arrived there.

When he reached Mr. Moorhouse's abode, Tisdale opened the door and said, "Captain Giles. Miss Moorhouse is in the large parlor. Let me announce you."

"Thank you, Tisdale, but I am here to see Mr. Moorhouse, if it is convenient to him."

"I'm sure it is, sir; just let me tell him that you wish to see him."

In moments, Tisdale returned to say that Mr. Moorhouse would see Captain Giles in the library.

"Captain Giles," said Mr. Moorhouse as Giles was ushered into his lair by Tisdale, "it is very good to see you. Tisdale mentioned that you wanted to see me about something."

"Yes, sir. I want to ask for your daughter's hand in marriage."

"Have you asked her?"

"Not yet, sir. I believe that I will need your consent first."

"Oh, you are interested in her dowry, are you? I am surprised."

"No, sir. My own wealth is quite sufficient to meet all her needs. I, of course, own Dipton Hall and its estate, free and clear. I also have seventy thousand pounds in the funds and I have a good deal more prize money coming to me. I wish to marry Miss Moorhouse, and for that desire her dowry is irrelevant."

"Then why ask me first?"

"Because, sir, I understand that Miss Moorhouse believes that she needs to take care of you and look after your wants. I am sure that I would stand no chance unless you can release her from that obligation. We shall, of course, be living in Dipton Hall, so Miss Moorhouse can continue to oversee the provision of your wants."

Mr. Moorhouse burst out laughing. "Oh, dear, Captain Giles. Here we are, Daphne and me, hoist by our own petard as the Bard would say. Daphne's need to look after her decrepit father is a fiction we decided to spread around. Daphne was attracting too much unwanted attention from empty-headed ninnies who were more interested in her dowry than in herself: I am not a poor man, Captain Giles, though I do have simple tastes. I had become the target of any number of widows in whom I had no interest. So we adopted the fiction that I required her to look after me. That deterred unwanted suitors for her and the prospect of having Daphne as a step-daughter in the same house damped the ardor of most of the widows. But I never dreamed that it would be taken seriously by a suitor like you. Of course you may ask her. I cannot speak for her, but for my part I wish you success in your suit. Go and ask her. We can deal with the dowry if you can win her.

Giles found Tisdale loitering outside the library door. Before the butler could tell Giles that Miss Moorhouse wished to see him, Giles had asked to see Miss Moorhouse. Daphne had, in fact, been wondering about Giles's mysterious visit to her father. She would have been listening at the door of the library if Tisdale had not already been stationed there with his ear to the keyhole..

Daphne rose from her chair as Tisdale entered to announce Giles who was right on his heels. She hardly had time to curtsey in response to his bow when he strode across the room and sank to one knee.

"Miss Moorhouse... ugh...Daphne... may I call you Daphne?"

"Of course, Captain Giles I know it is against protocol, but I would like it. And may I call you Richard?"

"Of course! Daphne, I have come to ask for your hand in marriage."

Daphne had to suppress a nervous giggle at Giles's position and the formal way he asked. She had day-dreamed of his asking her to marry him, but had always rejected the notion as being beyond the bounds of possibility. She had trouble believing that she had found a man who was not intimidated by her outspoken manner and direct approach to problems. She also realized that here was a man whom she would be glad to obey as the marriage vows required – provided, of course, that his orders were reasonable.

"You will have to ask my father," she temporized. "I cannot leave him without his permission."

"I was just talking with him, and he gave me permission to ask you. I do know that my proposal may seem rather sudden, but I know in my own mind that I want to marry you. I have to go away again tomorrow, to the Admiralty, so I would like to give you some time to think about my proposal before I return."

"Oh, dear. I do not need any time to know my answer, Captain Giles… Richard. It is 'Yes'! Yes! Yes! Yes, I will marry you!"

At that point Mr. Moorhouse entered the room. He had been eavesdropping and had had no trouble hearing Daphne's enthusiastic and positive response. He coughed loudly to warn of his presence, causing Giles to rise to his feet immediately.

"Father, Captain Giles has asked me to marry him, even though he is going away again tomorrow."

"Yes, and what did you reply?"

"I told him 'Yes'. He said you had given permission. You did, didn't you?"

"Yes, my dear. And I am sure that you will be very happy."

"Oh, we will be! I am so happy! Captain Giles, it is so wonderful! Thank you! But you must tell your mother. I hope she will not be too disappointed. I believe she expected you to marry someone much grander than me. I'll just have to try to get her to really like me so she won't be too disappointed. Oh, Father, thank you for giving Captain Giles permission."

"You are welcome, my dear. It is exactly what I hoped for."

"Captain Giles, you must tell your mother, and your half-sister. Oh, I want to shout the news from the rooftops. I am so happy!

"Captain Giles, please go and tell your mother. Then you can come back here and we can plan and play music and talk and talk and talk. Father, let's have everyone to dinner tonight to celebrate. Lady Camshire, and Lady Marianne and her daughters and Lord David and, of course, Captain Bush and his mother and sisters. Oh, when they were here last night, I never dreamt that I could be so happy.

"Go now, please, Captain Giles, so I can see you all the sooner."

As Giles left the room to carry out Daphne's instruction, Mr. Moorhouse accompanied him.

"I am very, very pleased. But I think those requests of Daphne's are a fair indication what you will be in for."

"I hope it is. I have never liked women who are always very deferential to their men."

The reception of Giles's news was quite different when he returned to Dipton Hall. His mother was very disappointed.

"How could you?" said Lady Camshire. "With your new wealth and fame you could have had your choice of fine young ladies from the very best families. Miss Moorhouse's background is insignificant. Why she hasn't even been presented at court! Richard, you didn't think of your family obligations at all. Miss Moorhouse is all very well, in her way, but she is no match for a well-off knight of the realm and the son of an Earl!"

"Mother, she most certainly is entirely suitable. And you are singing a different tune than when I was a poor naval captain with nothing but a courtesy title to catch a rich heiress. Now, Mother, if you want to keep seeing me, you'll take Miss Moorhouse to your heart. After all, she is your only likely prospect of having grandchildren."

"Well, she certainly is different from the ladies I have considered for you. And I have to confess a great deal more interesting, even though she hardly seems to know how to curb her tongue. And I do wish she wouldn't take such an enthusiastic interest in the gardening and farming."

"That's part of who she is. You will just have to learn to like her interests and enthusiasm."

Lady Marianne was no more enthusiastic than Lady Camshire. She really did not want Giles to marry at all, for she did not want to have to share Dipton Hall with another woman, and certainly not one who would clearly and forcefully be in charge of all domestic arrangements. She felt that she was right back to where she had been when Giles's mother had become the Countess of Camshire and caused Lady Marianne to make her unfortunate elopement. Only now, she no longer had the bloom of youth and she did have two daughters whose only hope of a dowry lay with Captain Giles. She had already discovered that being surly to Miss Moorhouse was an ineffective strategy, so she decided that she would have to appear to be enthusiastic about the wedding; nothing she could say would prevent its occurring.

Giles left Dipton Hall glad to have the duty completed and that the reactions had not been nastier. He was sure that Miss Moorhouse could win over the hostile members of his family when he and she were married, and quite likely before that. That reflection made him remember that his next step should be to see his brother. He was not sure of who was supposed to arrange for the marriage banns to be announced, but he wanted to marry Miss Moorhouse as soon as possible, and making sure before he left that the banns were read would mean that whatever the Admiralty wanted would not delay their marriage by having to wait on his return. His brother, as vicar of the parish, should know how to get the banns announced. Lord David did, in fact, know the procedure and he was certain the Mr. Moorhouse would agree to making the announcement as soon as possible.

Giles returned to Dipton Manor and he and Daphne spent the afternoon together, talking, even playing some music. The celebratory dinner was a great success and when the ladies withdrew, the gentlemen discussed with foreboding the progress of the war, while the ladies spoke of the multitude of arrangements needed for a satisfactory marriage service.

Chapter XIII

Captains Giles and Bush woke to the hub-bub of Westminster on a busy morning. Neither was used to the city's roar. Bush had never before slept in town, his previous visits having only been to pass through on the way to or from Harwich to some naval port without sleeping in the city; Giles in the past had always stayed at his Father's town-house. They enjoyed a hearty breakfast in the inn near Charing Cross where they were staying. Their conversation at breakfast was idle speculation about what the Admiralty might have in store for them and what might be happening in Dipton.

They presented themselves to the Admiralty shortly before ten o'clock and were immediately ushered into the Second Secretary's room.

"Captain Giles," the Second Secretary greeted him, "Congratulations on such a very successful cruise. Captain Bush, you are looking well. I trust you are completely recovered."

"Yes, sir."

"Excellent. For we have a command for you. Ah, here is the First Lord."

"Captain Giles, your last cruise in *Patroclus* was invaluable," that officer started immediately. "We now have another task for you which will complete the good work. And Captain Bush, this duty will involve you also.

"We need to recover those three frigates and the merchant ships whose location you established. I doubt that it can be accomplished by just one vessel, even one led by a Captain such as yourself, Captain Giles. So we will be sending two frigates. That is where you come in, Captain Bush. I want you to take command of the thirty-two gun frigate, *Perseus*, to accompany Captain Giles. She is lying at Spithead right now, and has a full crew and officers. Her captain suffered a seizure and has had to give up his position. You will take command of her, Captain Bush. That is, if you feel healthy enough to take up the commission."

"Aye, sir, I do."

"Splendid! Captain Giles's report stated that he had learned that the ships' crews were imprisoned either at the dock or in some sort of facilities nearby. Those men need to be rescued! And the frigates and the other ships must be retaken. That is what I am ordering you to accomplish. The presence of those ships in France is a disgrace, a disgrace, I say! Newsome here has your orders. I'm not sending captains to command the frigates which you recover. Lieutenants will do just to bring them back. And you said that the French pirates shipped all the petty-officers with the officers, so we'll provide you with enough petty officers so that the ships can sail. They are more important than the officers in getting a ship safely to sea. You can rely on the captured crews for the seamen. Now, I must be off. Newsome can fill you in on the details."

The First Lord bustled out of the room. Giles and Bush turned to Mr. Newsome, the Second Secretary, for elucidation.

"There are a few details of your orders that I should go over. You may think that they are needlessly detailed, but there is a reason. We have learned from our spies in Brest that rumors have been circulating about suspicious naval activity where the river enters the ocean. Normally the Admiralty would order the ships to stay in the bay while the attack would be launched from boats, but the news from Brest suggests that your frigates should enter the river and proceed upstream at least as far as the point where they cannot be seen from the coast. Indeed, given the number of men you will need to land at the dock, not merely to regain our ships but also to control the area so that you can free the prisoners, I believe that you should take your ships right up to the dock. Your orders cover risking your ships in that way.

"If you hurry, and the winds are favorable, you should be off the mouth of the river by dawn in three days' time. The tide will be flooding until ten o'clock, so you should aim to enter the river at first light and proceed upstream as early as possible.

"Now, about officers. The First Lord thought that we should not appoint captains or even commanders to command the frigates once you have secured them. Capable officers who are not presently in a command are few and they would mostly have seniority to you, Captain Giles. The ships, both the frigates and the others will be commanded by lieutenants, of whom there are many first rate ones still on the beach. We have fourteen lined up with orders to join you at Spithead, Captain Bush. I believe that your first lieutenant is rather junior, Captain Giles, as a result of the fracas over Lieutenant Foster. Do you want a more senior one?"

"No, sir, Lieutenant Davis has come along very quickly. I want to keep him as my First."

"Very well, the other lieutenants are to take charge of the recaptured ships. They will only be in command until you return to Portsmouth, of course. Similarly, we have enough petty officers to make the journey reasonably easily. We are relying on the recaptured crews to man the prizes, for that is what they will be. If not, you will have to use your own crews. Both of your frigates have almost full complements, so that should not be an excessive drain since you are to bring all the vessels back to Portsmouth immediately. Because of the possible need to free captives who may be some distance from the ships, we are also sending one hundred marines under marine Lieutenant James Dudley, in addition to the ones you already have on board. For land duties, Lieutenant Dudley will be the senior officer.

"The extra men should already be on board *Perseus*, Captain Bush. I am afraid that you may find your wardroom to be very crowded, but it should only be for a very short period of time. You may want to transfer some of the people to *Patroclus* when you rendezvous with her.

"Captain Giles, the news from Butler's Hard is that *Patroclus* is ready to sail. They have worked very hard to get her ready. We've been trying to keep her armament a secret, but I have no doubt that the news must already be out, so on your return, you will also go to Spithead. But we have lightered around shot and powder to make up for what you have already expended – my, you really do go through military supplies at a fast clip, don't you? *Patroclus* has been resupplied with rations. So you should be ready to sail as soon as you arrive at Butler's Hard.

"Here are you orders, and your commission, Captain Bush, and yours Captain Giles. Good luck to you both. I am confident that you will erase the blemish on our reputation from the loss of the frigates before it becomes general knowledge!"

Giles and Bush found themselves ejected from the Second Secretary's room without further ceremony and out on the street before they could fully absorb all the information they had been given. They hastened back to their inn to collect their sea-chests and Carstairs, before seeking out the Portsmouth Coach. Bush was bursting with enthusiasm about taking command for the first time, and of a fifth-rate. Thanks to Giles, he had avoided the slow progress from lieutenant to captain via being a commander in charge of minor vessels. Even if this command was temporary, and the Second Secretary rather implied that it was not, it was a big step up for Bush.

The two captains arrived at the inn just in time to catch the coach for Portsmouth, arriving there in the early evening. Bush immediately took himself out to *Perseus*. He was immensely pleased to have the boatman cry '*Perseus*' when challenged, indicating that the captain of the ship was in the boat. He mounted the side with comparatively little difficulty, immensely proud to see that Jackson's artificial limbs and his own devoted practice with them had given him the confidence not to request a bosun's chair. He arrived to the twitter of pipes and read himself in. His evening arrival gave him a chance to meet his officers and make sure that *Perseus* would be ready to weigh anchor in the morning.

Giles and Carstairs hired a carriage to take them to Butler's Hard so that *Patroclus* could sail on the morning ebb. The two captains had agreed to rendezvous in the Solent at six bells of the forenoon watch, but Bush was off the mouth of the river by two bells and *Patroclus* arrived one bell later. Giles went across to *Perseus* and was pleased to see that Bush had been given a well-ordered ship, obviously ready for whatever she might be called upon to do. He had all hands assembled, including the lieutenants, petty officers and marines that had been added to the ships' company for this venture. When they were gathered, he explained to them what they were going to do, and then took half of the additional officers and marines back to *Patroclus* in the boats of the two frigates. He didn't need to assemble his own crew since he could rely on Carstairs to report reliably to the ship's network that invariably spread any news or rumors quickly, and he would gather his own officers together once they were under way.

The wind was fair from the north-north west and the two frigates made a good eight knots as they sailed down the Channel to round Ushant before turning towards their destination. *Patroclus* was somewhat faster than *Perseus*, but even so they were making good time. So much so that on the second afternoon, Bush signaled to Giles that he would like to slow down and have some gunnery practice before they got so close to the French coast that firing their cannon might warn of their presence. Bush took a leaf out of Giles's book and practiced with powder and cannon balls, even though he knew that he would have to pay for the expended materials if they did not encounter a genuine need to fire the guns.

Early the next morning, an hour before dawn, they had worked their way to within half a mile of the shore, the lead going steadily in the chains to warn of any unexpected shoaling. There was enough of a moon that they could make out the shore easily and the gap where the river entered the bay. The wind had freshened somewhat and was backing into the south and promised to make their trip up the river simple. And so it proved. They entered the river under only mainsails and jibs and were beyond the trees before the sun had risen. With any luck, their presence would not have been noted.

Patroclus led the way up the river. Before the last bend, Giles ordered the frigates to anchor. He took his barge to survey the landing cautiously. All was calm. There was no sign of activity either on the vessels or on the dock.

After cautiously returning to *Patroclus*, Giles formed his plans. The ships' boats could safely carry fifty marines in the quiet waters of the river. The boats would lead the attack with the marines with the object of securing the dock to prevent any rush from on shore to get to the ships. If they met with no opposition, they were to proceed to block all entrances to what had appeared to be a barracks. Meanwhile, the two frigates would come alongside two of the frigates that were at the dock, grapple with them and take them. The crews of *Patroclus* and *Perseus* were then to secure the third frigate, the brig, if it was still there, and the merchant ships.

All went according to plan for once. The marines had secured all entrances to the barracks before their presence was even discovered, and the frigates were greeted with bleary-eyed ship's watchers who appeared to be nursing the effects of late night drinking. The barracks surrendered without fuss. The guards on the prison block gave up equally easily, though the number of prisoners released was disappointingly small.

Things had gone very easily so far. A major part of their mission had been accomplished without a shot being fired and without any casualties. But now they ran into a road block. The released prisoners knew that there were several other places where other sailors were being held as slaves. But they were unsure exactly where the prisoners were held or how to get to them. They did know that the locations were some considerable distance away. None of the former captives had been to any of the other places. They were only aware of them from casual references which the guards had made to these sites, and even then what little they had gleaned might be unreliable because of their own inadequate understanding of French. In short, they had no real idea where these different prisons might be or how to get to them.

Giles was in a quandary. He could hardly send the marines marching all over the country side hoping to find the missing captured-sailors. But equally, he really couldn't leave the captives against his orders. Even without that consideration, he could not possibly abandon them when there was a possibility that they would be sold in the slave markets of Africa. To add to Giles's troubles, the wind was clearly freshening even as it backed further into the south.

Giles led more by encouraging others than by command. He decided to present his dilemma to his assembled officers, not just those from Patroclus and Perseus, but all the others they had brought along on this venture. A solution to the problem soon emerged.

Lieutenant Dudley of the marines spoke perfect French, and three of the naval lieutenants who were to take command of the recaptured vessels could make a good try at the language. Lieutenant Dudley suggested that he could persuade some of the guards to reveal where the captives were held and lead a rescue party to them. Giles looked askance at him, not seeing how he could be so confident of getting co-operation from any of the guards.

"Why, sir, they are not legitimate prisoners of war. They are pirates, plain and simple. I will point out to them that we see only two ways of dealing with pirates. One is to hang them immediately, the other and more lucrative one is to sell them into slavery. I suspect many would prefer to hang."

"But we can't do either of those," Giles protested.

"Of course we can't, sir," responded Lieutenant Dudley, "but they do not know that we are constrained from doing so. It is what they themselves have been doing. I am suggesting that we tell them that if any of them will assist us by leading us to the places where the prisoners are held, then those people will be allowed to stay behind when we leave and that we will simply forget that they are pirates as long as they do not fall into our hands again. I would be surprised if that threat does not get some volunteers to help us."

Giles did not like the idea of threatening the prisoners. He had, however, not thought about what he would do with them. They were not naval prisoners of war. They were indeed pirates, or the assistants of pirates and slave traders. If he took them back to England, there was every likelihood that they would be hung or transported to Australia, since they were hardly suitable candidates for the press gang. Dudley's suggestion had merit and he himself could think of no alternative that would get him out of his dilemma. So he gave Dudley his permission to try.

The marine lieutenant put on quite a show of being the fierce, blood-thirsty warrior. While Giles could not follow most of what he was saying, he got the impression that Dudley appeared to be offering the leniency to some of the prisoners only very reluctantly under his captain's orders and that he himself was hoping to be able to hang the lot of them summarily. After his harangue, several of the former guards indicated that they would be very willing to help. Dudley quickly determined that the prisoners were held in four separate locations, and he chose a total of twelve of the volunteers to guide them. He indicated to Giles that he thought that having three terrified people to guide them would discourage any of them from becoming courageous enough to lead them astray. Lieutenant Dudley's marines, together with the ones from *Patroclus* and *Perseus*, formed into four parties, each commanded by one of the French speaking officers. Dudley led the group that had to go farthest. The information gleaned from the volunteers suggested that it would be impossible to rescue those prisoners and return to the ships that day. At least two of the groups could hope to return only on the following day. In the case of Lieutenant Dudley's group, they could only be expected in the afternoon on the following day and they would have to take supplies with them to allow for a lengthy absence.

The groups set off immediately. But being marines and not infantry, Giles reckoned that he could not expect a speedy return. The remaining captured guards were ushered into the prison that had held the English captives. The seamen herding them, because they knew how cooperation had been achieved to get volunteers, delighted in acting as if they were vexed at not being able to hang their prisoners immediately. The remaining seamen, largely under the orders of the officers brought to command the liberated ships, went about examining the condition of the vessels and making sure that they were ready to sail when required.

The wind was steadily increasing. By mid-afternoon it was blowing a full gale, and Giles was glad that their orders had not left them at sea on what would be a lee shore if the wind veered and otherwise would threaten to blow them out to sea. He made sure that everything on *Petroclus* was firmly secured and suggested that the other ships do the same. In Bush's case, Giles was told, rather testily, that the appropriate orders had been given at least half-an-hour previously.

The first two groups returned late in the afternoon, bringing with them the sailors they had freed and their guards, including the guides to whom they had promised release, but they would not be turned loose until the ships were leaving. So far the results had been very satisfactory, though Giles felt some concern when the lieutenant in charge of one of the groups reported that he suspected that one of the guards who had been watching the prisoners work when Giles's men descended on them might have gotten away. There was nothing Giles could do as a result of this news; he still had to wait for the other two groups to return the next day, and the gale which was now blowing ensured that he could not safely take the ships from the dock.

The next day, all Giles could do was to try to clear the mountain of paper work that arose from even a short stay at the shipbuilder's yard for repairs and also that was generated by the new voyage, hiding his impatience and worry as best he could. Bush, on whose shoulders the responsibility for the success of their mission rested more lightly spent the time getting better acquainted with his command. The third group arrived at seven bells of the forenoon watch. Only as the last light was fading did the final party appear. They had also successfully freed the captured sailors and commenced their return with a new group of their own prisoners, those who had been guarding the English captives. But the marines were intercepted by a company of cavalry which harassed their progress until Lieutenant Dudley lured the enemy into a skirmish in which the cavalry fared very poorly and were eventually driven off.

It was now too late in the day to attempt to take the ships down the river and out to sea, even if the wind had permitted it. The light had faded completely and the sky was heavily overcast. Giles ordered that all ships be ready to sail as soon as there was enough light to see their way, and posted a strong defensive line in case the enemy should attempt a night attack.

Overnight the wind did ease. The ships slipped from the dock soon after first light. *Patroclus* was in the lead, followed by *Perseus*, then came the merchant ships, the brig and finally the three recaptured frigates. Giles had ordered all naval ships to clear for action before leaving their moorings. The wind had backed into the east and was light so they had no trouble ghosting down the river borne along as much by the falling tide as by their sails. The white channel markers were easily spotted and the calls from the chains indicated that the depths were as expected.

Just as the sun rose, *Patroclus* cleared the line of trees and rounded the last bend to give a view of the bay. The sight that greeted them could hardly have been worse. Beating up towards the river's mouth was a French ship-of-the-line, a seventy-four. She was on a course to cross the mouth of the river close enough to the shore to block any ship attempting to leave the river for the open ocean. She was certain to reach the blocking position before *Patroclus* could escape from the river. Farther out to sea was a French frigate that could take care of any ships that eluded the blockade by the ship of the line.

Giles could only proceed. The situation might not be as hopeless as it appeared. The French ship had probably slipped out of Brest when the inshore squadron had been blown off station by the gale. It was quite likely that her crew was not well practiced having been trapped, possibly for months, by the blockade of Brest. On paper *Patroclus* stood almost no chance against the stronger French ship. In reality, if the French gunnery was not of high quality, *Patroclus* might stand a very good chance of defeating the enemy, especially as *Patroclus*'s bow chasers were of a size that surpassed the individual guns of many battleships.

As *Patroclus* was passing to starboard of the final channel marker, she slid slowly to a stop with her bow slightly elevated. She had run aground! Giles immediately shouted a string of orders to let loose the sheets and to furl the sails, to get the bower anchor into a boat and taken astern so that they could try to pull *Patroclus* off the sand bank. Other orders involved shifting some of the cannons to the stern. Only when these matters had been attended to did Giles look questioningly at the master, Mr. Brooks.

"Sand bank must have shifted in that gale. They always wreak havoc on this sort of coast. Actually, it is probably mud more than sand.

We are hardly listing at all. It is just bad luck that we ran aground on a falling tide, but at least there should be no structural damage."

"Not until that Frenchie starts pounding us," retorted Giles mournfully. The bower anchor was taken out and the cable linked to the capstan. But even with as many men at the spokes as possible, stretching the cable to its fullest extent, *Patroclus* refused to budge.

"Stand by the bow chasers to fire when the enemy comes in range," Giles ordered. The French ship was already maneuvering to bring *Patroclus* within range of her broadside. Luckily, she was not aware of the special nature of *Patroclus*'s bow armament and her present course, which should have kept the ship-of-the-line well clear of the range of the usual bow cannon of a frigate, would render her a good target for *Patroclus*'s more powerful pair. Just as the enemy was crossing *Patroclus*'s bow, she too slowed to a halt, also having run onto a mud bank.

Giles ordered the bow chasers to fire, double-shotted and with double wads to increase the force of the recoil as much as possible. *Patroclus* shuddered from the recoil, but did not shift an inch. Giles did have the satisfaction of seeing the shot crash into the French ship just above the lower gun ports. Both of *Patroclus*'s cannons continued firing but only now with single balls, for the extra force with which the single cannon balls struck the enemy more than made up for their smaller number and produced a more gentle recoil. The latter consideration might be paramount since, as the worried carpenter explained, the recoil was having a more serious effect of *Patroclus*'s timbers than usual since it could not be absorbed in any way by slowing or even reversing the ship's progress through the water.

The French ship opened fire on *Patroclus*. Giles ordered all hands who were not involved in serving the bow chasers to get into the boats and take refuge behind *Patroclus*'s stern: there was no point in taking needless casualties among men who could not advance the battle at present. He did keep a total of six gun crews on board, so that the crews actually firing the guns could be relieved before they tired too much.

Although the French ship's aim was rather erratic, it should have been an unequal battle with the French ship firing thirty-seven cannon to *Patroclus*'s two. But the number of hits was almost even since *Patroclus* was firing more than two rounds for every broadside of the French and most of the French shots missed completely. *Patroclus*'s well directed fire was chewing up the side of the French ship and had already hit several of her cannon, putting them out of service. What the result of the duel would be hung in the balance, until a loud, tearing sound came from *Patroclus*'s bow. Peering over the side, Giles saw that several staves of his ship's siding had sprung free at the bow. Before he could stop the gun crews, they fired again, and the bow seemed to open like a walnut before the pressure of a nut-cracker.

Giles had no choice but to abandon ship. He ordered a collection of readily combustible objects on *Patroclus*'s deck to be gathered about the main mast and he set the resulting pile alight. *Patroclus* was finished, but Giles would make any salvage attempts by the French more difficult. When the pile was blazing fiercely, he joined the last of the crew members in the jolly boat and ordered all boats to row as hard as they could to be well clear of the ship before the fire reached the magazine and blew the hulk to pieces.

Meanwhile, Bush coming behind *Patroclus* in *Perseus* had seen how *Patroclus* had run aground. Promptly altering course to starboard, he had missed the hazard, and continued seaward. The other ships followed his new course. *Perseus* come broadside on to the French ship's bow just as the Frenchman went aground. Bush immediately anchored so that he could fire into the French battle-ship, hoping that his fire would turn the tide of the fight even though his heaviest guns were only eighteen-pounders and the range was too long for his carronades. He ordered the other ships to proceed to seaward as *Perseus* began to pepper the French ship with his guns.

When *Patroclus* split apart, Bush was faced with a dilemma. His shot was doing little real damage to the enemy; the guns were too small and the distance too great for the balls to be effective and he dared no try to get closer to the enemy because he already had almost no water under his keel. It was basically the case that the spent balls just bounced off the French ship with little harm, though they did have enough strength left to injure many of the enemy crew who were manning the guns. Now even that damage to the enemy would be less likely to occur and Bush had to worry about fending off a boarding party from the French ship. He could still try to disable the French ship or he could up anchor and first rescue Giles before joining the other ships and proceeding to England. The lack of officers on the other ships and the limited numbers of crew members made having them join him in an attack on the French ship an unlikely proposition. But Bush did not relish giving up with the enemy clearly in sight and vulnerable to attack.

His dilemma was solved by Giles showing up with Patroclus's boats. Bush had been presuming that *Patroclus* must have suffered heavy casualties, not realizing that Giles had kept most of his crew out of harm's way. This presumption was ended when a midshipman announced that several boats were approaching *Perseus* from astern. Bush's immediate reaction that these boats would contain French troops bent on capturing his command was quickly quashed when the usual challenge was answered by Carstairs booming out "*Patroclus*." Giles had arrived and he had brought all his crew in *Patroclus*'s boats

"Captain Bush. Would you ready a boarding party – as many men as you can spare? I am going to take that Frenchman!"

"Aye, aye, sir," Although Giles had couched his requirements as a polite request, Bush knew perfectly well that it was an order. Bush spat out a string of commands that would place as many of his crew and his marines in the boats, fully armed as a boarding party. At the last moment, he ordered his first lieutenant to stay in *Perseus* while he himself scrambled into the last boat. He was damned if he would let Giles have all the fun. Wide grins greeted him as he came aboard the boat. Even in the short time he had been in command of her, all *Perseus*'s crew realized that Bush wanted no special treatment because of his disabilities. The tales of how he had received his wounds had grown in the telling until Bush sounded like a veritable Hercules.

Bush's boat was the last to arrive at the ship-of-the-line. He decided to board through the gun deck on the starboard side, the one which had been badly mangled by *Patroclus*'s shot. With Giles, his shipmates from *Patroclus* and the rest of *Perseus*'s company engaged on the larboard side, Bush was able to lead his men without opposition onto the starboard side of the French gun deck. He himself would have no recollection of how he had scrambled into the ship, though he seemed to recall a friendly boost as he led the way on board. The tale of that attack formed part of the lore of *Perseus* that would be passed on from one crew to another even after Bush had moved on to other commands, getting steadily more implausible, until *Perseus* was finally broken up.

In fact, the fight was indeed the stuff of legends. The French sailors found themselves suddenly attacked from the rear, by a yammering crowd of daredevils led by a raging man with a peg leg who was wickedly swinging a cutlass and breaking any head that came near him with a special club that sprouted from his other arm. It was too much for them. Those in the rear of the main battle threw down their arms presuming that the appearance of this seemingly huge hoard signaled that they would soon be overcome and all they could do was surrender in the hope that the madmen would spare them. The panic spread forward so that the attackers with Giles found that the pressure of the defenders, which had been threatening to drive them back to their boats, eased and soon Giles found himself confronting the French Captain who tendered his sword in surrender.

Having accepted the surrender, taken the French officers' paroles and given orders to secure the surrendering seamen, Giles turned to face a hard breathing Bush whose fierce battle grin was fading to a more civilized smile. Giles noted that Bush's cutlass, the knob where his left hand should have been and both sleeves of his coat were badly stained with blood. His subordinate had never been one to lead from the rear, and Giles was warmed to realize that neither promotion nor the loss of limbs had dampened Bush's enthusiasm to be personally on the attack in a *mêlée*.

"Captain Bush, thank you for your help. Many men will sleep calmly tonight who otherwise would have been committed to the deep! But I thought I told you to stay on your command."

"No sir. Your orders were to bring every man I could spare. My First is perfectly capable of sailing *Perseus*, but he has had no experience in hand-to-hand fighting."

"But I expected that you would be keeping an eye on our fledglings. Speaking of which, where are those frigates?"

"They are midway between us and the French frigate, sir," piped up Midshipman Stewart. Giles noticed that his uniform also showed clear evidence of participation in a bloody fight. "I was about to tell you that *Impatience* just signaled. Her commander is, I believe, the most senior of the three captains of the frigates."

"And what did he say?"

"As far as I could make out -- they do not have any signal officers, of course, and I imagine it is some time since any of them were signal midshipmen – they are requesting permission to pursue and take the French frigate."

Giles normally would have reprimanded Midshipman Stewart for his lack of respect for those of superior rank, but this was not the time.

"Signal to them to close on this vessel – I wonder what she is called."

"*Le Jour de Guerre*, sir" announced the irrepressible midshipman Stewart.

Giles was starting to think that a visit to the gunner's daughter might be the appropriate recipe for Midshipman Stewart's cheekiness, but this was not the time to attend to it.

"Sir," broke in Bush. "I wonder if it might not be best to allow them to attempt to capture the ship."

"But they lack officers."

"True, but they do have all needed petty officers, and their crews undoubtedly have scores to settle with the French. And think of their commanders."

"What about them?"

"They have been languishing on the beach, despite the recall of the navy when the war started again. From what I have seen of them they are capable officers, lacking in influence rather than skill or courage."

"This voyage should help them."

"Yes, sir. But capturing a French frigate would help them even more."

"I suppose. All right. Mr. Stewart, signal to the three frigates. They are to pursue and take the enemy, provided they can keep *Perseus* in view. Captain Bush, you had better return to your ship with your bloodthirsty crew and follow the frigates. I will stay with this *Jure de Something* and get her afloat and patched up enough to see us to the Solent. We shall have to share a bottle of claret when things are calmer."

Chapter XIV

The collection of old sailors, petty officers and retired lieutenants, who haunted the Portsmouth Naval Yard, kept abreast of the latest doings at Spithead, and had a keen eye for ship movements, had a treat late in the morning a few days after Giles's victory over the French seventy-four. A procession of ships made its way up the Solent to Spithead. The parade was led by a French third-rate with the French flag flying below the Union Jack. The pennant at her mast head revealed that she sailed under Admiralty orders. Studying the larboard side of the ship-of-the-line, the onlookers could see no sign of damage, as if she had been taken without a fight. They were not able to see the ruined larboard side.

The French seventy-four was followed by the frigate *Perseus* which had sailed from Spithead only a bit over a week previously. Next came three merchant ships, all flying the red duster. They were followed by a captured French brig of war and a French frigate. Bringing up the end of the line were three more frigates, British ones that the watchers recognized as vessels that had disappeared and were presumed sunk or taken.

As the anchorage at Spithead came into view, Midshipman Stewart pointed out to Giles that one of the massive first-rates was flying the flag of a full admiral. Even as the first gun of the salute that Giles ordered banged out, a flurry of signals rose on the flagship's signal halyards. When they broke out, they occasioned a startled comment from the usually unflappable Mr. Stewart.

"Good God! Captain Giles, the Admiral is ordering the first-rates and frigates nearest to us to clear for action and to prepare to raise anchors."

Mr. Brooks laughed. "He must think that we may be some sort of French ruse designed to wreak havoc among the anchored fleet. I imagine that Mr. Stewart used *Patroclus*'s number when identifying us and we are most certainly not *Patroclus*."

A subsequent hoist was read more calmly by the signal midshipman. "Our number and *Perseus*'s, sir. 'All ships to anchor immediately'."

"Make it so, Mr. Davis. Let's hope the lieutenants in command of the four frigates are not caught unprepared. Their chances of finding employment may depend on how they respond to the orders, or even if they can read them."

"The signal numbers for the same ships, sir. 'Captains to report on board'."

"Acknowledge. Carstairs, my barge as soon as we anchor."

Giles scrambled up the tumble-home of the flagship, *Herodotus*, to be greeted by Captain Dowson, the flag captain whom he had not previously met. Giles was about to suggest that a bosun's chair be rigged for Bush because negotiating a first-rate's tumble-home was a challenge even for fit and able-bodied officers, let alone one who lacked both a foot and a hand. He was forestalled by the appearance of Bush's hat rising into sight.

"May I name, Captain Tobias Bush, sir? Captain Bush, this is Captain Dowson. Captain Bush was largely responsible for us taking *Le Jour de Guerre* with such little loss of life."

"Captain Bush, Captain Giles, welcome. Admiral Murphy has requested to see you with absolutely no delay. Incidentally, the First Lord is in the Admiral's cabin as well."

Giles and Bush entered the Great Cabin to find the two admirals seated behind a table with their backs to the windows through which the sun was streaming. It made it very difficult for the captains to see the expressions on their faces. The flag lieutenant was standing beside them and seemed to be pointing out something to the two august figures. Giles suspected that in fact the scene was staged, just to impress on more junior officers the importance and burden of flag rank and the comparatively unimportant role of captains who were all too prone to take liberties with their superiors.

"Captain Giles, I see you are back," barked the First Lord. "What have you done with *Patroclus*?"

"I lost her, sir. The details are in my report," said Giles, placing his report on the table in front of the admirals.

The First Lord ignored it. "Lost her? Lost her? How did you 'lose' her? You make it sound as if *Patroclus* were a farthing that you dropped in the stews at Cheapside."

"No, sir. We ran aground and then *Patroclus* split at the bow in our gun battle with *Le Jour de Guerre*."

"Gun Battle? *Le Jour de Guerre*? Is that the seventy-four you just arrived in?"

"Yes, sir."

"And *Patroclus* split at the bow. Were you firing your bow chasers?"

"Yes, sir."

"They always said that having those powerful bows chasers would not work. I suppose that they were right?"

"Yes, sir. But she was designed for lighter guns than our long thirty-fours. They were installed at the orders of the Ordinance Board, sir. The ship's builder was very skeptical that she could take that weight. And the calculations were all made without the provision that *Patroclus* would be hard aground, sir," protested Giles.

"I know. The Ordinance Board really should come under our orders, but they don't. This will, however, give the people on the Navy Board the excuse they need not to build another one."

"Surely that cannot be, sir", intervened the First Lord's flag lieutenant. "*Patroclus*, even though she did split apart, gave very good value for money. One ship- of- the- line captured, three frigates captured, one frigate sunk, three frigates recaptured. It sounds to me that the Navy is up six frigates and one ship-of-the-line as a result of *Patroclus*. That's seven ships that the Navy Board don't have to build."

"I am afraid that they will not look at it that way. That's seven ships for which they won't be able to issue lucrative contracts to their friends and not reap the tokens of appreciation that flow from such an activity. But enough of this. I want to hear Captain Giles tell us all that happened. I know it is in your report, Captain, but I want it from your mouth. All the details from the time you reached the French coast."

The admirals listened in fascination. They grunted with satisfaction when Giles told of how the marines had driven off a cavalry patrol and shared the worry when a gale threatened to delay their departure still further. They chortled with glee when *Le Jour de Guerre* also went aground and quite clearly were of the unrealistic belief that if *Patroclus* had not broken apart then her cannonade alone would have defeated the enemy ship. They looked at Bush with disbelief as Giles related how his intervention had ended the fierce hand-to-hand battle that had ensued when Giles led his boarding party aboard the French ship. Finally they nodded approval as the three recaptured frigates caught and subdued the French one, and even sympathized with the problem that none of those three ships had an officer to put in command of their capture with the honor going to Bush's first lieutenant.

"Congratulations, Captain Giles and Captain Bush," stated the First Lord again when the tale was finished. I wish all my orders were fulfilled as swiftly and successfully as these ones. There should be some special honors for you, but I can't speak to that. There also should be large amounts of prize money, though I am afraid we will have to wait for the lawyers to determine what the divisions of the bounty are to be. The fact is that the lieutenants were sailing as supernumeraries, so I don't know how the disbursements will go. But everyone should get something and you two will be rich – or in your case, Giles, I suppose I should say even richer.

"Now we have the issue of what do to with the officers. Captain Bush, your first lieutenant is quite experienced, I seem to remember, and should be rewarded with his step, don't you think?"

"Yes, sir." Bush had not in fact been impressed with his first lieutenant and would welcome a change.

"Captain Giles," continued the First Lord, "do you think that your First is ready for command?"

"Yes, sir. He is becoming very experienced in all the duties of a sea officer."

"Good, then one of the lieutenants from the rescued ships can be your new first lieutenant. You can also have another one. I suggest you take the ones with the most and the least seniority and Captain Bush can have the middle one."

"Aren't we getting a bit ahead of ourselves? I don't have a ship or a crew, sir."

"You are right. We need to get you a ship. How would you like a ship-of-the-line?"

"It would be an honor, sir. But I would prefer a frigate, sir."

"Why?"

"Battleships spend most of their time on patrol in formation, moving to the orders of their admiral. Even in battle, there is not much chance for innovation or initiative. The individual ships are cogs in the wheel, with fixed roles assigned to them."

"I'm not sure Nelson would agree with you. But I see your point, even though the big, strategic events are determined by the battle fleets, and the frigates only support them and act as eyes of the fleet to bring the enemy to battle. I suppose that you are really a frigate captain at heart and the extra prestige of a ship-of-the-line doesn't count with you. At least, I know that it is not prize money that drives you. You have already earned more than enough to make you a nabob and in your career, you have passed up certain prize money to fulfill your duty speedily.

"All right. There is a frigate, just finishing being fitted out here in the Naval Yard here. A French capture, of course, a thirty-six. Shallow draft, as most French ships are. Renamed *Impetuous*. I will assign *Impetuous* and *Perseus* to Admiral Granger's command. No, I know,

Murphy, you are always crying for frigates, but I think right now the greatest threat is from Boney's invasion plans and from the Texel. You can keep your crew from *Patroclus*, Captain Giles, so you should be ready to sail in two weeks. You can both have ten days leave and then join your ships"

"Sir, can I let my men have some time ashore before they report to *Impetuous*? They have performed well and should be given leave."

"Aren't you afraid that they will run?"

"No, sir. They are all volunteers who know me."

"All right, but on your head be it. I suppose that you want your crew to disappear as well, Captain Bush."

"No sir, I am still new to them and they do not have as strong reasons to stay in *Perseus* as *Patroclus*'s people have to follow Captain Giles."

"I suppose not, but you have been equally successful in finding them prize money, Captain Bush, in the time that you have commanded them.

"Well, that should do it. Again congratulations to both of you."

The interview was clearly over, but the First Lord's flag lieutenant coughed and said, rather reluctantly, "Sir, there is still the matter of the court martial."

"What court martial?"

"Captain Giles ran his ship aground and then had her destroyed in a battle with the enemy. There is no question that there has to be a court martial, even though the result should be preordained."

"Let's get it over with. Admiral Murphy, please ask Captains Dumphries, Callaghan and Macalistair to report for four bells of the afternoon watch. Captain Giles, can you bring your logs and your master and his logs for the same time. I guess Captain Bush should also attend. Conrad, assemble all the other requirements of a court martial by four bells," this latter directed to Admiral Murphy's flag lieutenant.

"Sir, is it legitimate to have the court martial so quickly."

"I don't see why not. No court will condemn Captain Giles for his actions and they wont censure his master either."

"But appearances, Admiral!"

"Hang appearances. I need Captain Giles to be ready for service unencumbered by silly legal requirements. Just get on with it, Conrad."

"Aye, aye, Admiral," responded Lieutenant Conrad.

"I am afraid that the court martial is a necessary ceremony," continued the First Lord speaking to the two Captains. "Be back at one bell of the afternoon watch. And Captain Giles, don't forget to bring your sword."

Back on *Le Jour de Guerre*, Giles's first act was to talk to Lieutenant Davis.

"Good news, George. You've got your step. You'll be promoted to commander."

"So soon? Do you really think I can handle it?"

"Most certainly I do. And I am sure that the Admiralty will find you a ship very quickly."

"Oh, and Mr. Davis."

"Yes, sir."

"They are giving me a frigate that is coming out of the Navy Yard in a few days. Called *Impetuous*. The crew of *Patroclus* is being transferred to her. I imagine that the Port Admiral will send people to take charge of *Le Jour de Guerre*. Keep only an anchor watch on board. The rest of the crew can have four days of leave. Tell them, though, that if they try to desert, I will have them flogged."

Davis had to struggle to suppress a smile at this command. In all the time he had served with Captain Giles, he had seen the cat let out of the bag only twice. Both occasions were for offences against other crew members, not against the discipline of the ship. Even so, only a dozen lashes had been administered in total.

"Now where's the purser?" Giles continued. "Ah, there you are. Each hand to get five pounds before he goes on shore leave. It is against his prize money. Of course, it comes out of my pocket, in the first instance. And no withholding any of it to cover what you may claim they owe you. Just see to it.

"Carstairs, get yourself ashore. I want you to engage a coach to take us to Dipton starting at about eight bells of the afternoon watch. And then go to my tailor – you know, the naval one – and order a dress uniform and a couple of working uniforms and some civilian clothes and all the rest of the gear to replace what I lost when we destroyed *Patroclus*. Have him send them to Dipton post haste as soon as possible. Yes, you won't be taking me in the barge to the court martial. Jones can take your place this once. And we'll have Mr. Stewart. The boat won't dare to go astray with him in charge."

The court martial assembled on time in the great cabin of Admiral Murphy's flagship, *Herodotus*. Captain Dumphries chaired it and moved the proceedings along swiftly. Giles gave his own testimony succinctly and answered only a couple of questions. Mr. Brooks then again recounted how *Patroclus* had gone aground. Captain Callahan took his turn to question him.

"Mr. Brooks, why did you believe that there would be enough water to starboard of the marker?"

"I had taken soundings at that place when we entered the river two days previously. There was ample depth then, and the tide at that time was lower than when we were leaving the river."

"Do you have any thoughts on why the French ship also ran aground?"

"We found the chart that her master had been using of the bay. It indicated considerably greater depth at that point than there actually was. That, incidentally, is what my own chart showed. I imagine that the gale had also raised the mud banks in that area."

Captain Bush's testimony was brief, explaining how he had avoided running aground by turning hard to starboard when he saw *Patroclus*'s predicament. He also had had every reason to believe that *Patroclus* was safely in the channel until she grounded.

Captain Dumphries consulted in whispers with his colleagues and then turned to face Giles. Before speaking, he reached out for Giles' sword, which had been lying on the table in front of the three captains, and swung the hilt towards Giles.

"Captain Giles, we find that *Patroclus* grounded because of an act of God and that neither you nor Mr. Brooks bear any responsibility for it. We also find that your actions and those of Captain Bush and your crews conformed to the highest traditions of the Service. We commend you and all those associated with you, including those in charge of your recovered frigates, with actions that had exceptional outcomes."

The three captains then joined Giles and Bush to shake their hands and comment at greater length about the battle that had been won. Very soon, however, the flag lieutenant intervened, "Captain Giles, Admiral Murphy wants to see you and Captain Bush."

Admiral Murphy, this time, rose to welcome the captains. "Congratulations. I never doubted the outcome of the court martial. Now I would ask you both to dine on *Herodotus* this evening, but I know that you only have a few days' leave, and I understand that you, Captain Giles, have pressing interests in the place where your estate is, what's it called?"

"Dipton, sir."

"You should be able to get there easily tomorrow if you start now. I suppose that you want to go too, Captain Bush?"

"Yes, sir."

"Then you must both must dine with me when next we have the chance. I'm sorry you are going to Granger. I could certainly use you."

Giles and Bush returned to their ships agreeing to meet at the landing as soon as possible. As he climbed the tumble-home on *Le Jour de Guerre*, Giles reflected on how much he preferred frigates to the somewhat unwieldy line of battle ships. As the twitter of the bosun's pipes ended, he turned to Carstairs.

"Did you make the arrangements?"

"Yes, sir. The coach should be at the steps now. And I placed the order with the tailor. On his recommendation, I also got some small clothes and other items which he suggested that you would need. He had a coat and britches that he said were almost your size. More of working quality than of dress quality, but probably very serviceable and certainly better than what you have on now. It is almost new. The owner may have worn it only once since he bought them. Mr. Jeffreys, the tailor, said that he could alter them to fit you immediately. I knew that you might need to dress properly at Dipton before the new clothes could arrive, so I told him to do it. They should be waiting for us in the coach. I hope that my action has your approval."

"Very well done, Carstairs. I can hardly appear in company in these old rags. They were only working clothes when we engaged the French and the fight has not improved them."

Giles gave his final orders to Davis, and then was rowed ashore. The coach was there and Bush arrived a few minutes later. After stowing Bush's sea chest securely, they were off. Both men, as well as Carstairs, were used to catching sleep whenever they got a chance, however uncomfortable the conditions; so they were asleep even before the coach had worked its way through the streets of Portsmouth. They were roused when the coach had to change horses, and staggered bleary-eyed into the inn for a hasty dinner of bubble and squeak and a bottle of very indifferent claret. Then back to sleep as soon as the coach had started off again.

Giles awoke to find the morning well advanced and soon recognized sights and buildings that told him they were approaching Dipton. Bush was left with his sea chest and coxswain at the Dower Cottage and Giles proceeded to the Hall intending to wash and change before going to Dipton Manor to see Daphne. Steves came out to meet the coach as it pulled up in front of the entrance accompanied by a footman to open the coach door. One would never have guessed that he had not been expecting his master's arrival, although it was only due to a housemaid's call that she saw a carriage approaching that he had had any warning. From Steves, Giles learned that the Countess had returned to Ashbury Abbey while his half-sister and her daughters had gone for luncheon to visit a new acquaintance who lived three or four miles distant.

Giles was about to enter, when Daphne came running towards him in a flurry of skirts. She had been supervising some further work on the garden when she heard the carriage arriving and had walked over to see who the visitor might be. When she saw Giles, all sense of decorum left her and she broke into a run. She did not stop until she had flung herself into his arms. Steves looked on with a bemused expression on his face: Daphne had already won him completely so she could do no wrong in his eyes, no matter how much she might offend the usual proprieties. Giles luckily had had time to brace himself so that Daphne didn't simply bowl him over. He returned the greeting as enthusiastically as it was given, and simply rejoiced that his fiancée was not inclined to be bound by standard etiquette when it got in the way of her expressing her happy nature.

"Richard! How wonderful to see you! How long is your leave?"

Giles laughed, "I've just arrived and you ask me when I am leaving, as if you can't wait to see the back of me. Are you sure you still want to marry me?"

"Of course I do! More than anything in the world. I only asked because I want to get married. Last time you were hardly here for enough time to get engaged, let alone married. I hope it is longer this time, but I know that with the threat of invasion, you may be needed very soon."

"You are right about that, but I do have ten day's leave."

"Good. That's plenty of time. The Countess understands why we may need to hasten the marriage and I've told my brother and my sisters that they have to be ready to come at short notice. This is better than I expected. Let's see. Lord David read the banns for the final time last Sunday. Today is Tuesday. We could inform your mother and my brother immediately, and with our grooms carrying the messages, they could learn about it tomorrow, and travel on Thursday. We can be married on Friday or maybe Saturday morning would be better. Yes, I think Saturday morning would be best.

"Oh, Richard, I know that I shouldn't take the lead, but I really do want to be your wife as quickly as possible. I hope you don't mind."

"No, Daphne, I'm delighted about how eager you are to arrange the wedding. I was afraid that we would have to wait months so that a really elaborate occasion could be arranged."

"Oh, pooh to that. As long as the people who really matter to us can be present, I don't want to wait for some silly elaborate preparations!

"Steves. Captain Giles and I will have luncheon in the small dining room. Now, Captain, you should go and change. Your travelling clothes are rather the worse for wear. Steves see to it. I suppose that a footman or Carstairs can help you.

"Oh, there I go again. I don't really intend to give you orders."

"That's all right. Especially since I have had a lot of experience obeying orders -- and of ignoring them."

Giles went upstairs to his dressing room. There he examined the new clothes that Carstairs had obtained for him. They were not really of the first quality, but they would have to do for now.

"Carstairs, I would like you to return to Portsmouth as quickly as possible. Take one of the horses to the posting inn. Tell Mr. Jeffreys that I must have the dress uniform by Saturday morning because I am going to get married in it. Wait there and hound him for it. And bring it back here the minute you get it. Don't worry about the expense."

Carstairs complied even before Giles was ready to descend to have luncheon with Daphne. Strangely, however, he paused for a few moments at the Dower Cottage and conferred with Captain Bush before galloping off towards Ameschester.

Lunch was a leisurely affair, with Daphne quizzing Giles about his adventures. He tried at first to make light of any difficulties he had encountered, but soon realized that lack of full explanation of any problems simply led to Daphne asking a series of probing questions; she was as quick to question prevarications as any senior officer to whom he had ever had to report. The one difference was that Daphne was quite clearly on his side and her questions arose from a need to know in the most sympathetic manner everything in which he had been engaged. It struck him that she seemed to be totally unaware of the prize-money implications of his adventures, unlike any of his fellow officers to whom he might tell the tale.

After lunch, the two lovers strolled together in the garden. Daphne recounted her accomplishments and her plans, explicitly soliciting his approval at every stage. He enthusiastically endorsed everything she mentioned. Next their conversation turned to the management of their estates and what needed to be done. Here Giles could take a larger part in the discussion since he had been mulling over in his mind all the changes that he would like to see to the holdings of Dipton Hall. Daphne listened to his ideas with interest. Most of them she had already thought of herself and when Giles's ideas agreed with hers, she praised them without letting on explicitly that they were things of which she had already thought. When Giles suggestions did not agree with Daphne's ideas, she very gently but clearly explained how there was a better way to accomplish his objective.

The afternoon wore on and all too soon it was tea time.

"I must go home and arrange for dinner," Daphne announced. "You are coming, of course, and I shall invite Captain Bush and his family. I will also invite your brother, Lord David. It is short notice, but everyone knows that your time here is limited. We can't spend every minute alone together, unfortunately."

"I imagine you will also have to send letters announcing when we are getting married."

"That is already done. I had already written all the important ones only leaving the day to be filled in. And I made copies of each of them which I kept here. I knew that the time might be very short. The letters are already on their way. I finished them while you were dressing. And I have told the organist what music I want and put the bell ringers on notice stating that they will be required for duty some morning soon."

For the next three days, Giles and Daphne spent as much time as they could together, finding endless subjects on which to converse, both of great import to themselves and their future and also of the most trivial but delightful nature. They were only interrupted by the need for formal dining with their family members. The Countess arrived in high good spirits, Daphne having won her over completely on her previous visit. Daphne's brother and sister-in-law arrived on Wednesday evening, accompanied by their children. Her sisters came the following morning, also with children and husbands. The pre-nuptial dinner was a large and lively affair, as various members of each family cautiously sounded out members of the other family, luckily finding that they could not only approve of them but also like them. Somewhat to Giles's surprise, both his mother and his half-sister were on this occasion more affable than haughty. He found that Daphne's siblings were intelligent and open minded. This finding came as a relief since he was more used to the pattern where some relatives could not endure others.

Saturday, dawned cloudy and windy, threatening rain, but it started to clear soon after dawn. Giles and Bush, who was supporting his former captain in this most momentous of events, entered the church through a side door. Giles was as nervous as a flea as he waited for the ceremony to begin, desperately hoping that nothing would mar the perfection of the day for Daphne. He vaguely noticed that the church was packed, but thought nothing of it.

Daphne's arrival was heralded by a loud cheer, a sound that did surprise Giles. He knew that many of the servants and tenants of both estates might have gathered for the wedding, but he had not expected such vocal exuberance from them. Daphne appeared with her father to walk down the aisle. Giles hardly noticed that she was wearing a yellow dress, very elaborate in its decoration. What he did notice was that she appeared to be radiant.

Just before his brother, Lord David, who was officiating at the ceremony, pronounced Giles and Daphne man and wife, there was a surprising shuffling among the congregation. As Giles and Daphne turned to leave the church and Daphne took his arm so that they could walk down the aisle, the organ broke out with a triumphal march from Handel and the church bells began to ring changes to celebrate the wedding in the uniquely English fashion. The surprise came for Giles when their progress reached the church door. There they emerged to find that they had to pass under a long arch of swords held out by naval officers. Giles recognized them as men with whom he had served over the years. Beyond them, he found not only his and Daphne's tenants but also most of his crew from *Patroclus*. He could not imagine how in the world their arrival for the ceremony and their presence at Dipton had been kept a secret from him. He was very touched to realize that his crew members had decided to use part of their precious leave to honor him.

The next surprise for the newly married couple was to find that the horses had been unhitched from their cabriolet and their place taken by stalwarts from *Patroclus*. Men who were used to hauling cannon up a sloping deck and breaking the anchor out of thick mud had no problem pulling the carriage on the short trip to Dipton Hall. That was also a surprise for Giles, for he had thought that the wedding breakfast was to be held at Dipton Manor. He hadn't known that Daphne, having been informed by Carstairs about the extra guests, had moved the wedding breakfast to Dipton Hall as being better equipped to handle the larger numbers of guests than originally planned. The only difficulty in arranging the switch was to prevent Tisdale, who had known Daphne all her life and believed it was his right to supervise her wedding breakfast, from coming to blows with Steves, who was gloating over the change. In the end, she had resolved it by putting Tisdale in charge of all the outdoor activities while Steves could supervise the indoor ones. Since the outside arrangements were harder to organize than the indoor ones, a reluctant truce had been achieved.

Dipton Hall was packed. Both the main and the small dining rooms were in use and Steves had had to make still further provisions so that all could be seated. He and Tisdale had also secured additional servants from other houses in the neighborhood whose masters had been invited to the wedding. Daphne had sent invitations to everyone of quality with a fifteen mile radius and since she was well liked and respected, even though she was thought to be a bit odd and lacking decorum, almost all of them had accepted.

Giles and Daphne spent most of their time circulating among the guests, receiving congratulations and making introductions. Daphne knew none of the naval officers and was happy to realize how they all seemed to be delighted that Giles had found his mate. Giles was astounded to overhear, as they approached groups with whom he had served, that there had been lively speculation on whether he would get married at all as well as when. He even learned that the odds had been five to four in favor of his remaining single. Giles also had to be introduced to many of his neighbors, who were all very curious about the hero who had come to live among them, and were delighted for the couple, even if Daphne had spoiled the hopes of some of their daughters...

When the time came for the married couple to leave the festivities, Giles realized that he had not thought ahead about where they would go when they left the wedding breakfast. They could hardly have the carriage driven down the drive only to turn around and come back. He should have known that Daphne would have planned for this part of the ceremony as well as all the rest.

"Where are we going?" he asked her as they settled into the open carriage.

"To Brighton," she replied smoothly. "I have rented rooms for us there."

It was only after they had passed through Dipton and were rolling along through fields which on each side of the road belonged to one or other of them that Giles asked, "How were you able to secure rooms in Brighton at such short notice?"

"It wasn't at short notice. I took them for three months when I realized that we couldn't plan our wedding far in advance."

"Three months?"

"Yes, husband – oh, I love calling you 'husband' -- I wanted our wedding to be as perfect as possible and the expense of holding the rooms didn't matter if it would guarantee that we would start our life together in a good place. I had noticed this house where our rooms are located as being particularly fine when I visited Brighton with my father, though I never thought I would begin married life there. In fact, I didn't expect ever to have a married life."

"I am very glad, *wife*, that you changed your mind on that subject."

Author's Note

This is a work of pure historical fiction. The main characters did not exist in reality and their actions did not take place. In particular, there was no French frigate, whether pirate or tolerated by the French governments seizing British frigates and merchant ships during the Peace of Amiens. Neither side developed ships with major fore and aft armament, possibly for reasons having to do with the ships not being constructed so that they could sustain the sudden loads that such armament would impose, but more likely because of the hide-bound nature of the naval authorities. It is curious that such weapons were not developed, especially for ships of the line where the relatively new tactic of splitting the enemy line would have been made easier if the attacking ships could have mounted significant fire as they approached the enemy, while the defending ships would have been in a stronger position if they could have replied directly as they were being raked. But whatever the reason for the absence of such armament, Giles has been lucky to have had the opportunity to employ this fictitious weapon.

Readers have remarked that some of the concerns and activity around Dipton remind them of Jane Austin. I hope no one thinks I have drawn overly on her very special works. She was describing life very close to the social strata of the principal characters in this tale during much the same period, the exception being that titled members of the cast who participate in the actions at Dipton are more grand than any whom Austen described. It is perhaps worth remembering that Austen had two brothers who were indeed engaged in the naval war of the period, even though that war appears only obliquely in her novels. Indeed, that in itself is strange for there is ample evidence that the war, especially when the threat of invasion was serious, engaged the interests of the class of people with which Austen deals.

I hope that readers have enjoyed this volume. Giles, Bush and Lady Daphne Giles, née Miss Daphne Morehouse, will have challenging as well as rewarding lives as the war stretches on for another decade.

I would like to receive your opinions of the book, either positive or negative. You may email me at jgcragg@telus.net or through Beach Front Publishing House at BeachFrontPress@gmail.com

Printed in Great Britain
by Amazon